HEARTS FOR HIRE BOOK THREE

RAQUEL RILEY

Copyright © 2022 by Raquel Riley

www.raquelriley.com

All rights reserved.

No part of this book may be used, reproduced, or transmitted in any form or by any electronic or mechanical means, including information storage and retrieval systems, without written permission from the author, except for the use of brief quotations in a book review.

This is a work of fiction. Names, characters, places, and incidents either are the product of the author's imagination or are used fictitiously. Any resemblance to actual persons, living or dead, businesses, companies, events, or locales is entirely coincidental. The use of any real company and/or product names is for literary effect only. All products and brand names are registered trademarks of their respective holders/companies.

This book contains sexually explicit material which is only suitable for mature audiences.

Edited by Elli at Clocktower Editing

Cover design by Raquel Riley

Proofreading by Mildred Jordan

For Reid,

Your strength and beauty astound me.

Keep putting one foot in front of the other as you journey on,

and keep your voice raised loud!

For Riley,

You are a superhero!

Don't ever forget it.

Thanks for keeping an eye on my Bunny.

CONTENT WARNING

Please be aware that there are homophobic slurs throughout parts of this book. This story contains graphic violent hate crimes involving physical and sexual abuse, as well as past trauma involving childhood sexual abuse which may trigger some readers. The issues raised here have a satisfying resolution.

CHAPTER 1
RILEY

I inhaled the clean scent of the warm body blanketing mine, sucking the fragrant air through my nose. Reid smelled like scented dryer sheets fresh from the laundry.

Heaven—I imagined this was what heaven would be like when I died.

Those ten minutes of blissful peace were the best I got every day. Which was why I was a morning person. I got to wake up like this, holding Reid in my arms, absorbing his body heat, smelling his enticing scent, and touching his smooth skin without looking like a creeper. As long as he stayed asleep, I could get away with it. When he stirred, I would have to let him go and roll over, pretending to be annoyed by his sleepy clinginess.

As if on cue, Reid rolled over and brushed his rump against my groin. As he nestled into a comfortable position, his bottom nudged me repeatedly, making my dick fill. When I groaned and snapped my hips back, he smiled sleepily.

Sometimes, I wondered if he did this shit on purpose to torture me. Lately, it seemed as if we were both more aware of the tension between us than ever before—which was definitely causing problems for us.

Relaxing my hips, I let my body come back into contact with Reid's backside. The heat his slight body radiated warmed me like an electric blanket, making me want to press against him—crawl inside of him.

It has always been like this between us. When Reid and I were in foster care together as kids, we shared a bed. Every night, I slept next to Reid to keep him safe and to comfort him. Knowing he was safe and resting peacefully comforted me as well. Unfortunately, that freed up a lot of space in our bedroom for an extra set of bunk beds. We were never alone—never had a minute of privacy growing up in the system. The constant chaos and distractions had their own set of pros and cons, which kept our problems at bay until we started college.

It wasn't until we attended Waltham University that we finally found ourselves completely alone in our bedroom for the first time in our lives. The newfound privacy made me much more aware of him than I ever was before. Reid took that as a green light to shed clothes little by little at bedtime. It started with him changing from sleep pants to boxer shorts. His long, shapely legs were definitely something to admire. Then he began sleeping without a T-shirt and I waited with bated breath to catch a glimpse of his smooth torso and pretty, pink nipples. Sometimes, during the summer, I would wake up to find him in nothing but a pair of skimpy briefs. He claimed I threw off too much body heat, like a furnace, and that he was sweaty.

It made me want to sleep in cotton flannel every night.

Then Reid started changing clothes in front of me. When my friend Lucky had asked us to move into his aunt's house with him and a few other guys, I felt relieved. I'd hoped it was the distraction we needed and that it would remind Reid to be more modest. But no such luck. Lucky was nice enough to give us the master bedroom with a private bathroom, which gave Reid permission to continue to cross all my boundaries.

My fingers traced over the curve of Reid's bare hip, and I had to fight the urge to pull him into me, to fill my hands with handfuls of his soft skin.

Did Reid have no clue he was pushing the line of decency? Or was he just enjoying his privacy for the first time in his life? The freedom to change your clothes in your bedroom instead of locking yourself up in the bathroom was a small thing to most, but huge to us. The freedom to sleep in less clothing on a hot night—normal things that people did when they had their own place. But lately, I'd questioned Reid's motives, which was a first for me.

The thing about Reid was, he looked like an angel, and usually acted like one, too, so it was hard to know if he ever had an ulterior motive slide through his thoughts. But sometimes, I would catch him watching me as he undressed. When he left the bathroom door wide open during his showers, I had to wonder if he was doing it on purpose.

Reid brushed his toes along the underside of my foot where I was most sensitive. *He had to be awake.* I pushed back against his foot and he stilled.

Things became progressively worse when I started working for Lucky Match last year. My roommate, Lucky, started an escort service, and my roommates and I escorted to pay our bills. Not Reid though. Like I'd ever let him escort—*over my dead body.* I had spent half of my life keeping him away from abusers and predators. There was no way in hell I would offer him up on a silver platter to horny lonely men with too much money who would like nothing more than to take advantage of him. Just thinking of it made me feel sick to my stomach.

Reid was a virgin, and he would stay that way until he fell in love with a good man that I approved of—which would probably be when hell froze over. He hated that I escorted but mostly kept his opinions to himself. Every so often, he'd throw a fit if I stayed out too late on a date. Several months ago, he had a meltdown when he said I came home smelling like sex. To be honest, sometimes I did it just to piss him off. To remind him I was a catch, and that men wanted me, even if he didn't. It was completely unfair of me, but sometimes, my hurt got the better of me.

That was when the tension started to build, and I could feel Reid pulling away from me. He made other friends at school, like Griffin and Ryan, which I did not handle well at first. I was still not handling Ryan well. He was a little shit, and I knew he had his eye on Reid. I burned with jealousy every time Reid said his name.

Testing Reid's reaction to see if he was truly awake or not, I scooted closer, pressing myself fully against his back. Every part of me, from my chest to my feet, was in contact with his body. The heat he generated warmed me straight to my heart. Bending my head, I buried my nose in his neck, breathing him in. In a minute, I would have to pull away, but for the next sixty seconds, I would absorb as much of him as I could to last all day until I could do this again tomorrow.

Closing my eyes, I let my mind drift to a time not so long ago when our relationship began to change. Things turned from bad to worse when we took on a new client through Lucky Match—an artist who painted abstracts of nude male bodies. Because it was a strictly hands-off arrangement, I let Reid tag along one night. He loved it, of course, and had been coming with me ever since. The man paid us well to pose for him once a month. It always felt like the longest two hours of my life. To sit there in his studio naked, locked in some intimate pose together while not moving or talking for long stretches of time, made me hyper-aware of Reid.

The artist gifted us with a painting of the two of us in a lover's embrace, which Reid hung above our bed. He said it was beautiful—and it was, because he was in it. Every night before I went to bed, I stared up at the painting and thought what a long night I had ahead of me—sleeping next to the beautiful body beside me while reminded of what it looked like naked.

But the straw that broke the camel's back happened just two weeks ago. My roommate, Cyan, recently launched his boudoir photography studio. Reid and I volunteered to pose for him so he could use the pics for free advertising for his website. That night in his studio, *my God.* It was like the longest foreplay edging session of my life. Removing one article of clothing at a time—taking a few sexy photos—removing another piece, and so on. Just remembering it now made me semi hard. Cyan had a stellar imagination and talent for setting a sexy scene, and I ended up popping a massive erection. Cyan spotted it and then suddenly had to run upstairs, leaving us alone for too long. I knew he did that on purpose.

My friends thought I was oblivious to my attraction to Reid. They must be fucking stupid. Like I could be oblivious to his beauty, his perfection. I was just not willing to act on it, which meant I had to pretend I was in denial. But that heated moment between us in the studio changed the tone of our relationship. Reid saw my erection. It wasn't like I could hide it in the barely there underwear I wore. He stared for too long at it without saying a word. When he gazed up at me, his mouth was way too close to mine for comfort, and I backed away. Which was the last thing I wanted to do.

It was easy to see the hurt and rejection on his face, and I used it to my advantage instead of comforting him. I tossed his shirt at him rudely and told him to get dressed. We hadn't spoken another word about that night since, but it hung in the air between us, thick like humidity.

Reid continued to twitch his ass against me like he had ants in his pants. Sighing, I climbed out of bed and raced to the bathroom to start my day the same way I always did, by coming down the drain of the shower as I imagined a whole different morning scenario with Reid than running away from him.

And people wondered why I was so grumpy all the time? The one person I craved most constantly riled me up with lust, unbeknownst to him. I lived in fake denial every minute of every day, and the object of my desire was always within arm's reach, but I could never touch him. Add to that the responsibility of taking care of both of us, working two jobs, attending school full time, and doing everything in my power to achieve Reid's dream of opening a camp for foster kids—I had a lot on my plate.

Thoughts of him swirled through my head as I lazily stroked my hard cock with a soapy hand, drawing out my pleasure. Reid was the sunshine in my cloudy sky. One look at his bright smile never failed to melt my hostility and set me back on the right track. He was my *everything*—except my lover—except my boyfriend. *Except for my future husband.* And therein lay the problem. All he could ever be was my best friend, my confidant, my business partner, and thanks to our shared last names and childhood history—my pseudo brother. It was the obvious conclusion people always drew about us.

To better our chances of staying together whenever we were placed in a new foster home, we begged our caseworker, Charlie, to change our last names. He was so good to us, always looking out for me and Reid. We still kept in touch with him. We spoke weekly and visited him on holidays and school breaks. Charles Morgan was like an uncle or a father to us. Which was why we chose Morgan as our last name.

I bit back a moan as I massaged my sac with soapy fingers. Warm heat gathered in the base of my dick. But Reid and I were not related by blood, only circumstance. People often said they thought we looked similar, which I guess was mostly true. But if you spent as much time staring at Reid like I had, studying everything that made him special, our differences would stand out like a sore thumb.

His hair was a lighter shade of blond than mine, with natural platinum highlights. My highlights were darker, like caramel. He was four inches shorter than me and much more slender. My body was broad and packed with muscle. Reid's blue eyes were a much lighter shade than mine, like topaz. Mine were darker, like sapphires. His nipples were smaller and pink, while mine were larger and brown. His smooth, twiggy body reminded me of a ballet dancer, while mine resembled a jock. Everything about Reid was pretty and graceful and sexy, like a seductive siren. I felt like a bulky, lumbering bull next to him.

Thinking of his beautiful body and pale skin as I stroked my cock pushed me over the edge, and I came with a shout, spilling over my hand. Reid must've been listening through the door because as soon as he heard me cry out, he opened it and breezed into the bathroom to brush his teeth like he hadn't a care in the world.

"Almost done with your shower?" He rinsed his toothbrush and placed it back in the cup next to mine. Side-by-side, like everything was with us. We sat side-by-side as we drove, slept side-by-side in our bed, sat side-by-side in our classes and watched movies side-by-side on our couch. We ate side-by-side in the dining room. I spent my whole life beside the one man I couldn't reach out and hold.

Frustration boiled over inside of me. "Can't you wait until I'm finished? Can I not have five minutes alone? Fuck!" Cue his look of hurt disappointment. I felt like an asshole as I watched him storm off, slamming the bedroom door on his way out. It was always like this with us lately. Reid would push my boundaries until I snapped back, causing him to run away, then I would have to go and smooth his ruffled feathers. Overcome with a deep sense of exhaustion that my life would continue down this path for years to come, I sat heavily on the edge of the bed, wrapped in a towel, with my head in my hands.

We couldn't keep going like this...something had to give. I couldn't lose Reid, but our current situation wasn't working anymore. If I was being honest with myself, I could admit it hadn't been working for a long while.

CHAPTER 2
REID

Well, that backfired on me. I only had myself to blame for having pushed him. It started out innocently with my inappropriate case of the wiggles. But when Riley rushed out of the bed like it was on fire and raced to the bathroom, I knew I had affected him. His shout when he came in the shower was loud and clear. It made me feel empowered, knowing I had caused his erection. The little devil that sat on my left shoulder told me to open the door and invade his privacy so he'd know I'd heard him—that I knew what he was doing in the shower.

Who would've guessed he would snap like that and bite my head off? Now, I sat moping over a mug of steaming coffee at the dining table as I waited for Riley to come downstairs and acknowledge me. I couldn't start my day without knowing things were okay between us, because I was a codependent moron and everything in my world revolved around Riley—what he was doing, where he was going, who he was with. Was he thinking of me? Missing me?

I had no life outside of Riley. He was the only guy I had ever been attracted to or interested in, and I couldn't imagine that ever changing for me. Sure, I could point out an attractive guy in a crowd, appreciate his hotness, but no man had ever made my dick hard.

Except Riley Morgan.

His was the only face I ever conjured when I touched myself. When he laid beside me at night, it was hard for me not to wiggle my body against his.

Didn't matter, though. Riley wasn't interested in me. Well, maybe he was, but he wasn't interested in a relationship with me. I'd tested him many times, and he had the perfect opportunity during Cyan's photo shoot to kiss me. But he always turned away and rejected me. Every gosh darn time. It was like he wouldn't allow himself to be happy.

And if Riley wasn't happy, neither was I.

Some might say that it was unfair that he could date and I couldn't, but the simple truth was, I didn't want to. I was glad that Riley put his foot down and refused to let me work for Lucky Match because I had no desire to get anywhere near other men in a romantic capacity. Maybe I was overstating Riley's job by saying romantic—more like a sexual capacity. I'd probably freeze up and piss myself if anyone but Riley tried to touch me sexually—and he knew it—which made it doubly unfair of him to continually deny my advances.

Coudn't he throw me a bone? *Literally.*

I took a sip of the steaming coffee, feeling it wash down my throat with a delicious burn. Despite being the same age, I'd always looked up to Riley—he was my protector, my hero—a role he loathed. I'd often wondered if that was why he turned me away, because he felt like maybe he was taking advantage of someone who placed him on a pedestal. He thought I didn't see his flaws, but I saw everything about Riley. Which was why I was a hundred percent convinced he was the best person I knew and he would remain on that pedestal for the rest of his life.

"Hey, booger breath. Why do you look so mopey?" Murphy, Lucky's little brother, didn't wait for an answer as he breezed by me in search of coffee.

We were down to just the three of us now. Lucky moved out last summer to live with his fiancé, Hayes. Cyan recently moved in with his boyfriend, Griffin, who was my closest friend. Even with us three, the house felt empty. It was too quiet without Cyan's off-key singing and Lucky's loud mouth and dirty jokes. Not having them here every day left me too much time alone with Riley with no much-needed distractions.

The solitude ripped the bandage off our relationship, exposing the tension between us like a black light on a stain.

Riley bounded loudly down the stairs and I looked up, feeling hopeful. He rushed by me on his way to the kitchen, calling out, "We're leaving in five minutes."

I felt deflated—disappointed. When I entered the sunny kitchen to dump my empty coffee mug in the sink,

I saw Riley and Murphy laughing together. A feeling of unease settled in my stomach, bothered that he could be so casual with everyone but me. We used to laugh like that, always joking with each other, little touches and easy smiles, until recently. Now, it seemed Riley couldn't get far enough away from me fast enough. Ignoring them with a frown, I grabbed my backpack and headed out to warm up the car.

We shared a quiet ride to campus until the silence became too awkward for Riley. "Reid?" He said nothing more than my name. Checking on me without trying to instigate a conversation.

"I'm fine. Just thinking about how I miss Cyan and Lucky living with us. The house is too quiet." *And I miss you. I miss us.* Turning away from him, I gazed out the window at the vast blue ocean as we drove over the bridge that led into Charleston.

Riley cleared his throat. "Me too. Maybe we could plan something for this weekend where we could all hang out together—like old times. A club or Limericks Bar?"

"Yeah," I agreed, never taking my eyes off the water. "That sounds great. I'll ask Griffin and Cy—you hit up Lucky and Hayes." The idea of sitting around the house all weekend tiptoeing around Riley's mood didn't appeal to me. I'd much rather be out having fun with our friends. It was the perfect distraction.

Riley followed me to class and sat down next to me, as usual. Not so much for my entertaining company as it was to keep others away from me. This would be our last year attending the same classes before we branched out into our respective majors. I was earning my bachelor's degree in social work while Riley focused on early childhood education, with a specialty in camp management. Our goal was to cover all the bases that our camp for foster kids would entail.

Charlie was going above and beyond to help us set things into motion. He promised we would have funding and grant money ready to open our center as soon as we graduated. If not for Charlie, I don't know what Riley and I would have done—we probably would have been separated years ago. Charlie found a nonprofit organization that paid education grants to former foster kids, interest free. That was the only way me and Riley could afford to attend a private university like Waltham.

Ryan approached us and took the empty seat to my right, and I snickered, thinking it was a shame Riley couldn't clone himself. Ryan was a nice guy who befriended me because we had two classes together. We often studied during my lunch break at the Roasted Bean, the campus coffee shop where Riley and I worked after school. Riley didn't seem to like Ryan very much, and his grumpiness intimidated Ryan. He swore Riley always gave him the evil eye over my shoulder, which he probably did. I pretended ignorance because I would always stick up for Riley first, no matter what.

Sure enough, I could hear my human rain cloud grumbling under his breath as I conversed with Ryan, making plans to study after school. Riley casually touched my thigh to get my attention, his thick fingers claiming his territory. He was resorting to caveman mode.

"Reid, do you have our notes from yesterday?"

Of course, I had our notes. I'd outlined and highlighted them to keep Riley organized. School has always come easier to me than Riley. He excelled at sports, whereas I couldn't kick a soccer ball two feet. Long ago, we made an unspoken agreement to help each other in our weakest areas, because that's what partners did, and Riley and I were partners. A team. A united front through thick and thin.

Just not in the sense I wished us to be.

Excusing myself from my conversation with Ryan, I reached into my backpack to extract our notes and passed them to Riley—then promptly ignored him again, returning my attention to Ryan. It had to pique his ire to be ignored like this, but he deserved it after the way he snapped at me this morning.

Even though I was wrong for invading his space. *That's besides the point.*

What bothered me was that he hadn't apologized yet, so we could make it right. Riley knew it caused me anxiety to be at odds with him, and he was purposely letting me stew in it, which wasn't fair at all. The old me would have begged him to forgive me. Usually, I apologized even when I was not in the wrong, just to smooth the way between us. But lately, I'd been standing my ground, forcing him to come to me. So far, the results were unclear whether it was working. It depended on his mood and how long I froze him out.

Ryan's delicate voice cut through my thoughts as he gushed about a guy two rows up, who he said looked mouthwatering in tight jeans and a fitted shirt. I didn't share his enthusiasm, because compared to Riley, in my opinion, everyone was kind of ugly. I responded with a bland, noncommittal noise to pacify him.

Of course, he didn't let it go. "I thought you were into tall skinny guys. I've seen you check them out before."

Hardly—I often watched people out of curiosity, not because I was mentally auditioning them for dates. But Riley must have taken his comment personally, because his next words stung, and not just because they were a lie.

"That's not what you said in the shower this morning. You said you liked my broad shoulders and large size." His eyebrows rose when he referred to his size, creating innuendo.

Angry and embarrassed, I squeezed my eyes shut to hide the sudden rush of tears. Emotions swirled in my stomach, causing a physical reaction in my body. Usually, when Riley went alpha-possessive on me, I didn't mind because I knew he did it out of either love or concern for my safety. But this time, it hurt. He lied and tried to twist our situation into something it wasn't, just to make it look as if he had some claim on me which he didn't. He'd embarrassed me by making us sound inappropriate and scandalous. Like I was the kind of guy who casually showered with just anyone. Nothing could be farther from the truth.

Nobody besides our roommates and closest friends

knew we shared a bed, a room, and a life together in a non-sexual partnership. I felt outed. Degraded. My face heated with shame and anger, hot pin-pricks tingling my skin.

How dare he say such a thing about me!

He was supposed to have my back, not be the one to throw me under the bus. Narrowing my wet eyes, I glared at Riley as he smirked at Ryan like he'd won. *This wasn't a contest!* There was nothing to win. Certainly not me, because Riley already had my heart, and Ryan never would. Riley had to know that.

He was acting like he didn't respect me enough to consider my feelings, my privacy, or my reputation. I felt used for the sake of his selfish pride.

If I had actually been in the shower with Riley this morning, we wouldn't even be sitting here right now because there was no way I would ever have let him out of our bedroom afterwards. I scooted closer to Ryan, completely ignoring Riley. Anxiety churned in my stomach, making me want to run and hide and lick my wounds, but Riley would only chase me, and I didn't want that right now.

When I felt attacked or rejected, I curled up inside of my shell like a turtle and waited for the storm to pass. My only choice right now was to check out and disassociate so I could try and stow my feelings until later, when I could process them in a safe space.

And there would definitely be a later—as soon as I had a minute alone with Riley.

CHAPTER 3

RILEY

I was fucked. *Fucked so bad.*

Like always, I'd said the wrong thing at the wrong time to the wrong person. Because I was a petty, jealous asshole. I'd humiliated him. Acid churned in my stomach, burning a trail straight to my heart. Reid was the last person in the whole world I wanted to hurt. I'd spent years protecting him from harm, and I went and did it deliberately.

I was lower than pond scum. Shame suffused me—my self-loathing at an all-time high.

There was no chance to make it right until we were alone, so I stayed quiet. When I risked a peek to my right, I saw Reid with his head bent low over his textbook, hiding. Looking past him, I saw that fucker Ryan smirking at me. Was he gloating because I'd pushed Reid away? Did the stupid idiot actually think that was possible?

Not likely, *dumb Harry Styles wannabe.*

Righteous fury replaced self-pity. Nothing was ever going to come between us. Nothing and no one! Reid was *mine*. He was my—whatever—he was mine. Not Ryan's. We would get past this after I groveled and made it right.

The rest of the day stretched out—long and brutal—as I stewed in my remorse, worried about how much he hated me. I sat through two more classes where a subdued Reid kept his head down in his book. I kept waiting for him to look up so I could catch his eyes and plead with him to forgive me. Then, at the café, I handled most of the workload as Reid shuffled around the stockroom in the back, killing time. He used his break to study with Ryan, who kept darting glances in my direction, probably checking to see if Reid's continued avoidance was affecting me. Of course it was. I felt lonely as fuck, but I refused to give Ryan the satisfaction of knowing it.

Finally, we arrived home, and Reid promptly bolted from the car. By the time I made it through the front door, I heard our bedroom door closing loudly. Reid was going to hide out in bed, convincing himself I was a horrible person.

In the kitchen, I grabbed a beer from the fridge and parked my ass in front of the TV to give him time alone to decompress. We had the house to ourselves—Murphy was out who-knew-where doing God-knew-what. Or, more accurately, doing whom? Tilting my head back, I chugged the last dregs of beer before mustering the courage to go upstairs and face Reid. Dread pooled in my stomach, thick and sour like cottage cheese gone rancid.

Standing in front of our bedroom door, I wasn't sure

whether I should knock first or just walk in, which was ridiculous because it was my room, too. I gripped the brass knob and opened the door softly, peeking my head inside to make sure the doorway wasn't booby-trapped and nothing was going to fly at my head. Everything was quiet as I entered, shutting it behind me. Reid lay face down on the gray bedding, curled in a fetal position, clutching his bunny, Benny. It was a gift from his grandma when he was six, and it was the only thing he brought with him into foster care when she died and left him alone.

Reid clutched it tightly to his chest like I'd seen him do a thousand times when he needed comfort and strength. The kids in foster care bullied him relentlessly for it, which caused me to have to fight a lot. In the end, Reid ended up with the nickname Bunny, and I'd earned the nickname Hero. We were the only two who ever used the names, but they'd stuck for six years now.

Silently, I padded over to my side of the bed and sat. Reid's muffled sniffles gripped my heart painfully—which triggered my tears. *Fuck!* Reid was the only person in the world who could make my damn eyes water.

Stretching out next to him, I rubbed small circles on his narrow back. He stiffened but didn't pull away. Despite him being right beside me, I felt lonely, completely untethered from our connection. We lay like that for several minutes until he had his tears under control. What could I say to make him stop hurting? When I finally spoke, my voice sounded broken and scratchy.

"Bunny? I'm sorry. I'm a jerk, and I hate myself for what I said. I regretted it instantly, but it was too late to take it back." He started a fresh round of sniffling, causing my heart to clench. My mind whirled in panic. What if he told me to fuck off? What if he didn't forgive me?

My fingers continued to soothe him as my lips pressed a soft kiss to his neck. His skin tasted as sweet as it smelled and I resisted the urge to latch on and suck hickeys into his creamy skin. Some primal urge inside me wanted to mark him—to reclaim him as mine—to erase my doubts that he didn't want me any longer.

"Please don't cry. You're killing me. I'm so sorry. Do you know how sorry I am?" I wrapped my arms around him, scooping him up and cradling his slender form to mine. "Clutch me like Benny, so I can make you feel better." That earned me a sniffly chuckle.

Reid buried his face in my chest. "You're not my Benny, you're my Hero. You always make me feel better." He snuck a peek at me with his wet topaz-blue eyes, looking shy but hopeful.

My forehead connected with his, tethering us together. "Not today, I didn't. I failed you today. And I'm so sorry. I swear to God I'll never degrade you like that again."

Reid rubbed his nose against mine. "I believe you," he whispered, his voice raw.

"Would you feel better if you hit me?" I gave Reid a lopsided smile in hopes of drawing one out of him.

He shook his head, sadness seeping from his pretty eyes. "*Never*. But I would like to know why."

My sigh was loud and laced with frustration—because I was mad at myself and because he wasn't going to like my answer—but there was no way I could lie to him. "Because he's no good for you and you don't see it."

Reid's full lips drew into a tight line, draining the color from them. "Ryan is a drama queen and a bit shallow, but he's nice to me, and besides, we're just friends."

Anger clawed its way up my spine. "*Bullshit*. You may not see it, but he's into you. He's just trying to butter you up with that friend crap and then he'll make his move. Just you wait and see."

Reid rolled his eyes, dismissing me. He tried to sit up straighter, to pull away from me, but I wasn't having it. "No matter what his agenda is, you went about it wrong. You embarrassed me with your lie. You made it sound as if we have a relationship, like we shower together."

The old familiar feeling of rejection flooded me, turning my voice bitter. "I know what it sounded like. Would that be so bad? Jeez! We're not actually brothers or anything."

Reid's face flamed. "You made me sound slutty."

God forbid! "Oh, right. I got us mixed up. I'm the slutty one. You're the virginal angel."

Reid sat up straight, anger stiffening his spine. "So what if I'm a virgin! I'm not saying that makes me better than you. You aren't a slut, Ry. You escort to support us. I appreciate everything you do for me.

Anyway, I'll probably die a virgin because *you* won't let anyone near me."

Swift, hot fury replaced the blood in my veins. "Because nobody's worthy of you! I'm doing you a favor, *trust me*. I promise you every dime I own, Ryan isn't good enough for you, and he's not worthy of your body or your time."

Reid's eyes blazed with blue fire. "Good! Because he'll never have it. I'm not attracted to him. I told you that. I just wanted to make some friends. Is that something you think you should be in charge of? I don't tell you who to sleep with or who to be friends with. I don't tell you *anything*!"

It wasn't often that Reid was this angry with me. The feeling of being scolded came to mind, and I tried to defend myself. "There's two reasons for that. One, nobody is trying to take advantage of me. And two, I don't have any friends besides our roommates. *Only you.* And I don't get to choose who I sleep with either. It's work, and if I start getting picky and turn people down, we'll be broke."

Reid jabbed his finger angrily. "You have all the answers, don't you! You know everything, and I know nothing. I'm just your dumb dependent who weighs you down with unwanted responsibilities."

Swallowing hard, I bit back my next words because I finally could hear everything he was trying to say. Reid wasn't angry with me. He was angry at himself. He felt vulnerable, and he felt responsible for all my burdens. He thought *he* was a burden. My heart broke, for him, and because I'd inadvertently made him feel that way. It was the last thing I wanted. Why weren't my actions enough to make him see how much I loved him and cherished him instead of making him feel like I was selfish and overbearing?

Crawling over his legs to straddle his thighs, I pinned him in place. My arms snaked around his back, drawing his face against my chest. I held him while silently rocking him back and forth. "You're not a burden, Reid. You're the best thing that's ever happened to me. Without you, I would be lost."

His stiff body loosened in my hold. "You mean it?" His words were muffled against my neck, sounding faint and distant.

"Swear to God. You have no idea how much I need you."

"Need you too, Ry."

He focused his watery eyes on me and I'd never been more tempted to kiss his sweet lips. Reid was the glue that held together all my broken pieces and I was the umbrella that shielded him from the shitstorm life rained down upon us.

That night, we lay in silence for an hour with no chance of sleep—we both had too much on our minds.

"Ry? What if we lived in Maine?"

I should have expected he would play the 'what if' game tonight. It was something we always did when we needed to escape our current reality. We would make up a fantasy life with fantasy jobs and pretend we could be happy somewhere else, living as other people.

"It's damn cold in Maine." We lay side-by-side, facing each other.

His beautiful pale blue eyes sparkled with imagination. "You could work on a fishing boat and wear those rubber overalls like the guy on the fish sticks commercial." The small smile that teased his lips made them look irresistible to me—I wanted to kiss him so badly.

Instead, I snorted at the ridiculous image. I was definitely not cut out to be a fisherman. "And what would you be doing while I slaved away on a boat all day?" At least we were smiling now.

Reid licked his full lips, and the movement drew my eyes. "I would be home, growing veggies in our garden. Or is it too cold to grow veggies there? I'll have to Google it. I could bake you a pie or make a casserole so you have something warm to eat when you get home. Oh! I could bring you coffee in a thermos and pack your lunch and meet you at the dock."

His fantasy was getting sillier by the second—*I loved it.* "So, I have to bust my ass smelling like old fish and you get to be my house husband? That doesn't seem fair."

Reid paused, as if he was about to tell me something I didn't already know. *Fat chance.* "I don't think I'm cut out for hard labor. Maybe I could work in a coffee shop?" He wrinkled his nose adorably, staring at the ceiling while he thought about it.

Gathering him up, I rolled over him, crushing him with my weight as I broke into a hysterical fit of laughter, my abdominal muscles contracting with each twitch. "You definitely weren't made for hard labor. And since you already work in a coffee shop, we might as well just stay here."

Reid joined in, laughing as hard as I was. When I got him good and worked up, he usually snorted as he laughed, which always made us laugh harder. Eventually, we settled, my forehead rested against his. The air between us thickened with our faces pressed so close together.

"I said what I said because I was afraid Ryan would take you from me. Drive a wedge between us. But my petty bullshit divided us farther than he ever could. I'm sorry."

Reid kissed my forehead and squeezed me as tight as he could. "No one could *ever* take me from you. We're forever."

CHAPTER 4
REID

On Saturday, I asked Riley to drop me off at Griffin's bookstore, *Fairy*tales, on his way to meet his client. Riley was somebody's plus one at a wedding. We spent the afternoon drinking coffee, stocking bookshelves, and waiting on customers. Griffin hosted a children's story hour every Saturday afternoon, and today, he let me choose the book and read aloud. Spending time with the little ones was thoroughly enjoyable. It made my life feel meaningful, like I was born for an important purpose, and all of the suffering I've endured wasn't for nothing. I longed to finish my degree so that I could open up my summer camp and work with kids.

At seven o'clock, we closed up shop and headed upstairs to Griffin and Cyan's apartment above the store. Tonight, we were meeting our friends at the club, but first, we planned to grab some dinner. Because Murphy and Riley were out with clients, they promised to meet up with us later. The store had provided a wonderful distraction for me all day, but now that it was time to get ready to go out, my anxiety returned tenfold. I enjoyed meeting up with friends to go dancing, but the atmosphere in the clubs and bars always put me on edge. Random drunk guys groping and grinding on me—*bleh!* Their attention was always unwanted.

Sometimes, I felt broken inside, but I knew it was more likely because of past trauma. When a good-looking man paid attention to me, it didn't make my stomach flutter with butterflies. It didn't make my heart race or my blood sing. It made me feel panicked and nauseous, triggering my fight-or-flight reflex. It was hard for me to enjoy myself in that kind of scene because I was always hyper aware of the strangers surrounding me, crowding and suffocating me with unease.

Griffin tapped my shoulder, pulling me back from my thoughts. "Are you ready to get all dolled up? Wait until you see what Cyan is wearing."

I chewed on my fingernail, waffling. "I'm having second thoughts about going."

Griffin swatted my hand from my lips. "Hey, you're going to be surrounded by your closest friends. You'll be just fine. We'll be safe, and we're going to have fun."

Griffin always knew the right thing to say to put me at ease. He understood me so well, which is why he was my closest friend. The knot of tension that gripped my stomach unfurled. He rifled through his closet, fingers trailing over each piece of clothing until he settled on a charcoal gray vest. I noticed he didn't choose a shirt to wear underneath. With his arms bare and his smooth chest peeking out, he would look so hot. I wished I had his confidence. Maybe I could borrow a dash of it for one night.

"Okay. Make me pretty." I batted my lashes playfully at him, making him giggle.

Griffin smiled, his dimple making an appearance. "You already are, Reidsy. I'm going to make you gorgeous. *Irresistible!*"

Cyan's reaction the moment we stepped out of the bedroom should have been my first clue that I was making a huge mistake. "Damn, Baby Boy! You look smokin' hot!"

He assessed my sex kitten vibe with an appreciative eye, circling me as he took in my appearance. Griffin had chosen for me a garnet colored crop top and tight black pants that rode so low on my hips it was impossible to wear underwear beneath. He added black liner to my eyes and tinted gloss to my lips.

Then Cyan turned his attention on his boyfriend. His hooded eyes said everything he was thinking. "Penny, baby, are you sure you want to go out? We could stay home instead." Cyan eyed his boyfriend with deep interest.

Griffin looked hard-pressed to decide as he drooled over his guy. Cyan wore a black satin bustier that barely covered his nipples, black fitted formal pants, and a string of pearls around his throat. He lined his arresting aqua eyes with kohl and painted his full lips bright red.

Cyan was known for his gender fluid attire, and he always nailed the look perfectly.

"How about we compromise and leave early? You're even more fun with a few drinks in you."

As I listened to my friends fill the silence with their banter as we drove, I remained quiet in the backseat. We stood in a long line in front of the club for about thirty minutes before we finally made our way to the front door. The closer I got to the entrance, the stronger the feeling of dread became in my stomach. The club's bouncer stamped Cyan and Griffin's hands, marking them as legally able to drink. I received an orange wristband proclaiming that I was still underage for another three months.

The Playground was packed with writhing, sweaty bodies grinding to the pounding beat of techno music. This was my first time here, but I'd heard all about it from Cyan, as he frequented this place often with his clients. Sometimes, they had special events like drag nights or fundraisers where they auctioned men off for dates. We skirted the perimeter of the club looking for our friends, spotting Hudson, Lucky's soon-to-be brother-in-law, sitting near the bar. He waved us over to his table, a semicircular booth upholstered in purple velvet.

"Hey, Hudson! Glad you decided to join us. I know this isn't your usual scene." Cyan snickered, clapping him on the back. Hudson, Hayes's younger brother, was straight as an arrow and quite the lady killer. "Are Lucky and Hayes here yet?"

"They just texted—they're waiting in line to get in." Hudson looked us over, taking in our appearance. "Wow, don't you boys clean up nice? It's an odd feeling being in a place like this and knowing I'm not the popular one who's going to take home a date."

Griffin laughed, appreciating Hudson's tight jeans and fitted black Henley shirt. He looked rugged and sexy with his blond hair and blue eyes. "I have a feeling you're going to be plenty popular tonight. Whether or not you decide to go home alone is up to you." Even I had to laugh when I saw Hudson realize what Griffin was suggesting. He blushed all along his chiseled cheekbones.

"I'm good, thanks. Is Murphy coming tonight, by any chance?" Hudson asked, searching the crowd.

"Probably already has, more than once," Cyan joked. "He'll be joining us shortly." When Hudson's face soured, Cyan added, "He and Riley both had dates tonight."

That news didn't seem to sit well with Hudson, his brows drawn tight. "He's too young to be escorting." I hated the tension between them. We could all feel it and it fed my anxiety.

"Nonsense. He's the same age as Lucky and I were when we started, and Riley, too. He's fine. Rather good at it, actually. The boy was born to fuck." Cyan continued to make jokes, oblivious to Hudson's irate expression. With a sigh, I gave up on the idea that we could all be friends and get along tonight.

Thankfully, Lucky and Hayes arrived, diffusing the tension. Except, when Lucky got an eyeful of my getup, I froze all over again. "Oh-ho-ho, Baby Boy. Wait until Riley sees you. But no matter what he says, you look incredible." He pointed me towards the dance floor and smacked my butt. "Go, dance and have some fun before big brother shows up and ruins your night."

Griffin grabbed my hand and tugged me towards the crowded dance floor— smiling as his head bobbed back and forth—where we danced together, with Cyan at his back. I was having a great time, thoroughly enjoying myself as my body flowed to the music, when I felt a pair of hands grip my hips. Assuming it was one of my friends, I nestled into their hold, making myself at home in their arms... Until his voice spoke in my ear, cutting through the music.

"Can I buy you a drink?" I didn't recognize the deep rumble of the man behind me, and I twisted my head in his direction.

Definitely not one of my friends. I vaguely recognized him as one of the many jerks from Alpha Sigma Rai, the extremely homophobic fraternity on our campus. They've been cited numerous times for violence and inappropriate conduct, but never disbanded because the president alumni was the brother of the Dean of Students. This winner, in particular, had caused trouble before in the café where Riley and I worked. He probably hadn't recognized me because I looked so different from my usual style.

I felt slightly panicked just being this close to the man. Pulling away from him, I scanned the crowd for my friends. Cyan and Griffin weren't far, but we'd gotten separated by two other couples between us. I shouted for Cyan, who looked up, immediately recognizing I was asking for help. He grabbed my hand and led me back to our table.

"Hey, Baby Boy. You okay? Who was that guy?"

Griffin spoke over Cyan's shoulder. "I know who he is. He's an Alpha-hole from Sigma Rai. Was he threatening you, Reid?" Griffin looked concerned but fierce, like he would challenge the guy himself, despite the hundred pound difference between them. I wished I could be brave like him.

"No, I don't think he recognized me. He wanted to buy me a drink."

Hating how small my voice sounded, I tried to borrow some of Griffin's courage. Panic was clawing its way up my stomach into my throat. Soon, it would choke me, stealing my voice. It was a familiar feeling I'd experienced since childhood. Looking around, I searched frantically for Riley but didn't see him anywhere. How was it possible to feel so completely alone when surrounded by so many people? It felt like falling down a tunnel. I could feel myself slipping away from the present, back inside my shell to hide in safety.

I needed Benny. I needed my Hero. Snippets of conversation flowed around me, sounding distant and faded.

"I knew that guy was gay!"

"Most likely, the entire fraternity of ball-lickers are gay, they just don't know it yet."

"Explains the homophobia."

"I knew those guys who attacked me were looking me over a little too enthusiastically before they beat my ass."

By the time Riley arrived, I had almost completely checked out. He got right up in my face, gripping my cheeks so I could focus on him. "Reid, look at me. Focus, Bunny. I'm here, you're safe." The loud music and noise dulled my senses, making it difficult to snap out of my dissociated state.

I was vaguely aware of being pulled through the crowd as I stumbled over something in my path, causing me to snap to as I flailed for balance. "Slow down, Ry!"

He stopped and turned to me. "Are you okay? I want to get you out of here." The worry on his face etched deep lines in his smooth skin, aging him. But then bad turned to worse when the guy from earlier found me again and approached.

"Hey there, I thought you were going to let me buy you a drink. Don't leave yet. We're just starting to have fun." He reached for me with his enormous hands, one gripping my hip as the other landed on my back, creeping up my crop top. "I love the way you dance, backing that pretty ass up on my dick. You ready for another round?"

My heart beat so hard it hurt. Like maybe I was having a coronary or something. I felt dizzy and sick, swaying slightly as I leaned into his embrace. Riley snatched me back with one hand and reared his fist back, hitting the guy square in his face with his other hand.

"I'll go another round with you, motherfucker! Come on, *let's dance.*"

Hudson and Lucky pulled Riley back, dragging him outside as Griffin and Hayes guided me out behind him. When we had gathered outside on the sidewalk, my eyes watered, and fat, salty tears slid down my cheeks.

"Please, Ry. Take me home," I whispered brokenly.

He gathered me up in his arms and bustled me across the street to his car. We drove in silence as more of my tears fell. I hated my weakness. I hated I couldn't be strong like Riley, feisty like Griffin, brave like Lucky. Instead, I was a mess, a slave to my past, to my fears—always needing rescuing, and it always fell to Riley to save me.

My Hero.

My greatest fear has always been that one day, he'd tire of being my hero and would want more. Something different—*easier*—with someone who could take care of themselves. It would happen eventually. And I would be left alone to fend for myself.

Without Riley. My rock. *My everything.*

CHAPTER 5
RILEY

There were no words to describe how much I hated myself.

If I hadn't been out on a date with someone else, I'd have been there when Reid needed me. Instead, I'd failed him. I knew better than to let him go near a place like that without me. That club was a trigger paradise for him. That den of wolves couldn't wait to get their hands on a pretty little twink like him, and that Alpha asshole, a known violent repeat offender, had targeted Reid. I was sure I hadn't seen the last of him. Of course, punching his stupid face hadn't helped. But it sure felt fucking fantastic. I'd wanted to get my hands around his throat since day one of school, but I couldn't jeopardize our scholarships.

But off campus? All bets were off.

And what the fuck was Reid wearing? Someone had dressed him like a twinky Club Ken doll . "Who put you in those clothes?" Frustration, fear, and self-loathing caused my tone to sound sharper than I intended.

Comparison, Reid's voice sounded small, like a sullen mouse. "Our friends. Why?"

He knew why! He couldn't even meet my eyes.

My gaze traveled down to his exposed waist. I had practiced the art of self control around Reid for years, and if I was having trouble controlling my urge to reach out and unwrap him like a snack, I could only imagine what those guys would've done to him.

"Are you even wearing underwear? They did you no favors. A crop top and makeup? Seriously? What have I told you about drawing attention to yourself?"

Reid hung his head as he answered. "That it makes me an easy target."

My fingers gripped the steering wheel tightly, turning my knuckles white. "And, did it?" God, I was so beyond pissed off. If he had just worn his plain clothes, he might not have stood out and garnered that asshole's attention.

Reid's fists balled in his lap. "I shouldn't have to hide just to stay safe! What's wrong with wanting to feel good and look good for a couple of hours? Is that so bad? It's not a regular thing, just every now and then." More tears escaped, and he wiped them away before they could fall.

My anger deflated like a popped balloon. "No, Bunny, it's not so bad to want to feel good. But you lack the tools necessary to feel okay when you get noticed by men. You clam up and can't defend yourself. Every time you leave my side, I worry."

Reid turned his wet, pleading eyes on me. "But that's no way for either of us to live. Maybe I should get help and finally talk to someone. We went years hiding everything because it was us against the system and anything we told them might have gotten us separated. But now, we're our own people. Now, we can ask for help. I mean —I c-can. It's my problem, not yours." He sniffled, wiping his nose on the back of his hand.

Reaching over, I rubbed my sleeve over his gunky hand, wiping away his mess. "Anything that concerns you, concerns me. If you think you're ready to talk to someone, I'll find you someone to speak to. I'll drive you there myself and sit in the waiting room reading a magazine until you finish, then I'll drive you back home."

Neither of us said another word until we got home. Upstairs, I sat him right on the edge of our bed and removed his clothing piece by piece. "Go take a shower and wash the club off you. And scrub that shit off your face." I ducked into the bathroom to start his shower, laying out a fresh towel for him.

With my ear pressed to the door, I listened for sounds of more sobbing, but all was quiet. I'd bet Reid was retreating into his shell again. After his shower, Reid pulled on a pair of pajama pants and a tank top and crawled into bed, reaching for Benny. I showered quickly, enveloped by the lingering scent of Reid's strawberry scented body wash. Closing my eyes, I inhaled the smell of him deeply, letting it soothe my anger away and wash it down the drain with the suds. Joining Reid in bed, I scooted up close to him to spoon his body from behind. I wrapped my arms tight around his stomach, squeezing him to me.

Reid pressed closer. "Ry? Did you think I looked nice? Before I washed my face clean? Did I look like someone you would have asked to dance with tonight?"

Fucking Reid. This was the only reason I missed having a room full of foster kids to share my bedroom with. We never had to have these awkward conversations until we got our own room. Was I supposed to tell him the truth? What kind of position would that put me in?

Reid hooked his foot around my ankle. "Just once, I'd like to hear you say it. But only if it's the truth."

Damn! The truth was, with the way he looked tonight, I would have fucked him six ways from Sunday. I tugged on his hip, rolling him over to face me, searching his face to make sure he really needed this before putting myself out there. *He needed this.* Reid felt alone and lonely. He was reaching out to me, the only person he trusted, to tell him what he needed to hear. Although he had no plans to ever act on it or use it to his advantage, Reid needed to hear he was desirable and sexy and beautiful and wanted—*by me*. That I would have chosen *him*, and not because of our history and what he means to me. That I would have wanted him out of desire and not obligation.

Reid needed to feel validated, and to me, that came way before my pride.

Leaning into him, I placed little kisses over his eyelids, his nose, his cheeks, and his chin. In between each kiss—ignoring his giggles—I told him the truth. That he was beautiful, sexy, desirable, and hot as fuck. The latter compliment made him snort. "It's not that I don't like to see you looking so good, Bunny. As long as I'm the *only* man who sees it." *For your sake and mine.* "More than anything, I just want you to be safe."

Reid gazed into my eyes. "I'm sorry you had to hit that guy. Does it hurt?"

"I'm not sorry. I've wanted to do that for a long time. It hurts a little, but it should be fine by tomorrow." Reid gripped my hand and kissed each knuckle, making my heart melt.

"Thank you for saving me *again*," Reid repeated. I rolled my eyes because, of course, I'm going to save him —every damn time. Reid rolled onto his back and raised the back of his hand to his forehead in a classic southern Belle move. "Why, how ever will I repay you, handsome stranger?" His dramatic southern accent made me smile, easing much of my guilt and fear.

I rolled on top of him, tickling him as I held him down without mercy. "You can do my laundry for a week. That's how you can repay me." He laughed so hard he did that snort thing again, which started a whole fresh round of giggles.

The following morning, I let Reid sleep in, figuring he must feel exhausted. After washing my face with cold water and rinsing my mouth, I went downstairs in search of coffee and ran into Murphy. He looked worse for wear, with red, bloodshot eyes, messy hair, and unshaven ginger stubble on his cheeks.

"Late night? You're not just getting in, are you?" He'd been picking up a lot of extra dates lately to make up for us losing Cyan as an escort.

Murphy scrubbed his hand over his face, rubbing his tired eyes. "Got home about twenty minutes ago. I'm just grabbing some coffee and a shower before I pass out for a few hours. I have to be up at six tonight for another client."

My frown showed my concern for him. "Are you sure you aren't overdoing it? You look exhausted."

"I look exhausted because my date and his husband kept me up all night, playing games. If I die of sleep deprivation, I can't think of a better way to go."

His dreamy smile said it all. Murphy was enjoying being a single nineteen-year-old with no responsibilities and a job that paid him for sex. In his opinion, he was living the high life. I couldn't blame him.

When I raised my mug to my lips, hot coffee sloshed over the rim, burning my scraped knuckles, making me hiss from the sting.

"What happened to your hand?" Murphy looked mildly curious.

"I punched an Alpha Sigma Rai in the face."

His eyes widened. "No way! I can't believe I missed it. You'll have to do it again when I'm watching."

"Gladly."

I'd like to hit that douche bag every day of the week

and twice on Sundays. After preparing an extra cup of coffee for Reid, I brought it upstairs to wake him. I set the mug on his nightstand and sat on the side of the bed, running my fingers through his silky blond hair. It was longer on top, the tips of his bangs falling into his eyes. He was so beautiful. Reid possessed a feminine, ethereal beauty that set him apart from other guys. Hell, he was prettier than most girls I'd seen. I fought the urge to lean down and taste his sweet lips.

"Bunny, wake up. I brought you coffee." Smiling warmly, I gazed down at him, waiting for his eyes to open, thrilled that I would be the first thing he'd see. Sure enough, he rewarded me with a bright smile that chased away all the storm clouds hanging over my head. "I have plans for us today, so wake up and drink your coffee. Then grab a shower."

"You don't have a client today?" He scooted up into a sitting position and reached for his mug, rubbing the sleep from his eyes with his other hand.

"Nope. I'm all yours." I had, in fact, booked a client today, and another one tonight, but I traded them with our newest escort, Adam. The guilt I carried over being on a date and absent last night when Reid needed me most was killing me. I wouldn't make the same mistake twice in two days.

"Where are we going?" With his knees drawn up to his chest and his sleep ruffled hair, he looked fourteen again, reminding me of the boy he was when I met him.

"You'll have to wait and see. Just throw on a pair of jeans and a t-shirt and grab a jacket."

~

As soon as I parked the car, Reid knew exactly what I had in mind. "You brought me to watch the boats?" His effervescent smile told me how excited he was.

Relief settled over me, knowing I made the right call. The little park next to the river was Reid's favorite spot. "Yup. Boats, a picnic, and I brought your favorite comic book." Reid tackled me with a bear hug, hanging off my back like I was giving free piggyback rides.

"Thank you, Ry. I didn't realize how much I needed this."

Watching him enjoy himself and relax as his stress melted away helped relieve a lot of the guilt I carried. I might not always be present to prevent every disaster in his life, but the least I could do was to repair the damage I caused by being absent.

Reid dug into his ham and cheese sandwich as he pointed out a cruise ship off in the distance. His eyes reflected the sun, sparkling bright with happiness. His ability to shrug off his troubles and stay positive always amazed me. I certainly didn't possess that superpower.

"That one's going to Aruba. I bet the water is crystal clear, and it's sunny every day." He pointed to another large boat, a private yacht. "That one is headed to the Mediterranean. They're going to scuba dive and eat grapes and cheese on their sundeck and have lunch with a sheik."

I had to laugh at that ridiculous assumption. "A sheik? Why is he in the Mediterranean?"

Reid shrugged. "Beats me. That's where rich people go on vacation." He loved to play out these fantasies in his vivid imagination. It was another variation of our 'what if' game. Reid created lives and destinations for each of the boats that sailed by. Because as a child, when you lived a shitty life, it was easier to pretend to be someone else, even if only for a few hours. "Look, Ry! A cargo boat. I bet it's headed to the Bering Sea."

My gaze followed where his finger pointed over the dark blue water. "Well, if it is, it's going in the wrong direction. I'm going to guess the Panama Canal."

Reid looked satisfied with that answer and returned to reading his comic book. I took a moment to study him, watching the soft breeze ruffle his silky hair. In these unguarded moments where I allowed myself to feel, it was so easy to open my heart to him and think of all the feelings he stirred in me, things I wished to tell him that I could never voice out loud. Like how the way he allowed me to care for him gave me purpose. I wanted to show him how complete he made me feel by being a constant presence in my life. I wanted him to know that when he laughed or smiled, he made me want to smile, like it was contagious.

I wished I could find the courage to tell him that without him, I would be lost, set adrift like an unmoored boat floating out to sea. Reid made me a better person. Not as good as he was, but good enough to matter. Without him, I probably would have ended up being a juvenile delinquent. But because of him, I had no time to go down the wrong path, because he depended on me to be strong for the both of us, to do the right thing.

I had a mission, Reid's mission, to open a camp for foster kids and give them a place to shine, grow, and challenge themselves. A place they could dare to dream of bigger things. Without Reid, I had no vision of my own. No goals. All I'd ever wanted was to make a better life for Reid, to give him everything his childhood lacked, and to provide him with all the opportunities he missed out on growing up.

Reid Morgan was my motivation, my only goal in life. He was my whole world.

He felt my eyes on him and glanced up from his comic book with a curious smile. "What? You're staring. Do I have mayonnaise on my cheek?"

I smiled harder when he began swiping his cheek. "No. I was just thinking."

Setting his comic book down, Reid asked, "Oh yeah? About what?"

The hearts in my eyes were probably beaming out like the beacon of a lighthouse, calling Reid back home. "About you. About how you are the best thing that's ever happened to me. I'm glad you're feeling better today. You want to stop for ice cream sundaes on the way home?" It was his weakness. Ice cream sundaes were something we missed out on in foster care. Reid liked to go all out with sprinkles and a cherry on top. He said he was celebrating his missed childhood—though it was probably just an excuse to eat more ice cream.

"Ice cream? You bet. Let's go!" When we packed

everything in the car and were on our way to the ice cream shop, Reid reached for my hand across the console. Shyly, he looked over at me and said, "You're the best thing that's ever happened to me, too, Hero. Thank you for giving me this perfect day."

It wasn't the day that was perfect—it was just Reid. He made everything better.

CHAPTER 6
REID

The hot water felt incredible cascading over my shoulders and back. My wimpy muscles were sore from defending myself and my dumb stuffed rabbit from the new kid who moved in and felt he had something to prove. His name was Derek, and he was in tenth grade, a year ahead of us. He played football, like Riley. Riley told me to keep my head down and steer clear of him, and after yesterday, I aimed to listen.

The doorknob rattled, like someone was trying to force it open. Hesitantly, I peeked around the shower curtain to check the door, but all was clear. The rattling stopped. Considering there were six of us kids here, there was always someone trying to get into the bathroom. We had a five-minute shower limit so as not to use up all the hot water and run up the water bill, so I quickly rinsed off before my time was up.

Just as I stepped out of the shower and wrapped a towel around my bony hips, Derek burst through the door, shoulder first. He'd barged through the locked door too easily, making a mockery of my illusion of privacy. Derek looked me over hungrily, eyeing my mostly naked body. Blood surged to my ears, whooshing loudly. Panic clawed up my throat, thickening it, clogging my voice. I tried to speak, yell for help, but no sound escaped my lungs.

Derek laughed at me cruelly as he locked the door behind him. He snatched my towel away and grabbed for me, pulling me roughly against him. The coarse denim of his jeans chafed my skin, still sensitive from the hot water, as he ground his erection into my limp groin. "I'm going to bend you over this sink, pretty boy. If you scream, I'll make sure it hurts. If you fight me, I'll knock your fucking teeth out." He pushed me forward until my knees banged into the cabinet under the sink. Derek applied pressure on my upper back, bending me into position.

Fear froze my muscles. Derek was four times bigger than me. There was no way I could fight back and win. He spit on his dick and pulled my cheeks apart so wide it made my hole burn as it stretched. My head felt heavy and foggy, and I felt so panicked I was on the verge of passing out.

Derek wrenched my arm behind my back, and as he reached for the other arm, I struck out in reflex, knocking over the contents that crowded the counter. A glass jar that held our toothbrushes crashed to the floor, making a loud sound as it shattered. Riley knocked on the door. "Reid? You okay in there?" When I didn't answer, he tried again. "Reid? I'm coming in. Cover yourself if you can." Riley burst through the door much the same way Derek had, only this time, I felt nothing but relief.

Riley froze as he registered the scene. "You fucking fucker!"

He pounced on Derek, who was slow to defend himself because he was trying to pull up his pants. Riley took him to the ground, pounding on his face and ribs until he spilled Derek's blood all over the grimy, white floor tiles. I jumped back into the shower to avoid getting hit, covering myself with the mildewed curtain. Riley was relentless in his vengeance, but I wasn't scared to witness his destruction. It made me feel safe. Riley would take care of it, and everything would be okay. He was my hero.

"My Hero. My Hero." I rolled on the bed, scissoring my legs to find a cool spot in the sheets. "Hero. My—" My desperate whimpers roused Riley from his sound sleep as I flailed, reaching blindly for him.

"Bunny. Wake up." Riley shook my shoulder, speaking directly into my ear. "Wake up, Bunny."

"Nooooo," I groaned, reaching under my head to grab my pillow and stuff it over my head, blocking my ear from him and shutting out his voice.

"You're having another nightmare. Sit up and drink some water. Clear your head."

Huffing a frustrated sigh, I removed the pillow and sat straight. Riley handed me a cool glass of water, which I gulped. My throat felt parched, and I remembered how it had closed up in my dream, rendering me mute.

"Which one was it this time?" Riley knew the drill. Nightmares of my childhood plagued me at least once a week, if not more.

"Derek. I'm okay now. Thanks for waking me. I hate

being stuck in the dream and having to relive the entire episode."

After Riley split Derek's face open, Derek was sent to the hospital to have his head stitched back together and his broken nose set. Anthony, our 'foster dad', didn't report the assault because he was afraid someone would be removed and his check would diminish. Derek, to avoid facing charges, lied about his injuries. And Riley and I didn't speak out for fear of being separated if we were placed in another home.

After that incident, it was many years before I showered alone again. Riley always sat perched on the bathroom counter, keeping watch over me while I was vulnerable and exposed.

I felt so tired of reliving the worst days of my life every time I closed my eyes. And tired of living in fear of it happening again. By refusing to face my fears, I was crippling myself. "Ry? Remember the other day when we talked about therapy? I think I'm finally ready."

Riley released a deep breath, the air rushed from his lungs. "I think you're right. It's way past time. I'll call Charlie today and ask if he can recommend anyone he trusts."

Of course, Charlie knew someone board-certified who just happened to have an available appointment for Monday, because everybody liked Charlie, and everyone seemed to owe him a favor. After our last class, Riley drove me to the brick office building in downtown Charleston where Dr. Webber's office was located. We didn't have to wait long before the receptionist called me back.

Riley sensed my hesitation, and he grabbed my hand and squeezed. The heat and pressure from his hand bled into mine, grounding me. "I'll be waiting right here when you finish. If you need to take a break, ask for one. Don't hesitate."

Nodding my head, I stood and followed the receptionist through a maze of hallways until we reached a door with a gold nameplate that read Dr. Nathan Webber, ABCFP, LCP.

I wasn't sure what all those letters represented, but I hoped they meant he was a good listener, because I had twenty years of things to say I'd been storing up.

When I entered the small but organized office, I took a seat across from his armchair. This would be my talking chair, my hot seat. It was covered in maroon leather and looked out over an impressive view of the city. We were high enough up that I could see clear across Charleston to the ocean. Dr. Webber looked like a normal, non-intimidating guy with short brown hair, rimmed glasses, and a friendly smile. His style screamed university professor/academic chic.

"Hi, Mr. Morgan. I'm Dr. Webber. I'm so glad you could make it today on such short notice." He tried to put me at ease by making me feel like I was doing him a favor and not the other way around. I returned his smile and leaned forward to shake his outstretched hand. "If you feel comfortable calling me Nathan, or even Dr. N, please feel free. Or come up with something that makes you comfortable."

I appreciated his attempt to calm my nerves, but until I felt like I knew him better, nothing I addressed him as would feel comfortable yet. But I definitely didn't feel comfortable being called Mr. Morgan.

"Please call me Reid."

"Great! So, just to be transparent, Charles Morgan sent me your file from when you were in the system. It doesn't say much, other than the various families they placed you with, legal documentation of your surname change, and notes about school grades. Also, a request that you be placed with Riley Morgan at all costs. According to your file, he also received the same surname change you did. So, not much to go on. We have a clean slate between us and I'm hoping you will fill it up for me. Let's start by taking several deep cleansing breaths, and when you're ready, you can begin anywhere you want."

Closing my eyes, I focused on the soft whir of the white-noise machine, on my inhales and exhales until my erratic heartbeat slowed. Then I opened my eyes and the first thing that came to mind, as always, was Riley. So that's where I began. After all, if Dr. Webber wanted to know the real me, he would have to get to know Riley, too. We were interchangeable, connected, our lives intertwined too deeply to separate.

I explained the nature of my relationship with Riley, leaving out the details of how my heart was completely wrapped up in him, and touched on the nightmares that prompted me to seek out help.

"Reid, can you tell me more about these nightmares?"

With my hands folded in my lap, I rubbed my fingers back-and-forth over my knuckles, rubbing the skin raw. "They always center around an attack from my past. I usually have one or two a week."

Dr. Webber focused on my hands but chose to ignore the action. "Can you talk to me about the first time you remember being abused?"

That familiar feeling of panic, the tightening in my chest as my heartbeat quickened, returned, and my skin flushed with heat. Breathing deeply through my nose, I tried to rein in my anxiety and recount my story from an objective viewpoint. But there was nothing I could do to keep my fingers from twitching in my lap.

"I think I was seven. My mom's boyfriend touched me when I was taking a bath. He said he was washing me and making sure I was super clean. He called it the 'cleanliness check'. I knew what he was really doing to me." Dr. Webber never rushed me. He never looked at the clock and made me feel I was on a timer.

Nervously, I rubbed my palms together until the heat burned and the skin felt raw. "That continued for two years until he and my mom ran off. They left me with my grandmother, supposedly overnight, but they never came back. The second person who abused me was my grandma's neighbor. He was around my grandma's age, and he used to babysit me while my grandma played bingo or went out with her friends. He liked for me to sit on his lap while he read to me. But he always rubbed me through my shorts. That continued for three years until he died."

Dr. Webber took notes, and I felt he was listening intently. Not once did he interrupt me or placate me with false sympathy, which made it easier for me to continue. "When I was fourteen, my grandma died, and the state placed me in foster care. I was tiny for my age, and I just looked like the kind of kid you wanted to pick on. I was an easy target. I met Riley on my first day in the new home. When I had moved in with my grandma as a little kid, she gave me a stuffed bunny that I carried everywhere I went and slept with, and I got teased a lot for that when I was older. Riley stuck up for me."

I took a deep breath and gazed out the window. "The third time I got beat up, Riley was home, and he saved me. That night, I had a nightmare, and I woke up crying. Riley and I shared a bunk bed. He came down to the bottom to check on me and ended up lying next to me until I fell back to sleep. Somehow, it turned into a nightly thing. To this day, he still sleeps next to me every night." A rosy blush stole over my cheeks. It felt like the most natural thing in the world to me because we've been doing it for six years, but I understood it sounded odd to others. Dr. Webber never batted an eye at the admission, just made a note and asked me to continue when I felt ready.

"The next person who attacked me was a kid named Derek. He was older than Riley and I." I described to him the attack from my nightmare the other night. "Two years later, in another home, the man who was my foster dad attacked me while I was sleeping. It was the middle of the day, after school, and I was taking a nap, and Riley was at football practice. He came into my room and laid on top of me, and I woke up when I felt him taking my pants down. Of course, like every other time, I froze like a sheet of ice. I couldn't move or speak or anything. He was almost inside of me before Riley came home and saved me. He put the man in the hospital."

Dr. Webber offered me a bottle of water, and I paused to take a few sips. My throat felt dry from the emotions thickening it. "Most recently, Riley and I started attending Waltham University. Last year, we had a serious homophobic problem with one fraternity. They cornered me in the hallway and harassed me and gave me a black eye. They've also stopped in the café where Riley and I work on campus and harassed us several times. Riley won't fight back because he doesn't want us to lose our scholarships, but the other night, I saw one of the men in a club. A *gay* club. He didn't recognize me, and he started dancing with me, feeling me up aggressively. He wanted to get me drunk. Riley showed up in time to get rid of him. He actually hit the guy in the face." I was silent for a minute before adding, "I guess that's all." I squeezed my hands together, trying to still my fingers.

Dr. Webber's face showed sympathy and concern. He seemed to be a very understanding and patient man. "That's all, huh? Any one of those incidents is more than most people ever experience. For you to have endured that many, some of them prolonged, is more than I can fathom. You are very strong, Reid. It's only natural for you to experience anxiety and fear from everything you've faced. I'm going to help you empower yourself by teaching you the tools you'll need to overcome your fear. Also, I think it would be a wonderful idea for you to consider taking a self-defense course. I can give you some information about several classes nearby at the rec center. Is that something you think you have time to fit into your schedule?"

Immediately, I liked the sound of that. It felt like a very take-charge thing to do. "Yes. I definitely could. But even if I learn some cool new ninja moves, I don't think I have the strength to fight anybody off."

Dr. Webber smiled. "You'd be surprised what you can do in a moment of adrenaline-fueled mania. It's more about feeling prepared mentally to face an attack and feeling empowered rather than actually hurting someone. It may give you the strength you need not to clam up and freeze so that you may call for help or buy yourself a few extra minutes until someone comes along and helps you."

My hands finally relaxed at my sides, brushing against the cool leather couch. "That sounds good. It actually makes a lot of sense." Everything Dr. Webber said made sense because he was a smart guy and very good at his job. By the time I left his office, I was actually looking forward to returning.

When I returned to the waiting room, I brushed past Riley and headed for the door, afraid that if I fell into his arms like I wanted to, I would fall apart. Riley didn't speak to me until we were in the car. "So, how'd it go in there?"

"Surprisingly good. I like Dr. Webber. He's really easy to talk to. He suggested I take a self-defense course, and I think it's a great idea."

His eyebrows raised inches higher. "So do I. That's fantastic. I'm glad you two hit it off. So, this self-defense class, is that something you want me to sign up for with you?"

Taking a deep breath, I steeled my spine, gathering courage. "Um, would it be okay if I said no? Nothing personal towards you, but the whole point of taking the class is to feel empowered. I feel like this is something I have to do for me to be stronger, and it makes more sense for me to try to do it on my own. Can you understand that?"

His small smile made me feel like he was proud of me. "Perfectly. I agree with you completely. Can I drive you there and wait in the car?"

I laughed at his attempt to coddle me while encouraging my independence. "Of course. Who else would I ask to support me but you?" When I winked to show him I was teasing, he smiled back. "Ry? Can I have a hug now?" Riley looked relieved that I sought comfort from him as he pulled me into his arms across the console.

"Full disclosure," Riley admitted hesitantly. "I invited our friends over for a drink and to hang out while you were in your session. I figured you might want the distraction and their support. But if you aren't up for company, I can cancel. Just say the word."

"No, that's fine. I don't mind hanging out for a little while. But just for a bit, okay?"

It was really generous of Riley to plan ahead to cheer me up, but I was feeling drained and emotionally exhausted from reliving everything Dr. Webber and I had discussed today. Despite relaying such horrible memories, I actually felt in high spirits. For the first time in years, maybe in my entire life, I felt hopeful.

Maybe it was possible for Dr. Webber to teach me how to conquer my fears and make peace with my past.

CHAPTER 7
RILEY

All the changes happening with Reid had thrown me off my game, and I was not sure how to feel about it.

First, he made new friends that were not friends with me, then he started therapy, which I'm not involved in, and now, he was taking a self-defense class without me. These were all positive steps for him that were way too long in coming, but I didn't know how to describe the feeling I was left with. Slightly panicked? Displaced? Confused and ungrounded? Yes, to all of those. It was like he was trying to re-define our relationship.

I'd been nothing other than his *everything*. If Reid moved forward without me, I would have no identity.

Realistically, I understood he was not trying to move forward without me, he was only trying to grow stronger and seek his own identity, which I fully applauded. But damn if I didn't feel left out. I was not going to whine and cry about it like a baby because Reid would feel guilty and throw himself into my orbit and forget all about his positive changes. That wasn't what I wanted for him, but I couldn't help hating the way this felt, like I was being left behind.

I'd taken the last few days off from escorting to focus on Reid because he needed me, but I couldn't put it off any longer. Tonight, I had to return to work. For all that I pretended to like my job, I actually loathed it. I'd never been an overtly sociable guy who loved to party and hang out. If given the choice, I prefered to stay home eight out of ten times. Just a quiet night at home with Reid, watching movies and making dinner together. But I earned more money escorting than I ever had at another job, so I couldn't afford to turn it down.

Tonight, I was seeing a client who had taken me out once before. David was the man in charge at some high-falutin' bank in the city. He dressed in custom-tailored suits, drove a car that cost more than the house I lived in, and was absolutely boring in conversation and the bedroom. Nice, but boring. Tonight, he planned to wine and dine me at an overpriced dinner club that I had to wear a jacket to. He said I was in for a treat because they were playing live jazz music while we ate.

I could hardly wait.

If I was still awake by the time we finished dinner, I got to sit silently by his side while he entertained clients from the bank.

Then, if I was a good boy, the kind who keeps his mouth shut and says nothing to embarrass David in front of his clients, he'd take me back to his overpriced condo, which reminded me of a museum, and lay as limp as a fish out of water as I fucked him. If I was lucky, I'd get to leave right away when I finished and not have to stick around for an extra hour of cuddling and schmoozing. But, hey, for the thousand he was paying me, I was going to smile the entire night.

Murphy also had to work tonight, and I hated leaving Reid alone, so I arranged for Cyan and Griffin to come over and stay the night. They'd sleep in Cyan's old bedroom, but I had no doubt Griffin and Reid would stay up half the night playing with makeup and painting each other's nails. I swear to God—they reminded me of a couple of preteen girls at a sleepover. It wouldn't surprise me if they prank called boys for shits and giggles.

But I was glad for their friendship. It'd been good for Reid. Griffin was a sweetheart. Almost as good of a guy as Reid was, but he had fire and sass and an independent spirit that I was hoping would rub off on Reid. Just a little bit, not too much. The last thing I needed on my hands was a stubborn brat.

Hours later, as I followed David into his bedroom, I wished for a pack of antacids in my pocket. My stomach roiled because I was about to stick my dick in the very last man on earth I wanted to get naked with. I'd endured his idiotic games for hours, calling him sir, playing the obedient submissive. Now that we were alone in his bedroom, he wanted to turn the tables on me, pretending to be the meek choir boy as I topped him. Hell, I wasn't even sure I'd be able to stay hard the entire time. That was how little interest I had in this man. I didn't appreciate being made to look stupid or inferior in front of his rich pals like I was too dumb to wrap my head around their fancy financial terms and big collegiate words.

Fuck him and his friends.

As I stripped his designer clothes from his body, I disconnected myself from the here and now. Instead, I pictured the only body I dreamed of touching. It probably made me as twisted as David was to imagine Reid while I touched this asshat, but I knew from experience it was the only mind trick that would get me through this night while maintaining my erection. Imagining that I was stroking Reid's baby soft skin. Teasing his tiny pink nipples. Tonguing the little mole on his flat stomach before dipping my tongue into his navel—going lower to take him into my mouth.

Reid was one of those magical twinks whose dick size was completely disproportionate to his body. In direct opposition of his twiggy lanky limbs, he had a thick, long cock with a fat mushroom head. Not that I gawked at it, that he was aware of, at least. But when you shared a room and a bed and a bathroom with the same guy for six years, you were bound to catch a glimpse here and there. And when it looked as good as Reid's, it tended to stick in your memory.

Everything I did to David, I imagined I was doing to

Reid instead, which kept me hard enough to finish the job. After he came in my hand and I came in a condom, I collapsed, pretending to feel overcome with exhaustion in hopes he'd take pity on me and send me home sooner. And he did, but not because he cared about me. He said he had an early morning ahead of him and needed to turn in. That suited me just fine. I kissed his bearded cheek and reminded him to call me the next time he felt like having company.

As much as I despised sleeping with men I didn't give two fucks about and had zero attraction to, I never felt dirty and degraded when I left. Usually, I just felt numb. Maybe because I checked out during the act and went to my happy place, mentally, or maybe because I already hated myself and couldn't sink much lower. It disgusted me to bring Reid into it, even if only through my imagination. But not as much as I hated myself for having filthy thoughts about him to begin with. It felt like I was dirtying him up without his permission—stealing his innocence without his consent, and that made me worse than the scum who had abused him, because I claimed to love him.

When you loved someone, you didn't think about making love to them while you were fucking someone else. You just didn't. That wasn't love. It was using the idea of them for your own selfish gain. And I'd just used Reid to make a thousand bucks.

By the time I arrived home, the house was quiet and dark. When I walked into my bedroom, I spied a Reid-shaped lump under the covers. Passing the bed, I left him sleeping as I tiptoed quietly to the shower. The scalding hot water burned away all lingering traces of David's scent on my body, replaced with the sweet strawberry smell of Reid's body wash. Then I slipped on a clean pair of pajama pants and crawled under the covers to join him. His muffled voice cut through the silence like a knife.

"Did you have a good time?"

He wasn't asking because he hoped I had. The question was more rhetorical than anything. "Depends on what you consider a good time. In my opinion, no, I didn't. Did you?"

Reid threw the blanket off and sat up, rolling his eyes. His beautiful blond hair was a mess, twisted into several short braids that stuck straight out like porcupine quills, each secured with a different colored rubber band, creating a rainbow effect. He'd already washed the makeup from his face, but I could still see the red dye staining his lips, making them look like forbidden fruit, and traces of glitter stuck to his eyelids. When he held out his rainbow-painted nails, I couldn't stop the laughter that bubbled from my throat. After the sheer distasteful misery of my evening, it felt good, almost cathartic, to come home and face such a simple silly situation such as this—Reid's makeover from hell.

Feeling grateful to Griffin for keeping Reid occupied, I vowed to wake up early and make pancakes for everyone.

"Don't worry, I'll remove the nail polish and the braids tomorrow before I leave the house." He was trying to assure me because I usually vetoed anything that drew attention to him and made him a target, such as nail polish and braids.

I kissed the tip of his nose, allowing my lips to linger for a second too long. "You look beautiful, Bunny. I'm glad you had fun. I know it's late, but I'm in the mood for a snack. Are you hungry?"

"I could eat, I guess." Reid clutched Benny to his chest. He looked completely endearing when you considered the hairdo, glitter, and nail polish.

"Come downstairs with me, and I'll make us something." He slipped into his bunny slippers, white and fluffy with a stuffed head and a cotton tail on his heel, that I'd bought him last Christmas, and followed me to the kitchen.

Grabbing the ingredients from the cupboard, we sat at the table where I poured two bowls of cereal, and as I dug in, I heard a key in the door. "Must be Murphy."

It wasn't strange for him to arrive home this late when he was out with clients. But it was strange that I heard two voices. Murphy would never bring a client home, no matter how hot the guy was. Reid and I exchanged a look and dropped our spoons at the same time, heading into the living room for a peek.

Hudson, Lucky's younger brother, was standing in the hallway, arguing with Murphy as he held him steady on his feet. "Again? Is this becoming a regular habit?" This was the third time Hudson had dropped Murphy's drunk ass off at home. Seemed he had a habitual designated driver.

Hudson gripped Murphy's bicep. "Caught him trying

to use another fake ID. Guerrero Martinez." Murphy giggled, oblivious to Hudson's stern expression. "How could they mistake him for Hispanic? He is as white as Casper the ghost, but with freckles and auburn hair."

"For forty dollars, I look a lot more Hispanic," Murphy sassed, swaying on his feet.

"What you need is a babysitter and a short leash," Hudson snapped.

"Oh, kinky." Murphy raised his auburn eyebrows, clearly interested.

"You need to grow up, Murphy." Hudson pushed him aside.

Murphy's hand dropped to his belt. "Would you like me to drop my pants and show you just how big I am?"

"Dick size doesn't equal maturity." Hudson rolled his eyes, clearly fed up with Murphy's bullshit. I couldn't blame him. Babysitting Murphy Maguire was a full-time job.

"I'm willing to try anyway just so you can prove me wrong." Murphy grinned, clearly thinking himself witty.

Hudson cracked his neck from side to side, sighing loudly. "Go to bed, Murphy. Maybe I'll see you next weekend when you try to pass yourself off as Santa Claus."

"Are you going to pretend to be my naughty elf?"

It was like watching a tennis match, the insults and innuendo being volleyed back and forth. If I didn't intervene, they might have continued all night. "I think it's past your bedtime, Murphy. Let's get you upstairs and into the shower." I handed him off to Reid and returned my attention to Hudson. "Thanks for bringing him home safely. Again. How do you keep running into him when he's out? Is it pure coincidence?"

"We always end up at Limericks at the end of the night. I'm usually there with a date or after a date, same as Murphy. Tonight, we both happened to be alone. I still have to drive all the way back to the city, but I wanted to make sure he got home safely so I didn't worry about him all night. Of course, he's completely ungrateful, not that I expected any less."

"Thanks, Hudson. I appreciate it, and so does Lucky." I waited until he was seated in his car before shutting the door. Then, I headed upstairs where I could hear Murphy and Reid in the bathroom, preparing the shower.

"What the hell happened to your hair?" Murphy asked excitedly. Reid giggled, followed by another question from Murphy. "I love your nails. Can you do mine like that?"

I loitered in the hallway because we couldn't all fit in the bathroom at once. Griffin and Cyan poked their heads out of their bedroom door to see what was happening. "Murphy came home trashed again. Hudson dropped him off."

Cyan rolled his eyes and tugged Griffin back inside, shutting the door on our drama. When I peeked in the bathroom, I saw Reid sitting on the counter, with Murphy behind the shower curtain. He was singing off key, butchering a song I used to like until now as Reid laughed. I left the door open and leaned against the wall in the hallway to wait, thinking how much I wanted to knock sense into Murphy, drag Reid back to bed, and go to sleep sometime before the sun came up.

~

The following morning, Reid and I slept in. Feeling guilty for breaking my vow to cook, I offered to treat him to breakfast at the Apple Blossom Bistro, a quaint little café here in town. Reid had a soft spot for their chocolate croissants.

After breakfast, we spent a few hours volunteering at Over the Rainbow, the LGBTQ+ youth center downtown. Reid and I went most weekends and, sometimes, our friends joined us. I tossed the football around with some kids while Reid gathered up his usual pep squad and cheered us on. Twice, I fumbled the ball while imagining him dressed in a cheer uniform. Then we all gathered on the mismatched sofas in the community room and watched a movie.

Every time we came to volunteer, Reid seemed to be floating on air when we left, stuck in dreams about our future. He truly loved helping others. Reid was selfless like that. He possessed the kindest, most generous heart of anyone I'd ever met. Sometimes, I felt pure pride at his ability to love so freely after being hurt so many times as a child. Not that he didn't carry scars, but they pertained to his love life and trusting men with intimacy. When it came to empathy, sympathy, and acts of kindness, Reid had come through unscathed. He shined brighter than any star in the sky at caring for others.

There was nothing I wouldn't do to make his dreams come true. No man I wouldn't sleep with, no amount of coffee I wouldn't serve to homophobic assholes, no luxury I wouldn't forgo in order to save a dollar so that Reid could have his damn foster camp.

I would succeed or die trying.

CHAPTER 8
REID

Seated in Dr. Webber's office, I gazed out the window at the city skyline. His soft, soothing voice broke through my thoughts. "Reid, last week you described to me several instances of sexual contact that were initiated by other men. Can you tell me of an instance when you were the one to initiate sexual contact with another man?"

For a moment, I racked my brain, searching for a time in my life where I went out of my way to flirt with someone. *Nope, nothing*. I couldn't recall a single time I'd ever made a move on anyone. I wasn't sure how to feel about that, but I wasn't surprised.

"I've never consciously initiated sexual contact with anyone. I'm not entirely certain I've ever approached someone intending to flirt with them, either. I have never sought attention from another man."

As the reality of that hit me, I couldn't help but feel

lonely and isolated, like a man standing alone on an island. How have I gone twenty years without wanting to be touched by another person when I craved people's energy? Weird, considering I genuinely liked other people, and I often felt energized by making connections with them. Somehow, I was this weird mix of shy introvert and a people person. It was like I wanted them to draw me out of my shell.

"So, do you have any ideas why you think that might be?" Dr. Webber knew the answer he was seeking—he just wanted me to arrive at the conclusion on my own. That was how therapy worked.

"Because I'm afraid?" Sliding one shoe over the toe of the other, I avoided looking at him.

"Are you? It seems to me you have no problem befriending strangers and striking up a conversation. Do you find yourself afraid to approach people?"

Just look up. Look him in the eye. "Not really, no. I enjoy meeting new people and making friends."

"So why would it be different to seek sexual attention? If you trust someone you barely know enough to spend time alone with them and open up about who you are in a friendship, what would be different about kissing someone in that setting or flirting with them?"

Why in the heck was he asking me? If I had the answers, I wouldn't be here. "I guess if I felt safe with someone I considered a friend, I could, but I've never had the desire to. I honestly just don't feel attracted to people. I don't feel sexual desire when I look at an attractive person. Though, I would definitely feel safer if it was my choice to start contact rather than feeling blindsided by it, like I did at the club the other night."

Dr. Webber scribbled a note on his pad. "Good reasoning. Can you recall a time you have ever felt desire for someone? Or has it never happened before?"

My cheeks flamed under his scrutiny. I was no stranger to feeling sexual desire. My dick got hard several times a day, naturally. But I was being honest when I said I'd never experienced sexual desire for another person. *Besides Riley.* He didn't count because he was Riley, though I suspected Dr. Webber knew I was twisting the truth. Before I could even tell another lie, he cut to the chase.

"Tell me about that time. The one you're thinking about right now that you'd rather not talk about."

Damn, he was good! It was like he could see into my head. Reclining further into my chair, I sighed deeply and gathered my courage. Maybe it would feel freeing to finally admit this to someone, seeing as I never have before.

"The only person I have ever been attracted to is Riley. He has caused many of my erections and starred in most of my fantasies. Okay, all of them." Dr. Webber patiently waited for me to continue as he made notes on his pad. "But I've never initiated anything between us. I've never been kissed or touched in any way of my own free will."

He adjusted his thick frames higher up on his nose. "What do you think makes Riley different from other men that you find attractive but feel no desire for?"

Everything. Instead of meeting his eyes directly, I focused on the small potted plant sitting on his desk. "Uh, our history, maybe? I don't know. I feel safe with Riley. I trust him with my life. He knows all the parts, the good and the bad, and he likes me in spite of it all. Also, Riley is the best person I know. He's amazing—well—I think so. I'm attracted to every part of him, inside out."

Dr. Webber smiled knowingly at me. "There are a myriad of different sexual identities. Are you familiar with any of them?"

That question hit me out of left field, leaving me off-center. "Well, I know I'm gay. Without a doubt."

"Have you heard terms like asexual and demisexual? There are many variations of either of these words."

"Yes, I'm familiar with the terms." I wondered where he was going with it.

Dr. Webber set his pen down and steepled his fingers as he regarded me. "Reid, do you think you have any connection or similarities to either of those words? Does either one of them feel like a good fit for you, or even a partial fit?"

I turned the words around in my mind, trying to fit them like puzzle pieces into my identity. For the first time in my life, I considered being something other than just gay. "I wouldn't say I identify with asexuality because I definitely feel desire for someone, often. Like, a lot." Dr. Webber smiled and nodded for me to continue. "Demisexuality seems to describe a lot of what I feel. Or don't feel, in this case. It makes so much sense."

Dr. Webber smiled warmly. "Excellent. I would never

presume to label anyone in any way, but I think it makes so much sense for you because, friendships aside, you've never experienced the kind of bond with anyone that you have with Riley. From what you've told me, it goes deeper than most people experience with their partners. You and Riley live together, sleep together, rely on each other, confide in each other, and trust each other. You have what is called a non-sexual partnership. The fact that you wish that were different, that you experience sexual desire for Riley, tells me you want to have a complete relationship with him, but something is holding you back. We can discuss that later, but for now, I think it's safe to say that what sets Riley apart from your other friends is the reason you feel desire for him and not anyone else. You have a deep emotional connection with him, or he's just your soulmate. You're one and only. Your first and only true love."

A giggle escaped me because I felt giddy with hope and all my feelings for Riley were swirling around my head and heart, flooding me with endorphins. "I'm going to say it's both. But I'm curious to know, does it matter why I'm demisexual? I mean, was I born this way or is it because of my past trauma?"

Dr. Webber considered that for a moment. "I don't think it matters, Reid. What matters is *what* you are capable of feeling, not *why*. Your experiences may have shaped who you are or you may have ended up that way, regardless. What matters is, this is who you are, and I don't see that changing, nor does it have to."

My fingers curled into my jeans, gripping the denim

like a lifeline. Maybe I wasn't defective or broken after all. Maybe there was a valid reason I'd never been attracted to anyone but Riley. "I feel a hundred pounds lighter. Thank you so much for listening and understanding."

Dr. Webber returned my smile. "That's wonderful. Next week, we're going to address why you keep your feelings toward him bottled up. So enjoy your good mood while you can." He smirked, the first I'd ever seen from him, knowing I wasn't looking forward to our next session.

Riley was waiting for me in the parking lot. It was difficult to meet his eyes while feeling like I was keeping secrets from him now that I knew something he didn't. I'd always known that I was crazy about him, but admitting it out loud to Dr. Webber felt like a confession, like I was finally coming to terms with the idea.

I was in love with Riley Morgan, the only boy I'd ever been attracted to.

For some reason, I felt nervous, like a hundred butterflies were fluttering around inside my stomach. After six years of spending almost every moment together, suddenly I had no idea how to act around him. And the most unsettling part was Riley was going to figure out in a second something was wrong with me. No way would he let it drop—he would twist and tug until I spilled my secrets.

If that happened, I tried to imagine the worst-case scenario. What would Riley say if I finally admitted to him I was in love with him and had been hiding it for years? Would he be surprised? Disgusted? Did he already have some idea? If he didn't feel the same, it would cause an uneven balance in our relationship. Just like our washing machine, when one side was heavier than the other, the balance was out of alignment and the whole thing shook loudly until it shut down. An uneven distribution of weight would throw the whole cycle out of whack. Would that be what happened with Riley and me?

If I risked telling him how I felt, then I risked our relationship. I was not willing to gamble with Riley because I'd die if I lost him. I didn't know how to be me without him.

"How'd it go? You look upset. Did you have to discuss stuff that was hard for you?" His face was full of genuine concern. Nobody cared for me like he did.

"Nothing too upsetting, more like a revelation. Dr. Webber helped me realize that I'm probably demisexual. He said it doesn't matter if it's because of my past or if I was born this way, the result is still the same. Apparently, I'm only able to feel desire for men that I share a deep emotional connection with, that make me feel completely safe."

Riley was across the seat in a heartbeat, tugging me into his brawny arms, squeezing the breath from my body. "I knew this therapy stuff would be good for you. Look how far you've come in just two weeks. Demisexual, huh? You know I love you no matter what you are, right?"

Nodding, I swallowed down the lump of emotion

clogging my throat. It didn't matter to me I had no family, no close blood relations. I had Riley, and his love equaled that of ten people. I felt truly blessed.

"Although, it sucks since I'm the only person you have that kind of bond with. I guess that leaves you right back at square one—single as a Pringle."

Seriously? Ugh! He had to be the densest guy I knew. If I ever decided to tell him how I felt, I was going to have to draw him a map and connect the dots for him.

CHAPTER 9
RILEY

Another weekday, another behavioral studies class, and another shift at the Roasted Bean. As I ran the cleaning cycle on the espresso machine, I prayed to God to give me the strength not to cut Ryan's left hand off with a dull, rusty knife. The little snot rag was extra handsy today, touching Reid every chance he got.

Falsetto laughter rang out, piercing the relative quiet of the café. Its shrill sound grated on my last nerve and made me jump, causing me to drop the ceramic mug in my hand. Everyone clapped when the cup shattered.

"*Fucking Ryan*," I muttered under my breath. It shouldn't be surprising that he had the most off-putting laugh I'd ever heard. Matched his personality.

Never would I admit this to anybody, especially not Reid, but Ryan wasn't a bad guy. Annoying? Yes. Shallow, full of himself? Definitely. But from what I'd seen, he was a good friend to Reid. None of that frenemy, put you down so I can feel better about myself bullshit. I was still positive he had a crush on Reid, but the more I saw them together, the more convinced I was that Reid wasn't interested. As long as I felt secure that I was still Reid's number one person, I could put up with the little shit.

Reid and I didn't have friends growing up. We only had each other. There were no sleepovers, birthday parties, hanging out at the arcade after school with our best buddies. It was easier not to make friends who were just going to leave you. This was important to him—he needed this validation and acceptance, the inclusion. Reid was a social butterfly, and he bloomed under the attention of others. I had no such needs—I only needed Reid. Though I appreciated the friendships I'd made since starting college, I didn't need them like Reid did.

After I finished sweeping up the last shards of broken ceramic, Reid approached the counter. "Can I get another double shot macchiato for Ryan?"

My irritation mounted as I glared at him. "Does Ryan have legs? Or are you his official errand boy now?"

Fuck Ryan. He could take his ass down the street to Starbucks and get his own damn macchiato. Turning my back on Reid, I emptied the dustpan into the large industrial garbage can behind the counter.

Reid narrowed his eyes, his lips flattening into a straight line. "I wonder why he's hesitant to approach the counter himself," he added sarcastically.

Matching his expression, I donned the same skeptical look of disapproval. "Are you going to be on break the entire shift? Or do you plan on helping me out?"

Reid made a point of surveying the café. "We have three customers. Is that too much for you to handle?"

Not at all, I thought as I held a mug under the espresso machine, smelling the delicious steam that wafted into my face. *Watching Ryan flirt with you and touch your leg is too much for me to handle.* He was lucky I didn't scald his balls by dumping this steaming macchiato into his lap.

"Charlie texted me about Thanksgiving. We're still planning to join him for dinner, right?"

I handed Reid the mug, brushing my fingers against his as I transferred it to his grip. "Of course. Just like we do every year. I'm excited to tell him about my therapy. Don't forget, we have to choose a song for the Black Friday karaoke battle with the guys."

Ah, yes... the second annual Black Friday karaoke showdown. Last year, my roommates started a tradition on Black Friday. We made a buffet of Thanksgiving left-overs and paired off into groups for an epic karaoke battle. Cyan took the top prize, a bottle of Jameson and a week off kitchen cleanup. Reid and I gave it our best shot with our performance of '*Holding Out For a Hero*' by Bonnie Tyler. "Sure, think of a couple of songs, and we'll choose one tonight."

I couldn't care less about the damn karaoke. What mattered to me was teaming up with Reid and feeling like a partnership again. Reid returned to his study session with Ryan, and every time I heard his high-pitched tinkle of a laugh, my eyelid twitched. I had no customers to serve, and without the distraction of work, I hated that he commandeered my attention.

Screw it, if you can't beat them, join them. Except... I just thought of a way to do both. When I approached the table, I leaned over Reid's shoulder, getting right up in his personal space just to show Ryan I could.

Petty? Absolutely. "Hey, Reid, you think you can rub my back tonight? I pulled something when I was stocking those boxes earlier. I feel a twinge right here."

I pointed to a spot just above my waistband, about two inches from my asscrack. Reid placed his hand there, checking to see if I felt pain at his touch, and I cringed—well, fake cringed. There wasn't a damn thing wrong with my back, except that Reid's hands weren't all over it.

"Sure, Ry. After your shower tonight, I'll rub some muscle cream on it. Maybe you should take a pain reliever to hold you over until then. Do you need me to cancel my class?"

Cue the instant remorse. Reid was scheduled to take his first self-defense class as soon as we finished our shift. He was so excited to begin and here he was offering to cancel because of my fabricated back injury. He was so kind and selfless and just—Reid. I hated lying to him, but what was a guy to do when another guy wouldn't keep their damn hands off your man?

"No way. You are not canceling that class for my sake. I'll be just fine until we get home."

The door swung open and in walked Simon, a TA in

the engineering department that was also a client of mine. I'd been on two dates with Simon. The first time, I was his date to his ex-boyfriend's wedding. We had a great time in an awkward situation, dancing and laughing and pretending to be madly in love as we fed each other bites of cake. The second time was a week later. He called me back to tell me what a great time he had at the wedding and asked if he could take me to dinner. Dinner led to a tour of his apartment, where I topped him for two hours. That was last month, and I hadn't heard from him since, but maybe that was why he was here.

"Simon? How are you? You look great." I met him at the counter, and he pulled me into his arms for a hug.

"Not as good as you. Which is why I'm here, besides the coffee." He laughed, revealing his dimples. Simon was a good-looking guy. He had much the same body type as me, but where I was fair in hair and skin, he was darker—brown eyes, brown hair, and tan skin. "I was wondering if you're busy this weekend?"

His hungry eyes raked over my body, revealing his intentions for our date. It didn't do a thing for me. "I'm definitely available for you. Text me with the details." I filled his to-go cup with espresso, topped it with whipped cream and served it with a smile. "I look forward to hearing from you."

When he left, I noticed Reid and Ryan staring at me. They had probably listened in on our entire exchange, which made me slightly uncomfortable for different reasons. I didn't like to broadcast to anyone but my roommates what I did on the side for work. And I did not like the way Reid was looking at me, like he was hurt or upset. I was not supposed to be the guy that made him look like that. I was supposed to be the one who fixed it.

I was always careful to keep the details of escorting to myself. That wasn't something Reid and I ever talked about. But one of those details' names was Simon, and he'd just walked into our café. Apparently, Reid didn't like it shoved in his face. Not that I could blame him, seeing as I was having a hard time accepting his study buddy, Ryan.

As if my day wasn't already shifting downhill, a loud-mouthed pack of Alphas walked in. The antagonistic Sigma Rai fraternity loved to come into the café and stir up trouble, targeting Reid and I with their homophobic rhetoric. The university had always held a conservative reputation, probably because of the Dean of Students and the president of the largest fraternity on campus, the Alphas, being brothers and extremely anti-inclusive.

Their bigotry reigned supreme for far too long until last year when the faculty and students united, along with a considerable amount of support from the community, and held a large rally on campus. The Rainbow Rally said to all the haters, we were here, and we were queer, and if you didn't like it, find another school. Things had improved considerably since then, but Waltham University still had a long way to go before it could be considered an all-inclusive and safe campus. Another rally was being coordinated for after the Thanksgiving break, and I remained hopeful that things would continue to get better.

But today wasn't one of those days. Three of them walked inside. One stood guard at the door. The other two approached the counter, banging on it loudly with their fists to get my attention, like I didn't see their asses coming. "Hey, Laverne, where's Shirley? It's time to get to work in the kitchen and make your man some coffee." They snickered at their humor. "Wait, we're missing one. Shirley! Come give me some sugar, baby."

I swear to God I was going to kill this fucker in a second. With my bare hands. He craned his neck over my shoulder, looking for Reid. His friend spotted him and Ryan sitting at the table.

"There are a couple of pretty ladies sitting right over there. Is that your girl?" I recognized the loudest mouth from the club the night he hit on Reid. The other two I'd seen in here before causing trouble.

The loudmouth made his way over to Reid, who ducked his head in his lap, probably hoping to disappear. This was the kind of shit that caused Reid to have panic attacks. I tried to follow him, but his friend blocked me, getting right up in my face. "Try me, motherfucker," I threatened.

Standing behind Reid, he laid his hand on Reid's shoulder. Reid shrugged it off, shoulders going rigid. "Did you miss me, pretty baby? I should stop in more often to say hi. Who's your sweet friend? Are we having a threesome?"

I couldn't let this continue, even if it meant fighting with this douchebag who was still in my face. Palming my phone, I punched out a text message. "I alerted campus security, and they're on their way. Better leave now, boys."

The two guys nearest me split, walking out the door as they called to their friend. Bigmouth watched them leave, then bent down to Reid's level, getting right up in his face.

"I guess you'll have to save me a dance, sugar. Don't think I don't recognize you from the club. Say one word about me and it will be the last time you use that pretty mouth for anything, whether it be to suck a dick or tell a lie about me." With one last warning look aimed at Reid, he took off, running toward the student parking lot.

"Reid!" I ran to him, hugging him tight. With his gaze fixed on his lap, he wouldn't even meet my eyes. "It's gonna be okay. They're gone now." God, I was so angry. The fear of losing our scholarships made me feel powerless to defend him. "Fucking bastards!" When I gripped his chin to urge him to look at me, Reid startled in my arms, and tears streamed down his face.

"Stop yelling. You're scaring him worse," Ryan admonished, making me scowl. He chose now to prove he had a set of balls?

"Reid, sweetheart, I'm sorry. Listen to me, I'm going to lock the doors and clean up. Give me fifteen minutes and we'll leave. Can you sit with Ryan for a few more minutes if I lock the doors?"

Reid didn't answer, but Ryan shooed me away. "Just go, hurry up. I've got him."

My lips brushed his cheek, wet from his tears, and I

squeezed him tight. "I'll be right back. You're going to be fine."

"Right back, Reid," I reiterated as I ran to the back of the café. After making quick work of locking up the till and totaling receipts, I forwent cleaning up. I grabbed my backpack and ran back to the dining area.

Ryan was packing Reid's book bag as he continued to sit woodenly, staring at nothing. Scooping him up, I wrapped my arm around his narrow waist and gently hauled him to our car. "Thanks, Ryan."

He handed me Reid's book bag. "I'll text him later to see how he's doing."

Alone together in the car, Reid's tears came harder. "I hate myself."

He looked so broken and miserable with his arms folded across his chest. He was sinking into a pit of self-hatred, one I knew all too well. "No, Bunny. Don't say that." I pulled him into my arms, letting him sob into my chest.

"I'm a c-coward." He sniffled, wiping his eyes on his sleeve. "I'm weak! I couldn't even speak. I was so angry I wanted to hit him, but I felt frozen again. I thought I was getting b-better." He hiccuped into my shirt, leaving a snotty trail of mucus across my pec. I didn't care. All that mattered was Reid. I refused to let him fall into despair.

"Reid, sweetheart, you just started therapy. It's going to take a while before you can face a situation like this and not hate your reaction. Please don't beat yourself up. I wanted to take you home, but I think instead, I'll take you to that class. You really need it. Let's get you calm and cleaned up, okay?"

He nodded and sat up, staring out the window. He was in his head again. "I'm here, Reid. I'm always going to be here. You aren't alone. If that guy had approached you anywhere but on campus, he'd be waiting for an ambulance right now."

I hated that Reid felt like an easy target at school because we didn't want to jeopardize our scholarships by fighting. Most of the guys in that fraternity were well connected, whereas Reid and I were nobodies, just lucky to be here on the good grace of the Fostering Knowledge Foundation who provided our tuition.

When we arrived at the rec center, Reid went ahead while I stayed behind in the car. Palming my phone, I placed a call to campus security and filed a report, stating what happened in the café. After what seemed like an empty promise to look into it, I left a message on Dr. Webber's voicemail briefly explaining that Reid had been threatened and asking if he could fit Reid in again this week for another session. It was intrusive of me, but I'd always taken care of Reid like that. In my opinion, he needed to keep talking about what happened, so he didn't backpedal and pull his little turtle-in-the-shell routine.

I'd be damned if Reid was going to erase his hard-earned progress because that asshole was afraid of his own sexuality.

CHAPTER 10

REID

Exhaustion hit me hard, both emotionally and physically, robbing my energy and focus. First, the ordeal in the café and then the self-defense class. We didn't learn much, it only being the first class, but I loved being there. It felt empowering. Of course, Riley knew what I needed, choosing not to let me skip. He was struggling the same as I was. Whenever I had a bad day, or as he called it, went turtle on him, he blamed himself. I hated to see him struggle with his guilt. None of this was his fault.

There were a million things I wanted to say to him as we lay in the dark in our bed. This was the safest I'd felt all day. The lack of light provided a false sense of security. He couldn't see my face or look into my eyes, but I knew he could feel my heart and hear my thoughts.

His next words confirmed that. "Can I touch you? I feel like I need to bridge the gap between us because you feel a million miles away from me."

I reached for his hand and he grabbed onto it like a lifeline. He was drowning, and he needed me to anchor him. At the same time, I felt lost, like I was floating away from my body as it was weighed down to the bed with all my fears and anxieties. My mind just wanted to drift, to get away from it all and be free. Leave it all behind. I could start over, like in my 'what if' game. I could choose any one of those fantasies and make them a reality and be a whole different person, a different Reid, who wasn't afraid. Who could defend himself as a strong independent man that didn't have to rely on his other half to get through each day.

The only problem was, none of those imaginary lives were worth living without Riley by my side.

"Do you blame me?" Riley whispered so softly I could barely make out his words.

"Don't say stupid things. You know it's not your fault."

"I do. I blame myself." His thumb rubbed circles over the back of my hand.

"Just like I hate myself? We aren't to blame. You have to let this go."

He toyed with my hand, stroking each finger from base to tip before moving on to the next. It was oddly both soothing and erotic.

"Before everything happened, that guy that came in, was he a client?" Even with all that had happened since to distract me, curiosity was burning a hole through my mind.

"Yes." Riley's hand stilled.

"Have you slept with him?"

Normally, I never asked private questions or details about his clients. It wasn't my business, and I didn't want to know, but I'd also never seen their faces before or watched as they flirted with Riley right in front of my eyes. That was an unfamiliar experience, and I didn't like it, not one bit. It caused me to feel insecure and insignificant, and although it was absolutely absurd, it made me question my place in his life.

Not to mention the raging jealousy.

"There's no way I'm discussing this with you, Reid. It's inconsequential and makes no difference, so drop it." He tried to pull his hand away, but I tugged it back.

"I could never be that. I can't ever give you what he can."

Sometimes, we skirted the parameters of our relationship like this, calling out the inevitable truths without recognizing that we were actually talking about being a couple someday. We could discuss it hypothetically while leaving it to remain unspoken.

"What? Why would you even say that? Why would you want to be him?"

"He was a good-looking guy, Riley. Built, strong, and brave like you. Does he work at the University? He probably has a good job. Does he have his own place? I'm sure you've seen it. Is it nice? He probably doesn't suffer from panic attacks like I do. I bet he could lift a tire and I can't even lift a TV. I'm a skinny nothing of a mess and that guy has everything going for him. You need a guy like that, Riley. That's what you deserve. I'll never be that. I'm holding you back. I'm nothing but dead weight tied to your ankle." My eyes watered and I squeezed them shut to hold the tears inside.

Riley rolled toward me and propped up on one elbow, leaning over my body so he could see my face in the darkness. "You're assuming I'm attracted to that, but I'm not."

His warm breath ghosted over my lips and I parted them to inhale his breath, swallowing him into my lungs. My eyes popped open. "Really? I am. How can you not be attracted to that guy?" I was probably attracted to him because he reminded me of Riley.

"He's just not my type. Doesn't do it for me. I'll tell you another thing—I'm tired of hearing you talk down about yourself. It's okay to have a bad day once in a while, but the next time you call yourself a mess or nothing, just remember how far we've come. And you can remind yourself that you can't be *nothing* because you're my *everything*. Without you, I'd be nothing. Do you understand what I'm telling you?"

Smiling, I teased, "That you have horrible taste in men? Yes."

In lieu of the kiss that I craved, Riley ground his chin against mine, a completely brotherly move. "You say potato, I say patato. To each his own."

After a beat of silence, I asked, "So what's your type then?"

"Good night, Reid. Sweet dreams." He rolled over,

presenting his back to me. Moments later, his soft snores lulled me to sleep.

~

When I woke up, the first thing that occurred to me was that I never gave Riley his back rub. He was still asleep, so I straddled his hips as he lay flat on his stomach and kneaded the area he'd told me was sore. Light at first and then with more pressure, drawing tiny moans of appreciation from him as he slept. His skin was smooth and silky, stretched taut over well-defined muscle. It was hard not to appreciate the view spread out before me.

He stirred, half dreaming—half awake as I rubbed lower down his back. When he tensed as I tugged his pants lower, I knew he was fully awake. The more I rubbed, the more he squirmed under my hands. Either he made a miraculous recovery from the day before or he had been lying about his injury because the only thing affecting Riley right now was the hard-on he was trying to hide from me. I was glad for his discomfort as he tried to find relief from my wandering hands without rubbing himself into the sheets. He was stuck at an awkward angle, trying to get away from me and get away from the mattress beneath him without embarrassing himself.

Deciding to test his limits, my finger lightly traced down the top inch of his exposed crease, pretending like I was going to continue to draw his pants further down by tugging lightly on the cotton fabric. That did the trick as Riley muffled his laugh into his pillow, throwing me off by bucking his hips. I landed slightly off-balance by his side as he turned to peek at me.

"You weren't really going to take them off, were you?"

My eyebrow hitched in challenge. "That depends. Were you really injured? Some back injuries are connected all the way down the gluteus maximus, and massage is a key technique for relief."

Riley looked at me with an expression that said 'be serious.' "Of course I was really injured, but I'm feeling better now. No need to massage my gluteus maximus."

"Careful, Riley Morgan, when you lie, your nose grows, among other things." Reaching for his hips, I tried to roll him over to expose the other things about him that had grown, but he wouldn't let me budge him.

Riley jumped out of bed. "Okay, I lied!" he cried out as he ran to the bathroom.

As he ran, he cupped his erection with his hands to hide it from my view. Flinging myself into the warm spot he vacated, I buried my face into his pillow, kicking my legs victoriously. His musky scent filled my nose as I celebrated my small victory.

I was still lounging in bed when Riley came out of the bathroom with a towel wrapped around his hips. He was a sight to behold. Pure sex appeal. Shamelessly, I eyed him as he dressed with his back to me.

"So, I narrowed down our song choices for karaoke on Friday."

"No need. I've given it a lot of thought and come up with the perfect song."

He glanced over his shoulder and the teasing glint in his eyes convinced me I was being set up. But I was bowled over by his unprecedented attention and focus on our project, a very un-Riley-like thing. "What did you pick?"

He pulled his shirt over his head and came to join me, sitting on the edge of the bed. "Last year we sang Hero. So, I thought this year we could sing 'Little Bunny Foo Foo'. That way, we're both represented equally." He placed a kiss on my forehead as I spluttered and was quick to dodge the pillow I aimed at his head.

"Be serious! While entertaining, it's hardly a winning song choice."

"I don't know about that. Picturing you dressed up in bunny ears and a cottontail is very convincing. You definitely have my vote."

He tried tickling me and pinching the spot above my butt where my cottontail would be if I were a rabbit. I dissolved into a fit of giggles, twisting and turning to get away from his hands when a knock sounded on our door.

"Quit snogging and hurry the fuck up! Last day of class and you're driving. I don't want to be late." Murphy needed to work on his charm.

"Snogging? Where does he come up with these words?" Riley tore out of our room and set after Murphy.

By the time I made it down for coffee, I found Murphy in a headlock receiving a super noogie as Riley made fake kissing noises and threatened to lick his face. These were the kind of antics I'd missed when my roommates moved out. The teasing and constant laughter and banter between friends that filled up all the silence in our empty home. This was family.

Three days later, we spent Thanksgiving with Charlie, gathered around the dining table in his small suburban home. This was our fourth year of celebrating with him. He had no other family, no spouse, no children, just us. Charlie always said we were his boys, not his sons or his nephews or his friends, just his boys, and he was our Charlie. He didn't try to be a father or an uncle or anything he wasn't. He was just a friend, a confidant, a role model, and someone we could trust. He always came through for us and never let us down. Charlie Morgan had earned our trust and respect long ago, and he honored us by sharing his last name with us.

"Reid, I made those candied yams just for you, so eat up," Charlie said. Riley doubled my helping when I took only a small spoonful of the sweet potatoes. "Tell me about school. I haven't heard two words about your classes this semester."

We filled him in on our course load and our shifts at the café. He asked us about our volunteer work at the youth center, Over the Rainbow, and I told him about my new friends. When Riley nudged my leg under the table, I knew it was time to come clean about therapy. Charlie was over the moon happy for me. He had nothing but encouraging and supporting things to say about my progress. When Riley told him I had started a self-defense course, his eyebrows nearly hit his hairline.

Charlie forked mashed potatoes into his mouth. "Reid, you are just full of surprises today. I'm so happy you are thriving."

The look Riley shared with me said everything. In his eyes, I could see that he was not only proud of me but impressed with my progress. And underneath that, underlying everything spoken and unspoken, I saw the familiar look that said he loved me, that he would always stand by me. That we were forever.

Charlie continued, unaware of the current passing between Riley and me. "I just want you both to know that everything you will ever want or need is within your reach. Your dreams and goals, your future plans, and most importantly, the love you seek. It is within your grasp, both literally and figuratively. Reid, hold out your hand." Obediently, I extended my hand towards Riley, who was sitting closest to me. "Riley, hold out your hand as well." He reached for my outstretched hand, and I clutched it tightly. "Everything you seek, everything you need to survive and succeed, is within arm's reach. Don't ever let go of each other."

My eyes stung with unshed tears. Charlie was so smart, so intuitive. He was none-to-gently pointing out that Riley and I needed each other to thrive, which we did. I was sure it would be Charlie's greatest dream to see his boys end up together, happy and united. Heck, it was my greatest dream, too. But I couldn't write Riley's future for him. He would have to make his own choices about love and life. I could wish on every candle I blew out and every shooting star in the sky, but ultimately, it was Riley's choice. But when I chanced a look at his eyes, he didn't seem to be fighting it. Whether for Charlie's sake or to spare my feelings, I wasn't sure, but it was something, and it was a positive sign.

CHAPTER 11
RILEY

I hadn't meant to be so transparent, but in a moment of weakness, I let my guard down and Reid saw everything in my heart written across my face.

And the world didn't end.

It was still spinning on its axis, and the stars were still aligned, and life was carrying on around us, even though the awkward tension in the car was so thick I could cut it with a knife. Knowing Reid, he wanted to talk about it, but he couldn't bring himself to voice his questions out loud. I hoped he didn't. This was one time I prayed Reid wasn't brave, that he caved to his insecurities, because I couldn't discuss my feelings for him right now. They were too close to the surface and I'd spill my secrets like a perp under pressure.

Maintaining the status quo had worked for six years and it would continue to work. As long as I stuffed my feelings down deep, everything would be alright. "Let's go to bed when we get home. I'm exhausted and stuffed full."

"It's the turkey. It has a chemical that makes you sleepy." Of course Reid knows that, he loved to read. "Ry? You know I'm grateful for you, right?"

Glancing across the console, I saw Reid shyly peeking at me. "Yeah, Bunny. I'm grateful for you, too. Happy Thanksgiving."

When we were tucked into bed, Reid curled into my side and wrapped his arm around my waist, clutching me like he does his stuffed bunny. I ran my fingers through his silky hair, lightly scratching his scalp as he drifted off to sleep in my arms.

My chest expanded, unable to contain all the love I felt for him. A sense of rightness and peace washed over me like a wave. This right here, this was what made everything worthwhile. Holding the boy I loved, keeping him safe and showing him with my actions instead of words how cherished he was, how loved. I didn't need to make love to him to prove that. Words weren't necessary, as long as I could make him feel treasured as he fell asleep. If I continued to show him how perfect he was every day, I was doing my job. I only prayed this was enough for him.

~

"Alright, who's got a quarter for the coin toss?" Lucky scanned the group assembled in the living room. Griffin offered up a quarter.

We spread the leftovers out buffet-style in the dining room, the coffee table held shot glasses and whiskey, and everyone gathered on the L-shaped couch, waiting for the karaoke battle to begin. Like last year, Hudson acted as our impartial judge.

Lucky flipped the coin into the air and called heads as it arced. He caught it and declared himself the winner. "Heads it is. Come on, Professor, we're up first."

They queued up the karaoke machine and sang '*Don't Stop Believing*' by Journey. It was a brilliant performance, and they didn't suck. Of course, Lucky was a great showman. He had loads of charisma, but Hayes had the better singing voice. We all clapped for their effort and took a round of shots.

After another coin toss, Cyan and Griffin were up. They stole a brief timeout to prepare their costumes and came downstairs to the beat of '*You're The One That I Want*' from Grease. The kicker? Cyan dressed like Sandy, blonde wig, black spandex and all. He even had the platform heels. He was a smoking hot Olivia Newton John, I'd give him that. Griffin dressed as John Travolta in head to toe black, looking like a jock greaser with his gelled curls and shiny wingtip shoes. The choreography was spot on, and their voices sounded great. They were going to be hard to beat, for sure.

Reid and I were up next. I let him pick the song, and he kept with our Footloose theme from last year by choosing '*Let's Hear It For The Boy*' by Deniece Williams. I pretty much stood still while Reid danced around me, pretending I was *the boy* he wanted to give a shout out to. He sang how I watched every dime as he stuck his hands in my pockets and turned them inside out to show how empty they were. When we got to the chorus, I lifted him up by his waist and spun him around, adding a touch of flair to our routine. It was cheesy as fuck, but I thought it was really sweet of Reid to sing my praises. He always made me out to be some overachieving superhero when I felt like anything but.

It probably wasn't the winning performance, but it had loads of heart. As we waited for Murphy to ready himself for the final act, Reid cozied up to me on the couch, smelling like fresh laundry. His soft lips ghosted over the shell of my ear, sending tiny shivers down my neck.

"I don't care if we win or not, I'm just glad we have this family to be a part of. I'm grateful this is our life now." He kissed my cheek, and like a moron, I blushed crimson.

Fucking Reid and his pure heart. The only time I ever felt close to being the superhero he thought me to be was when I realized I was doing my job by making him feel blessed to live the life we ended up with. It sure as hell was a long way from where we started out.

I wasn't sure what to expect from Murphy, as this was his first year taking part in the karaoke showdown, but I was wrong to doubt him. To everyone's surprise, he strutted down the staircase looking like the ultimate sugar baby to Madonna's *'Material Girl'*. Murphy had donned Cyan's blonde wig and was dolled up just like Madonna circa 1980s, wearing a hot pink satin dress and a rhinestone necklace. It had to be some prom dress castoff from a second-hand store, but he pulled it off perfectly with his pale skin and petite frame. Personally, I thought Murphy made one hot chick.

Murphy sashayed around the living room in his black satin heels, paying special attention to the judge who sat shell-shocked, eyes and mouth wide open. Poor Hudson, he wasn't sure what to make of his nemesis, the constant thorn in his side. I couldn't blame him. The gender swap looked authentic and was confusing as hell. When the song ended, Murphy spun in a circle and landed in Hudson's lap, playing up the part of the love-starved sex kitten to perfection. Hudson blushed furiously, looking completely uncomfortable. He scooted away from Murphy with haste and stood, brushing out his pants as he fought to regain his composure.

"Who won? Tally up the scores, Hudson!" Lucky shouted, clearly excited.

"No need. I'm the reigning champ and always will be." Cyan smirked, feeling confident.

"I don't know, Sandra Dee. It looks like Madonna gave you a run for your money," Hayes taunted.

"Why do you have to wear a wig if you want a chance at winning?" Griffin held his hands up, confused.

The comments went on and on, volleyed back and forth between Cyan, Griffin, Hayes, and Lucky. Finally, Hudson cleared his throat and held out the prize, a plastic microphone spray painted gold, probably from a kid's toy at the thrift store.

"As much as it pains me to say it, the winner is Murphy. Also, I'm weirdly turned on by his wardrobe choice, but not confused. I know underneath that wig and pretty dress lies a dirty little leprechaun." He handed over the trophy, and we clapped loudly for Murphy, who executed a perfect bow, making his wig fall off.

It was comical and absurd, and we all dissolved into laughter as Griffin and Murphy took turns singing lewd lyrics into the plastic gold mic. Lucky poured another round of shots, and we toasted our friendship. It was the perfect end to a holiday centered around family and friends.

My phone chimed, and I retrieved it to find a message from Lucky. He met my eyes over the crowd, giving me a knowing look. The text was information for a date tonight, my hookup with Simon, the teaching assistant I ran into at the café. I nodded at Lucky, letting him know I was accepting the client, and headed upstairs to shower and get dressed. Dread settled over me like a weighted blanket, smothering the joy I felt just minutes ago. There was nothing I wanted more than to crawl into bed with Reid and tangle my legs up with his.

Reid walked into our bedroom as I slipped into my shoes. "Going out? It's kind of late, isn't it?"

Sighing, I tried to school my face to keep the disappointment from showing. "I have to meet a client. I'll probably be back late. No need to wait up. I believe

Murphy is staying home, but if he doesn't and you're bothered by being alone, I can ask Griffin and Cy to stay."

Reid stayed quiet, and I waited for him to figure out what he needed to say. After a minute, he sat next to me on the bed, his fingers toying with the gray blanket. "I don't need a babysitter. I'll be fine on my own."

He was holding back, but I didn't push him, half afraid of what would come out of his mouth if I did. Leaning in, I pressed my lips to his cheek, leaving a soft reminder of my love behind.

Reid's fingers traced over the spot my lips had just touched, as if trying to keep the kiss from fading. "Ry? Tonight was a good night. I wouldn't change anything about our lives. When I picked that song, I was thanking you for everything you do and saying loudly, I wouldn't change a thing about you."

His words moved through me, snagging my heartstrings and leaving me speechless. That was the second time today his beautiful heart caused me to choke up. There was no doubt I had to be the luckiest guy in the world, and here I was leaving him to go dick some guy I couldn't care less about. I felt possessive of Reid and our time together, of this moment that I didn't want to end but was afraid to let unfurl. Only one thought slid through my head as I gazed down at him sitting on our bed, looking so vulnerable and genuine.

Fuck my date, fuck my fears and my denial. If I let this moment slip away without turning it into a memory, I'd regret it forever.

Stroking my fingers along his jaw, I tipped his chin

up to meet my eyes. "Do you want to know the song I would have chosen for us?"

Reaching into my back pocket, I palmed my phone, pulling up the song on my music streaming app, then tossed the phone on the bed as I pulled Reid into my arms. He came willingly, and I held him close as he laid his head on my shoulder. My arms came around his waist and his back, keeping his body as close to mine as I could get him. His heat seeped through my shirt as we danced together. Our bodies swayed to the sound of Bryan Adams singing '*Everything I Do, I Do It For You*'. Keeping my voice down to a whisper, I sang the words softly in his ear as we moved together, and when the song ended, Reid looked up at me with tears pooled in his pretty blue eyes.

Scooping him off his feet, I laid him on the bed. My lips brushed over his forehead. Our eyes met and held a moment too long, and it turned from tender to heated in an instant as desire and anticipation pooled in my gut. Reid closed his eyes, forcing the tears to roll down his cheeks. I brushed them away and pressed the softest, chaste kiss to his lips. With a whimper, Reid chased my lips for more, but I pulled away and stood. My goal was only to show him how much I cherished him, not to start something I couldn't finish.

"You are the center of my world, Reid Morgan. Everything I do, I do for you, and everything I am is because you make me a better person. You are the key to my happiness. You are my past, my present, and my future." My thumbs swiped away the wet trails of tears that tracked down his beautiful face. "You are the most beautiful person I've ever met, and if I try for the rest of my life, I'll still never deserve you." I brushed his hair from his forehead and kissed his brow again before walking out.

As I shut the door behind me, I was shadowed by Cyan, who followed me downstairs. Couldn't get a moment of privacy in this house, and these people didn't even live here any longer!

"Why can't you tell Reid you're in love with him?" He dogged my heels with no intention of letting me get away.

Obviously, he wasn't mincing words—he aimed straight for my jugular, but I could be just as straightforward. "Because if I fuck up, I lose him and then we have nothing, not even what we have now. I just can't risk that."

Cyan paused. His handsome face tightened as he considered my words. "That's a valid point, but it's horseshit. There is no way you can fuck this up. Actually, there's a million ways you can fuck it up, and I'm pretty sure you'll nail every one of them, but it doesn't matter because no matter how many times we fall short of our own expectations, all that matters is that we tried. To the people who love us, usually that's all they want is to see us try. We don't always have to get it right—nobody is that perfect."

I scoffed, shaking my head. "Reid is that perfect."

Cyan laid his hand on my shoulder. "And that's why you love him, so go tell him. Because he deserves to be loved, and you are the only sad sack he'll let do it."

I shrugged his hand off and stepped back, putting some distance between us. "What part of this situation don't you see clearly? I'm on my way to go see a client. We're going to fuck for hours. I do this several times a week, with different people, and you want to paint me as some romantic hero. What about *that* does Reid deserve? Because, in my opinion, he deserves so much more."

Cyan shook his head, disgusted. "Your whole entire reason for existing is Reid, and his sole focus in life is you. You two have the most selfless, meaningful love I've ever seen. It's beautiful to watch—*gut-wrenching*. Someday, you two are going to find a way to come together, and when you do, it's going to be magic. It's the stuff fairytales are made of. The kind of thing they write books about. That star-crossed, written in the stars kind of love. *Once in a lifetime.* You're going to grow old with that man by your side, so stop wasting time and make it happen."

Fuck him! Everything he said was my dream. But it wasn't as easy as he made it seem. He didn't get to come dangle a carrot in front of my face, making me second-guess everything.

"Stop following me around with your unsolicited advice and fuck off, Cy. Just because you found your happy ending doesn't mean we all get one. My happy ending is giving Reid his fucking camp for foster kids, buying him a house someday, and making sure he realizes his potential. If I can achieve that, I'll be happy, *fucking ecstatic.* And so will he. We don't need more than that. Not every fairytale looks the same. And *do not* mention a word of this to Reid!"

A long time ago, I made peace with the fact that Reid and I would never be more than this. Because what we had now was better than not having anything at all.

CHAPTER 12
REID

Riley stared at Murphy like he had grown two heads. "I can't believe you're wearing that shirt to visit your aunt Sadie. I can imagine how her gossipy friends are going to react." Riley eyed Murphy's T-shirt which said, *Sounds Gay, I'm In*.

Murphy laughed it off. "Wait until you see what Griffin is wearing. The shirt I picked for him is even better. Also, my aunt's knitting circle made all of us rainbow beanies to wear, so put it on and smile, Riley. Don't piss my aunt off or I'll make you sorry."

The three of us were in Riley's car on our way to visit Lucky and Murphy's beloved aunt at the rehab facility where she lived. We visited most weekends. Aunt Sadie was like the grandma I didn't have—she lovingly adopted us all. She had a special fondness for me most of all, always saving the snacks she won at bingo to feed me, thinking I needed to gain weight. I would never mention this to anyone, but her unconditional acceptance of me and her warm hugs meant more to me than anything else—except Riley, of course. It replaced something inside of me that had been missing for a long time.

After visiting her at A New Day Nursing and Rehab, we were going to meet up with our friends at the Rainbow Rally. It was becoming an annual event put on by the faculty of Waltham University to spread the message about sexual and gender equality.

It did not surprise me to find Lucky and Hayes also visiting when we arrived. They were already seated outside in the gazebo by the pond, Sadie's favorite spot. As soon as she saw me, she opened her frail arms wide, inviting me into her warm and loving embrace.

"Aunt Sadie, tell us about your new roommate. Is she nice?"

"She snores like a freight train and steals my tissues, but she's a nice girl and she always saves me a place at bingo when I arrive late. Tell me about this new class you're taking, Reid. Are you learning how to defend yourself? Any good moves you can teach me?"

I laughed and patted her bony knee. "I don't think you're ready to learn my moves just yet, but I'd be happy to demonstrate them on Murphy."

"That sounds like it would be highly entertaining," Lucky quipped.

"You boys play nice," she admonished.

Aunt Sadie passed out our beanies, which I thought looked great, and reminded us to prune her azaleas. We lived in her Cape Cod style house in Cooper's Cove, looking after the place for her while she chose to stay at the rehab center. I remember the first day I pulled up to the house, when Riley and I moved in, filled with nervous anticipation, and the first thing I noticed were her prized azaleas and rose bushes standing proudly among the manicured beds. The wide porch with its wooden rocking chairs and the shuttered windows made her home feel warm and welcoming, just like her. It was the first time I've ever felt truly at home in a place I've lived in.

"The gardening is my job. I love getting my hands in the dirt. It's therapeutic and satisfying. Your azaleas have doubled in size since you last saw them. I promise to take good care of them for you."

Aunt Sadie clasped my hands. "My sweet boy, promise me you'll take care of yourself and come back to see me soon. Do you know what they say about friends? A good friend is like a four-leaf clover, hard to find and lucky to have."

She passed out hugs and kisses, lingering just a little bit longer with me, and we left her to head to campus. Visiting her never failed to buoy my spirits. Aunt Sadie made me feel loved. Kind of like my grandma had when she was alive. The others often teased me, but I didn't mind one minute of her doting affection.

When we arrived at the university, the parking lot was overcrowded and roped off, and campus security guards were directing traffic to municipal parking lots nearby. It was apparent the rally had doubled in size since last year. We parked several blocks away and walked to the courtyard commons in the center of campus to meet up with our friends. News vans and camera crews were covering the event as well as other colleges and schools, local businesses, families, students and faculty, and just anyone and everyone who was here to support us.

It was an amazing feeling to see so much positive energy after being targeted by so much hate recently. When you were living day to day under the microscope of public opinion and small-minded people, it was easy to feel alone and segregated. Being surrounded by such an awesome display of acceptance and support made me feel free to be me, strong and empowered.

Of course, there were plenty of people wearing red hats and holding protest signs with ugly slurs. They booed us and yelled nasty things as we marched by. It was nothing I hadn't expected to encounter, but it raised goosebumps on my skin to come face to face with such blatant and baseless hate. I couldn't imagine why they even cared who I was or who I was attracted to. How did it affect their life in any way? It was fear and prejudice in its rawest form.

The Alpha Sigma Rai fraternity was front and center, leading the charge *against* equality, and as I passed by a group of them, one stuck their foot out directly in my path and tripped me, smirking when I stumbled. Riley caught me and helped to steady me. Several feet away, another one spit on me as I walked by.

"Oh, look, it's your girlfriend from the café!"

I raised my head high and looked straight ahead, choosing to rise above such petty insults. But tears threatened behind my eyes. It wasn't personal—I mean, it was, but it wasn't. They didn't know me individually. They didn't know I was a good person with an enormous heart, that I would help anybody in need, give anything I had to make someone else's life easier. All they knew was that I represented something they didn't like or didn't understand, and that scared them.

If everyone looked upon each other through my eyes, our world would be a much kinder place.

"Reid! Hey!"

When I heard my name being shouted, I raised my head over the crowd to see Maya, Colton, and a few other kids from the youth center carrying signs, waving me down madly. We invited them to join us as we marched. My heart swelled with pride to see these kids team up to show their support. It couldn't be easy for insecure and impressionable teens to expose themselves to so much judgement.

We walked for hours, only stopping when the sky darkened. Murphy and another escort, Adam, had an after party to attend for Lucky Match. Riley declined, claiming he was exhausted, and I wondered if it had anything to do with the fact that he hadn't come home last night until after three o'clock. Three twenty-one, to be exact. I know because I stayed up watching the clock until I heard his key in the door.

Earlier, I'd seen Riley's friend from the café, Simon. From the way they looked at each other, I could tell he was more than likely Riley's client last night. It wasn't hard to put two and two together. Jealousy burned through my veins like wildfire—it was an ugly feeling that spread through me like a disease. I didn't experience it often, and it didn't sit well with me now.

It angered me thinking Simon had touched *my* Riley, maybe even brought him pleasure. Or that Riley touched Simon in a way I dreamed of him touching me. I wanted to be the only one—his one and only. I hated to imagine that they shared something intimate, that Riley looked into his eyes intently, the way he looked at me sometimes. Everything that Riley and I shared, I wanted it to be all for us, only us. It was not enough that we dreamed together and planned our future and slept together every night. I wanted *everything* he had to give, and I wanted to be the *only* man he gave it to.

In a perfect world, I would be the only man that turned his head. Because Riley Morgan is definitely the only man that turned mine.

Knowing he'd given away a part of himself that I craved and had never received left me feeling empty. And lonely. Maybe even slightly disillusioned. I was the guy he loved, but I would never be the man he was in love with. I knew without a doubt that Riley was the only man I would ever love. The imbalance was so unfair.

Riley and I drove home in silence. There was so much on my mind I was trying to process. The feelings that surfaced during the rally that left me feeling low and unaccepted, coupled with the unconditional love I'd received from Aunt Sadie. And the jealousy I felt over Riley and Simon. It wasn't even about Simon. If I was being honest, it was about all of Riley's clients, his escorting in general. It wasn't even fair for me to complain about it because I didn't have a claim on Riley, and moreover, he only did it to support us. What could I possibly say? I'd rather be broke than share you with other men? It sounded utterly ridiculous considering we were not dating.

Familiar feelings of inadequacy and worthlessness crept through my mind, crawling over my skin with cold fingers, and I felt myself clamming up and retreating into my turtle shell again, something I promised myself I would try to quit doing. But it was safe inside there, and quiet. It was easier to cope with the outside world when I wasn't *in* the outside world, at least not mentally. My body was physically there, but my mind was adrift.

Of course, Riley noticed. He placed his hand on my knee, squeezing gently. "Reid, come back to me. I can sense I'm losing you to your thoughts."

He knew me so well, if only he could see inside my heart and know what I feel for him. All I could do was reach out for his hand as I continued to stare out the window as we drove over the bridge. It was the only connection I could make as my mind continued to bury itself under layers of feelings and fears, thoughts and emotions.

Two steps forward, one step back. That was the speed of my progress. Baby steps.

~

Two days later, we were back in class, sitting through a lecture on microorganisms. I had plans to stop by Griffin's bookstore, *Fairy*tales, after school today and was eager to be finished with classes so I could sit and drink coffee with my best friend and catch up. My time with him usually left me feeling lighthearted and grounded—exactly what I needed today.

Riley dropped me off at the bookstore and said he was going to run errands while I visited before coming back to pick me up and take me home. Our house in Cooper's Cove was a good thirty-minute drive from the bookstore, and I didn't want Griffin to have to go out of his way for me. The smell that enveloped me as soon as I walked through the door—old leather and coffee—felt comfortable and familiar. This bookstore was a place I'd come to think of as my second home. Griffin joined me at the bakery counter where we munched on cookies and lattes while trading gossip.

"So, Ryan wants me to join a new club he found, the Manga Maniacs. It's for comic geeks like us, and I'm interested, but Riley hates the idea of me and Ryan having a *thing,* as he calls it."

Griffin snickered, biting into his chocolate chip cookie. "So, *having a thing* is code for being involved in something he's not a part of that includes Ryan?"

Smiling, I nodded. "Pretty much, yeah. I guess I've been undertaking too many new things lately, and he can't keep up. Do you think he's feeling left out?"

"Definitely!" Griffin's face lit up with a sassy smile. "Riley is burning up with jealousy, and here's why. Let me tell you about all the hot sex I have on Thursdays. What's the hottest hot you can describe? Inferno? Raging hellfire? Molten lava? It's all three of those combined. Now, you might ask what's so special about Thursdays? Well, I'll tell you, Reidsy. Thursday is my book club day where the Romance Readers of Waltham congregate here in my shop, and we discuss steamy swoony smut books. Also, Adam, the hunky twunk who is not only a member of my book club, but also escorts for Lucky Match, always sits right next to me. Every week when Cyan catches an eyeful of me and Adam with our heads bent over a dirty book, sipping coffee and laughing together, he takes me upstairs the minute they leave and pounds me into the mattress. Or the table, the wall, the couch, the floor, the shower door. Whatever surface we come across first. Coincidence? Hardly. So, tell Ryan you're dying to join the Manga Maniacs with him, because it might make Riley jealous, but that's a good thing. A *great* thing."

He winked at me like he'd just imparted highly coveted state secrets, and I giggled, thinking what a bad influence he was on me. But he definitely had a point. It wouldn't be a bad idea to stir the pot and see what would happen if I pushed Riley out of his comfort zone. A little jealousy wouldn't hurt him. But I wondered if the jealousy was nothing more than a possession game and not because he had real feelings for me. I was reminded of the day in the café where he pretended to have a fake back injury. That was jealousy, right? Was I brave enough to play head games with Riley? In my experience, these things usually backfired on me in a spectacular way because I lacked the finesse to play coy.

The following day, I was still trying to sort out the logistics as Riley and I were closing up the café. "Almost ready to head home? Your head is in the clouds today." Riley stood behind me, holding a large bag of trash.

"Sorry, I've just been thinking about things. If you want, I'll take the trash out while you sweep up." Grabbing for the black plastic bag, I hefted it over my shoulder and headed out the back door to the dumpster behind the café.

Because it was already growing dark, I failed to see the shadows cast over mine. Three shadows belonging to Alphas from Sigma Rai. I didn't hear their footsteps until it was too late to run.

"Hi, sweetheart. Did you miss me?" His cruel voice slithered over my skin like a poisonous snake, dripping venom in its wake.

I recognized him instantly, the guy from the club who harassed me last week here at the café. He was at the rally as well. He might be the one who spit on me. Backing up a step, two steps, I stumbled over a cardboard box, falling hard on my bottom and scraping my palms on the asphalt as they crowded over me. They wore menacing smiles and fear washed over me, drowning my reflexes. It wasn't just a feeling of doom—it was a primal fear that felt final. Something terrible was about to happen to me.

My heart rate spiked as adrenaline flooded my system. The buzzing in my ears sounded so loud I couldn't hear anything outside of my head. I felt dizzy as the bitter taste of bile gurgled up my throat, burning my mouth.

I tuned out their taunting words as they closed in on me. My primary focus was on their touch as rough hands tore at my hair and clothes. Nails scraped my skin, drawing blood. My vision was narrowing down to the width of a tunnel, darkening around the edges, blurring the details of my attackers. Futilely, I tried to cover my face with my hands, but the pain in my wrist was too great. I floated away even before I felt the final blow to my head. And then I felt nothing but blessed peace as the darkness consumed me.

CHAPTER 13
RILEY

Where in the hell was Reid? How long does it take to dump a bag of trash? When he still hadn't returned after I finished sweeping up, I went out back to check on him. Knowing Reid, I bet he found a stray cat feeding near the dumpster and was trying to nurse it. The idea that we might bring home a furry friend with us tonight had me walking a little faster, hoping to stave off the inevitable pleading puppy dog eyes Reid was bound to give me when he tried to convince me we should keep whatever he'd found.

Shoving the back door open, I peeked my head out, looking left and right, but I saw nothing. "Reid! Where'd you go?"

When I got no response, I walked fully into the alley, standing with my feet planted and my hands on my hips, scanning for Reid. "Reid! Come on, it's getting late."

The only sound was a cool wind that whooshed past

my ears. For whatever reason, my instincts had me circling the dumpster, wondering where he could have disappeared to. Curious and a little uneasy, I moved slowly. Define hairs on the back of my neck raised with caution, thinking Reid might jump out at me at any moment.

When I saw him, I didn't believe my eyes. I couldn't be seeing what was in front of me. It was like one of those horrific dreams where you want to run, but somehow your feet are frozen. And then my senses kicked back online, and I choked on a ragged cry.

"Reid! Reid, baby."

I ran to him, crouching over his prone body. There was a lot of blood, too much. His right eye was swollen and bruised, and his face was scratched in several places, a nasty gash above his swollen eye. His pink pillowy lips were split and caked with blood.

Reid's shirt was torn and hanging from one shoulder, and his jeans were unbuttoned and scrunched down around his hips. His underwear was torn. Nausea churned in my stomach, and I had to turn my head as vomit bubbled up my throat, choking me. I spit a mouthful of the remainder of my lunch out onto the cracked concrete. Reid was unconscious. I laid my hand over his exposed chest, feeling for a heartbeat. It was faint, but I felt the shallow rise and fall of his chest as tears filled my eyes.

"Reid, wake up. Baby, open your eyes. I need to see your eyes, baby. *Please*," I choked, sobbing through my words. "*Please*, Bunny. I need you. Don't leave me!" Reid stirred, his head moved to the side before going slack again. "Help! Somebody help me!"

It was then I remembered I needed to call 911. Why had that not occurred to me yet? Scrambling frantically for my phone, I shoved my hand in my back pocket, clutching it desperately in my fingers. It took me three tries to open my lock screen because of the blood coating my thumbprint. Wiping my hand on my jeans, I tried again. When I had the dispatcher on the line, I gave her the café's address and laid the phone down on the ground, putting it on speaker while I waited for help to arrive.

I tried gently shaking Reid as I sobbed brokenly but got no response. When I reached for his hand, I realized it was bent at an odd angle, probably broken. That made me cry harder.

"Reid, hang on, baby. Help is coming. You're going to be okay. I promise."

I made promises to him, to God, to anybody who would listen if he would just be okay, if he would just pull through this, I would give anything.

A frantic, desperate fear took hold of my mind. My blood curdled down to the marrow. What if he never woke up? What if he woke up but was never the same? There was no life outside of Reid. Not for me—not without him.

It seemed like forever but was probably only minutes before I heard the distant wail of sirens carry on the wind. They pulled right up to us in the alley, followed by police cars and campus security. While they tended to

Reid and strapped him to the stretcher, I ran inside to lock the doors and made it back outside before they even had him loaded up. There was no way in hell I wasn't getting in that ambulance with him.

The tears hadn't dried up, but they were silent now. Violent shudders that wracked my body, causing my shoulders to shake. Shock was setting in, and my system was overloaded with adrenaline. There was no outlet for my fear, my panic, or my anger. It buzzed through my body like a live wire.

I had no clue what they were doing to Reid as he lay strapped to the gurney. My mind was somewhere else and as my eyes raked his body, I catalogued the injuries that I could see. An EMT wrapped his broken wrist in a bandage with a splint to stabilize it, and they gave him a shot of something, probably for pain. God, he had to be in so much pain, and he would feel it all when he finally woke up. I wished I could absorb it for him so his body could be at peace.

My world was crumbling around me and I didn't know how to stop it. The dam holding back my tears broke, soaking me with wet misery. Reid's body had never been at peace. His beautiful broken body had suffered abuse his entire life. Would he ever know how it felt to be touched out of love?

When we arrived at the emergency room, medical staff rushed around us shouting orders—it was a confusing flurry of activity. Wherever they took Reid, I followed. There was no way I was letting him out of my sight—until we reached the double doors that led to the inner bowels of the emergency room. A doctor intercepted Reid and told me I had to wait outside while they took him to X-ray. My hands shook uncontrollably as I tried not to lose my shit.

A uniformed officer approached me and asked questions about what I had witnessed. My body gave out and I collapsed against the wall. Dropping my head into my hands as I bent over, I tried to clear my head. There was no way I could give a statement right now when I was this overwhelmed. It wasn't possible to concentrate on details when I had no idea what was happening with Reid. My only priority was making sure he was going to be okay—until then, nothing else mattered.

The cop led me to the waiting room. He pressed a cup of steaming coffee into my hands, and I stared at it blankly. "Mr. Morgan, can you tell me what happened?"

What happened? Yeah, I fucked up. I let the most important person in my life become a victim of abuse, again. I left him for dead while I swept a fucking floor. I'm a worthless, useless piece of shit.

My teeth chewed my bottom lip until I tasted the metallic tang of blood. "I'm not sure. I was inside closing up the café while Reid took the trash out. When he didn't return, I went out to look for him and found him laid out behind the dumpster. That's when I called 911."

"Okay, I have detectives and a forensic team at the scene, collecting evidence. I guess we'll have to wait for Reid to wake up before we get more answers. Can you think of anyone who might be angry with Reid or have a reason to attack him?"

"I'm not sure. Reid is the kindest person I know, but being gay makes you a target for all kinds of hate. Excuse me, I have calls to make." Pulling my phone from my pocket, I walked down the hall and called Lucky. He answered right away. "Lucky? Reid is in the hospital. He was attacked behind the café. I—I need you. *Please.*"

The plea sounded broken as I choked back deep gut-wrenching sobs. I ended the call before I broke down again. He would alert the whole group, so I didn't have to repeat myself. I felt ashamed to face any of them, but I needed their support, and so did Reid.

I sucked lungfuls of air through my nose, letting it fill my chest cavity, giving my heart time to slow its rapid beating before exhaling slowly through my mouth.

It wasn't long before a nurse in blue scrubs approached me. "Are you Riley Morgan?"

I fumbled my phone, almost dropping it. "Yes, how's Reid? Is he okay? Can I see him?"

"We have admitted him to a room. I'll take you to him. He's still pretty knocked out, but he's starting to wake up." She led me down a maze of corridors and finally stopped outside of a room at the end of a long hallway. "The doctor will be in shortly to discuss his condition with you."

Stepping cautiously into his room because I was afraid of what I'd find, I closed the door behind me before daring to look at the bed. My breath caught in a choked sob when I saw him lying there, broken and battered. They set his wrist in a cast that covered half his arm. His swollen eye had a thick gauze bandage taped over his brow, and his face and arms were covered in scratches. Someone had cleaned the caked blood from his split lip, but I could see how swollen it was. He had wires connected everywhere, snaking out from underneath his hospital gown. Machines beeped, monitors flashed data I couldn't begin to understand, and in the middle of it all, Reid looked so tiny, so frail, so at odds with the beautiful, graceful man I knew so well.

Coming closer, I stood next to his bed, unsure where to touch him safely. This all felt totally surreal. Just an hour ago, we were preparing to close up the shop and go home. We were going to order a pizza and watch a movie together. Now, everything had changed. It felt like someone had flipped my world upside down and I was living in a parallel universe, where nothing made sense. My heart was breaking, and the shattered pieces were floating around inside my chest, scraping my insides raw.

The doctor knocked on the door before walking in. "I'm Dr. Malone. Are you Riley Morgan?" I nodded, not able to manage much more than that. "I have you listed as his next of kin. Does he have any other family?"

"No." My voice sounded broken and raw. "I'm his only family."

Dr. Malone raised his clipboard to read the notes from it. "Alright. We took X-rays, CT scans, and did a full workup. Reid has a broken wrist, two fractured ribs, and a concussion. His brow needed six stitches, and he has a laceration on the back of his head that needed four stitches. The scans show his right kidney is swollen and the surrounding tissue is pressing on it. His urine will likely have blood in it for a couple of days, but he should heal nicely with rest and time. He's wearing a brace around his ribs, which needs to stay in place for a few weeks. Also, we were required to do a rape kit because his clothing was torn and his pants were taken down. We didn't find any evidence of sexual assault by penetration, but there is a deep scratch on his penis. We collected skin tissue from under his fingernails and sent it to the lab for testing. That information will be turned over to the lead investigator on his case. We'll need to keep Reid here for a couple of days under surveillance for his concussion and to monitor his kidney and to make sure there are no further complications. Do you have any questions?"

My head swam with the onslaught of information and I shook it in vain, trying to clear it. "Only a million. But I need to process everything first before I can think clearly. Just tell me if he's going to be okay."

Dr. Malone smiled, his kind brown eyes switching from me to Reid. "He will be. He just needs time to rest and heal. He's lucky. It could have been much worse, I'm sure."

Lucky? I barely restrained myself from grabbing his throat.

After that, I was left alone to absorb the multitude of Reid's injuries. Spotting a chair in the corner by the window, I grabbed it and pulled it up to his bedside. Exhausted and empty, I took his good hand into mine and cradled it protectively against my cheek. The weight of the day came crashing down on me. I laid my head down on the thin blanket covering Reid's lap and the next thing I knew, someone nudged my shoulder.

Opening my eyes, I sat up and focused on my best friends gathered across from me on the other side of Reid's bed. Cyan and Griffin, Lucky and Hayes, Hudson, Murphy, they had all shown up to support Reid. All I wanted was for him to open his beautiful topaz blue eyes and see how much they loved him.

Over the next hour, I fielded endless questions about the attack and Reid's condition until Reid finally stirred. His hand was nestled safely in mine when he opened his eyes. They were bloodshot, with broken capillaries, and I hated that I couldn't see his blue irises clearly.

"Ry?" He focused on my face, and I tried to focus on him through my tears.

"I'm right here, Bunny. Right here." My hands squeezed his a little tighter.

"Don't let go." He squeezed my hand pitifully, lacking his former strength. Then he closed his eyes again as consciousness faded.

"Ry, maybe you should—"

"Don't!" I interrupted Cyan, speaking more harshly than I had intended to. "Don't tell me what I should do or feel or anything. This is my fault, and I'm not moving from this spot until they tell me it's time to take him home."

It made me sick to see the pitying looks on my friends' faces. I wasn't going to entertain their bullshit for one second. Nor did I want to hear about how there was nothing I could do to prevent this, how it could've happened to anybody. It couldn't and it didn't! It happened to Reid because I wasn't protecting him like I should've been. A mistake I planned never to repeat because I would not leave his side. *Ever. Again.*

Cyan dropped his hand on my shoulder. "Ry? When Reid wakes up again, I don't want him to see his blood on your clothes. Go home. Shower and change and eat something, grab a coffee. Then come back. I swear to you we won't leave this room until you return. If he wakes, I'll tell him you're on your way." Cyan spoke so calmly and rationally despite my previous outburst. As much as it peeved me, he had a valid point.

My eyes traveled down my shirt, and I realized for the first time that I was indeed covered with streaks of Reid's blood. There was *no way* I was going to let him see that when he woke up. It was the only thing that made me move from his side.

"And bring Benny back with you for Reid," Cyan suggested. I resented that Cyan's level-headed thinking was doing more for Reid than my useless sniveling tears.

"I'll be back within the hour." My eyes narrowed, pegging each of them with a cold, hard glare. "Nobody moves from this room until I return."

CHAPTER 14
REID

The sun's warm rays kissed my body as I laid in the sand. Cool water washed over my toes, burying them deeper into the mushy sand with each wave. My eyelids squeezed shut against the harsh glare of the sun as a cool breeze blew over my heated skin, cooling me off.

"Would you like another drink?"

My eyes blinked open to see Riley hovering over me, holding a frosty colada. The sun glinted off his blond hair. I drank in the sight of his tanned body, packed with muscle, and suddenly, I was thirsty for something other than liquid refreshment. As if he could read my thoughts, his mouth descended on mine, tasting the lingering flavor of coconut and pineapple.

"Mmm, delicious. I could kiss you until the sun sets." Riley gazed into my eyes, blocking out the sun's glare and casting my body in shade. Goosebumps rippled across my sweat slicked skin.

"Let's cool off in the water."

He scooped me up and carried me into the waves, laughing as they crashed against us. Wrapping my legs around his waist, I clung to him as I licked the salty water from his neck. His hands slid under my bottom to hold me afloat, and I clung tighter to his body, my arms around his neck.

"You're so beautiful, Reid. You're my *everything*, Reid. Reid. Reid..." His voice morphed into a distant echo. "Reid. Reid."

Slowly coming awake, I opened my eyes to see Riley gazing at me intently. But there was no bright sun, only harsh fluorescent lights. Beeping machines replaced the sound of the seagulls' cries. I wasn't floating away on the waves—it was just dizziness. Everything hurt. My head throbbed, and my wrist pulsed with pain.

"Where's my beach?"

Riley's smile was brilliant and blinding. He looked so happy to see me. That felt even better than being at the beach. "I'll take you to the beach as soon as you're all better."

He leaned forward and pressed his warm lips to my forehead. It wasn't the passionate kiss I'd conjured up minutes ago, but I wasn't going to complain. I'd take his lips any way I could get them.

"I thought we were at the beach. I must have been dreaming." My eyes scanned the sterile room and then down the length of my body, taking stock of my condition. Memories of the attack came back to me, like photographs, one at a time, until they added up to a scrapbook of nightmares. "I thought I was dying. I thought they were going to kill me. All I wanted was to see you again, to say goodbye." Was that my voice? It sounded so weak, unfamiliar to my own ears.

I'd made him cry. Tears streamed down Riley's scruffy cheeks as he sniffled and mustered up a watery smile for my benefit. "No, baby. I found you lying behind the dumpster and called for help. You're in the hospital, but you're going to be fine. You never have to say goodbye to me. I'll never leave your side again. I'm going to fix you up and take you home." His fingers brushed the hair from my eyes. The gentle touch felt so good against my bruised skin.

My head swam with a heaviness that felt foreign to me, and I struggled to keep my eyes open. "Love you, Ry. I'm gonna go back to the beach now." I blinked and didn't open my eyes again until it was dark outside my window. Riley was still sitting by my bed, holding my hand.

Being in the hospital sucked. It was nearly impossible to get any rest. Someone constantly interrupted me every fifteen minutes or so. A nurse would come in and ask what my pain level was and distribute meds. The doctor would make his rounds. Nursing assistants came to take my vitals and copy data from the monitors into my chart. All I wanted was peace and quiet. I wanted to crawl under the blankets and hide. A nursing assistant walked in carrying towels and a fresh gown, and I guessed it was bath time.

She began running hot water in a plastic basin and prepping for my sponge bath until Riley jumped out of his seat like it was burning his ass. "Nobody touches him but me."

He snatched the towels from her and blocked her access to my bedside. Normally, I would have rolled my eyes at his overprotective attitude, except I was grateful for his interference. Being touched by anyone right now besides Riley was more than I could stand. Even the doctor's exam made my skin crawl.

"It's part of my duties to bathe him. You're welcome to assist me, though, if you want to be present and Mr. Morgan consents." She sounded like she was trying to explain math to a toddler. Her overly bright smile seemed patronizing.

Riley's rugged face hardened. "Let me be clearer. Nobody touches him but me! Though, if Reid consents, you may be present, but you may *not* assist me. Reid?" He looked to me for an answer. I shook my head in the negative. The last thing I wanted was an audience. "There you go, no consent. Thank you for dropping off the supplies. I'll take it from here." Riley completely dismissed her after that, paying her no attention.

"Okay. If you need my help, press the call button." Thankfully, she wasn't going to make Riley repeat himself. He seemed pretty adamant about the no touching rule.

Riley added soap to the water basin and set everything up on my bedside table. "It's time for your sponge bath, Mr. Morgan. I'm nurse Riley and I'd like to assist you. Let's get you squeaky clean before Nurse Ratched comes back."

He was trying to get me to smile, but I seemed to be all out of smiles lately. Riley dipped the cloth in the warm soapy water and wrung it out. He gently washed my face and neck before he untied my cotton gown and pushed it down. After wetting the cloth again, he washed my chest and shoulders. The warm cloth felt heavenly against my dry skin. Riley removed my dirty gown completely but kept me covered with the blanket so I wouldn't be cold. He washed my arms and hands next, paying extra attention to the dried blood under my fingernails before sliding his hand underneath the blanket to wash my stomach.

Knowing what came next, I became nervous. My eyes followed his hands as he bathed me. What was supposed to be a mundane task was becoming too intimate for such a sterile environment. Riley slid the bottom of my blanket up to expose my legs and dipped the cloth again to warm it before washing my feet and legs. But instead of getting to the awkward part, he switched things up and resettled the blanket. I wasn't sure if I felt relieved or disappointed.

"Let me help you sit up a bit so I can reach your back."

Because of my fractured ribs, I had no strength in my core. It hurt too much to contract my stomach muscles. Riley slid an arm under mine and braced my weight as he pulled me toward him, practically hugging me to his broad chest. He reached behind me and spent several minutes running the cloth over my back. The moan that escaped me told him how glorious it felt. If you've ever laid on your back for days, you would understand how itchy it got.

Before resettling me on the pillows, Riley spoke low next to my ear. "I bet that feels good, doesn't it?"

He had no idea how his words were affecting me, making my dick plump embarrassingly just before we addressed the groin washing issue. *Spectacular.*

He wet the washcloth again and looked me in the eye. "Reid," he whispered. "We have to wash—you know. Between your legs. I'm not sure you can reach without straining your ribs. What would you like to do? Is it okay if I wash you? I'll be quick and gentle, and I won't look."

What a pity. Am I the unluckiest bastard in existence? The one and only time I have a legitimate excuse for Riley to finally touch my dick and he wants to do it quickly and gently without looking. Moreover, I felt too depressed to even fully enjoy the situation.

"Do whatever you need to. I'm fine with it," I said dejectedly.

Spreading my legs, I stared out the window as he reached under the blanket. "I'm sorry. I can't do it like this. I have to move the blanket and look because I'm supposed to reapply the antibiotic ointment on your cut."

He was referring to the three-inch scrape along my

dick left by my attackers. I hated he would see the evidence of my being abused there, in the place I had reserved only for his hands, his eyes. He's the only man whose touch I've ever wanted, and I hated feeling like they took that choice from me. He was going to hate it, too. I could sense his mounting anger rising to the surface.

Everything was tainting this experience. What should have been a magical union between his hands and my genitals was not going according to my fantasies. Technically, it was just a bath and not a hand job, but it was the first time I was consenting to someone handling me down there and I just wanted it to go differently. Not just consenting to *someone*. Riley was the only guy I'd ever loved, ever dreamed of, and I wished we were someplace else and our circumstances were happier ones. I huffed a sigh of discontent, which Riley misinterpreted and started apologizing for. And here I thought things couldn't get worse.

"I'm sorry, Bunny. I'll hurry up. I'm so sorry." His hands worked quickly, his movements jerky. "*Goddamn bastards!* How dare they do this to you!" Riley grit his teeth so hard I thought they might chip.

Yeah, things were definitely getting worse. This ship was sinking fast. I couldn't even look as he cleaned me. I just wanted it to be over as fast as possible. But things went from worse to up shit's creek without a paddle as I felt the wet cloth pass over my hole. My body cringed, probably from the wetness and it being unexpected, but I effectively pushed Riley away with my unintentional action. He probably thought I was cringing from *his* touch specifically and would never try and touch me again. It wasn't possible to feel more miserable than I did right then. Next, he applied the ointment to my cut and then he tied a clean cotton gown around my neck and settled my covers back in place.

I continued to stare out the window as Riley emptied the water in the sink and dumped the wet towels in the laundry bag hanging on my bathroom door. He resettled himself by my side and kissed my hand. Such a platonic gesture, just what every guy dreams of after getting their meat handled by their dream man. How much more of this could I handle before losing my mind?

Two days later, they sent me home. Riley's ever-present hovering continued, and I knew it wasn't just concern, but guilt that drove him to steal my sanity. The only upside was that everyone who came to visit brought me emotional support gifts. Griffin brought me my weight in chocolate, and Ryan dropped off recent issues of my favorite manga. Charlie came to visit and gifted me with four new anime DVDs, which I'm positive Riley coached him on, and Lucky and Hayes dropped off a brand new MP3 player.

Days passed, and I could feel myself detach further from my surroundings, choosing to escape inside my turtle shell whenever possible. Dr. Webber reached out to me several times through online meetings, and we talked about the attack. He said I needed to process my feelings and my reactions, both in the moment and in the aftermath.

At night in bed, I didn't even want to feel Riley hold me. Usually, I turned away from him and laid a pillow between us. He must have noticed that I scooted away or tensed up when he touched me. The distance between us made me physically sick, but I didn't know how to overcome feeling afraid or disinterested in being touched. Of course, I knew that Riley's touch differed from anyone else's, and I craved his hands on me, but my head was in a dark place. Not even my Hero could pull me out of it and drag me into the light.

Riley scooted his body so close to mine, we were almost touching as we lay side-by-side in the spoon position, my back to him. "Bunny, please let me hold you. I feel so alone, and I'm worried about you. Can I wrap my arms around you?"

His voice sounded so quiet and sincere. If I wasn't so numb, it would have brought tears to my eyes. He wanted to bridge the distance between us as badly as I wanted to connect with him. Nodding my head, I forced myself to accept his touch. Riley snaked his brawny arms around my waist, careful not to squeeze my ribs too tightly. After a tentative moment of waiting for me to pull away, he squeezed me tighter and inhaled as he buried his nose in my hair. It hit me right in the gut. He sought my scent because it was familiar and comforting to him, and I realized just how far I'd pushed him away.

Carefully turning in his arms, I buried my face in his

chest, powerless to hold back the tears that finally fell. For the first time in a week, I cried while Riley held me safe in his protective embrace. Once the tears started, they didn't stop. Riley held me for a solid thirty minutes while I grieved. I cried for the loss of independence I had gained, for the self-esteem I recovered that I now felt was lost, and for the distance I'd created between me and Riley. I cried because I was tired of being a victim. And the more I cried, the more reasons I found to cry about.

I felt exhausted, and I wasn't sure I had the strength to recover. It might be easier to just give up and waste away. Riley would never let it happen, though. He would drag me kicking and screaming back into therapy. He would save me, even if I couldn't or wouldn't save myself.

His fingers stroked through my hair, soothing my ragged nerves. "Shhh, it's alright, Bunny. Let it all out. You're safe with me."

Riley pressed soft kisses to my head. His gentle reassurances softened the edges of my anger. I hadn't even realized I felt so angry until I cried in his arms. My heart thawed, the numbness receded. Dr. Webber assured me these were the stages of grief, and it was completely acceptable to feel this way. It felt symbolic somehow that it was Riley who was helping me begin to heal, because didn't he always?

My fingers curled into his chest, seeking a solid foothold to tether me to the present. "Why do men always want to hurt me? They're all so abusive in one way or another. I haven't met many that are nice. What is it about me that makes men act so mean to me?"

Riley made a tortured keening sound, like my question physically hurt him. "It's not you, Reid. Nothing you do causes anyone to act that way. That's their problem. You're not responsible for their shit. Any decent man would want to keep you safe."

My lips brushed across his chest. "Like you, Riley. You're the best man I've ever known. You're my Her—"

He bolted upright in bed, frustrated and angry. "Don't say it, Reid! Don't call me a hero. We both know I'm not. I'm just the first person you ever met that was nice to you. That's all. But you twisted it in your romantic mind to make me out to be something I'm not."

How had he come up with such a convoluted diagnosis of my feelings? Sitting up carefully, I tried hugging my knees to my chest, but it made my ribs ache. "You can say what you want, but I know better. You're my Hero for a million different reasons. You prove it over and over again every day, whether or not you want to. But I don't think you'd still be here with me if you didn't want to."

Riley jumped out of bed and paced back and forth across our room. "Can't you see? I'm no better than *them*! I think about doing the same filthy things to you they do. The same disgusting thoughts run through my sick head." He jabbed angrily at his head. "I'm not your fucking Hero, Reid! I don't even deserve to be near you."

His misplaced self-recriminations fell on deaf ears. The only words that filtered through my brain were how he wanted to do filthy things to me. "Do you mean that,

Ry? Do you really think about me like that?" Hope bloomed in my chest for the first time in years.

He finally stopped pacing, his head hung in shame. "God, Reid, I'm so sorry. I'm so, so sorry. Please don't hate me. I can't bear that." Riley pleaded with me, hands clasped in prayer. He looked genuinely disturbed by his desires.

Alarm pierced through the hope. Is this how he felt all along? Was this misplaced sense of morality what kept us apart all these years? "Riley, don't be ashamed. I've always dreamed of having you touch me like that. Like, not as a brother or a friend. But... *more*."

Riley fell to his knees beside the bed. His fingers gripped my thighs. "You don't mean that. You just haven't met anyone else nice besides me. When you do, you'll be glad you waited for them. I can't take that from you. It wouldn't be fair."

He thought I was confused and misguided about my crush. But it was not a crush, and I needed to find the right words to make him understand my feelings for him were real.

My fingers cupped his jaw, cradling his face in my hands. "I've been in love with you since I was fourteen. I've crushed on you since the day I met you. That first night I had a nightmare, and you held me and rocked me back to sleep, I fell in love with you. There's no one else in this entire world I'd allow to touch me, ever, and no one I dream of besides you. You're my *everything*, Ry. But most importantly, you're my *home*. Wherever we end up, I'm always home with you beside me."

Riley dropped his head into my lap. “Reid,” he begged, not allowing himself to believe me. “You don’t mean that. You don’t see me as anything more than your hero.”

My hand smoothed over his hair. “I’ve met lots of nice people besides you. I wouldn’t dream of ever letting one of them kiss me. But you, Ry, I dream about you almost every night. I imagine when you cuddle me, you might let your hands roam below my waist. I fantasize about when you kiss my cheek, that your lips might travel sideways, seeking my mouth instead. When you spoon me in bed, I can sometimes feel your erection pressed against me and I have to make myself lie still so I don’t rub myself against it. I purposely invade your privacy constantly just to catch a glimpse of your beautiful body.”

Riley lifted his tear-stained face. Hope and denial fought for dominance in his expression. “That’s not true. None of what you’re saying is real.”

Shaking my head, I smiled softly. “The thoughts I have about you when I touch myself are *very* real. The jealousy I feel when you sleep with other men is also very real.”

Riley winced with regret. “What are you saying? Are you saying you want more than what we have?”

My hand patted the covers, inviting him to sit next to me. “Is that so hard to believe? I’ve always wanted more from you. I just thought it was one-sided. I always believed you viewed me as an obligation. Like a brother you were responsible for looking after.”

Riley sat down on the bed, pulling me into his side. "Trust me, Reid, there's nothing about you I've ever seen as brotherly. That would be at odds with the thoughts I have about you. I've wanted you since the first time I slept beside you in bed. But I could hardly act on my feelings when you were so conflicted with nightmares. And then the abuse you suffered, like I said, I felt like I wasn't any better than them."

I hitched my leg over his thigh. It was as close as I could get to crawling into his lap. "There's no comparison. You aren't anything like them." Riley raised his other leg over mine and we fell back onto the bed, twisted together in a tangle of limbs. "We've wasted so many years. Promise me we won't waste any more."

He pressed his lips to my forehead, leaving a soft kiss on my skin. "Reid, this doesn't change anything. We can't do this."

My head snapped up. "What? Why not? You just admitted that you want me. What's stopping us?"

His hand landed on my back, just below the brace covering my ribs. "The same thing that's always stopped me. Our relationship. What if things don't work out and I lose you? I can't lose you, Reid. You're my only family, you're all I have. I can't risk it."

Like I was going anywhere. "You'll never lose me, Riley. *Ever.* Not only am I positive you are the only man I'll ever love, but even if you changed your mind about me, you could never change my feelings for you. My love for you is unconditional and eternal. You'll always have it. My heart belongs to you completely. I just happen to carry it around for you because you already have one."

Riley leaned in until his forehead touched mine. "Reid, sweetheart, the one I already have is yours. I was just holding onto it for you until I was sure you wanted it."

"I want it, Ry," I whispered, my words tickling his lips. "I want *everything*. All of you." What I wanted was to feel his lips on mine, but after years of conditioning, I lacked the courage to make the first move.

CHAPTER 15
RILEY

I didn't do it. I had the perfect opportunity to finally kiss Reid, and I froze. The longer I sat frozen, the more awkward the moment became, until I could feel his disappointment like a tangible object. Reid looked crushed.

Desire warred with my conscience, causing me to question not only my motives, but what was best for Reid. How could I contemplate touching him when he just suffered a sexual assault? On top of a long history of sexual abuse. In my heart, I knew he wasn't ready for more. But I was determined to do everything in my power to help get him there. Because I didn't know how long I could hold back, knowing that he wanted me, too. Reid and I had waited six years—we could wait a little longer—despite his protests.

Also, I was still sleeping with other men—regularly. There was no way in hell I could make love to Reid and then dip my dick into someone else. But to give up escorting would delay achieving our dreams for years. Then again, having Reid's love was something I never dared to dream of, but knowing I had it made everything else pale in comparison. I needed to sort out my priorities. *Our* priorities. For me, that was Reid, first and foremost. But first, I would need to figure out what his priorities were—the future plans we made, or finally embarking on our relationship.

Over the next week, I noticed a lot of changes—some small and others big. We stood side by side as we brushed our teeth, left the bathroom door open during showers, and snuggled a little closer on the couch. Reid developed a habit of letting his hands wander in bed as we spooned, brushing my nipple or peppering little kisses across my skin as he lay nestled against my chest. I loved every second of his attention and knew it was only going to get better as we allowed ourselves to be more intimate with each other.

As the week unfolded, our schedule was so hectic it was hard to find time alone together. Reid went back to the doctor to have his stitches removed. The detective handling his case came by the house to update us and ask more questions. She explained that Reid's attack was classified as a hate crime, and they were still waiting on the lab results to identify the DNA under his fingernails. Reid was determined to identify his attackers and even testify against them in court if necessary.

We fielded many visits from our friends and Charlie, and Griffin stopped by and stocked our freezer with casseroles. No one seemed to notice a difference in our relationship, which told me we must have always appeared closer than I imagined we behaved. I had a feeling nobody was going to be surprised when we finally announced our new status.

Reid still receded into himself when I wasn't engaging him with conversation or activity, so I tried to keep him busy each day. I painted his toes, removed his brace to massage his back, played board games, or invited him to help me in the kitchen. Today, I had plans to spring him from the house for a few hours of sunshine. We drove to the park to spend some time lounging in his favorite spot, the hammock by the river.

Instead of sitting apart from him on the picnic bench, this time, I nestled my large frame into the hammock with him. It felt perfect when he laid his head on my chest. I stroked my fingers through his soft hair as I listened to him wonder about the lives of the passengers on board the passing ships. The cool breeze that brushed over our bodies gave wings to his fantasies, carrying them out over the ocean to thrive.

Reid snuck his hand under my T-shirt, lazily tracing patterns on my stomach as he daydreamed. He became increasingly bolder with each sweep of his fingers on my skin, trailing his touch lower and lower until his fingers flirted with the waistband of my sweats. The devil on my left shoulder begged him to keep going as the angel on my right shoulder screamed for him to stop. I stilled his hand with mine, halting his descent, but he wouldn't quit.

"Bunny, we—"

"I'm just exploring. I have a lot to learn. Your body is like a map and I'm in geography class." His devilish smile tipped the scales in his favor.

"Ungh, you have no idea how that sounds."

His dirty innocence was going to be the death of me. Reid's slender fingers breached my waistband and followed the trail of blond hair down to the larger patch, tickling through the nest of hair. The anticipation of being touched by him made my dick rock hard. There was no way he didn't see the outline through the thin cotton material.

He ignored my cock like a seasoned tease, instead going for my inner thighs with the softest brush of his fingers. When I groaned in frustration, he smiled, his eyes glittering with hungry power, and I realized his self-esteem was multiplying with each second that passed. He felt emboldened and in control, two things Reid rarely was in a position to experience. It sounded so cliché, but the sexual healing was exactly what he needed.

Reid licked his lips, tempting me to taste his mouth. He studied my expression as he slid his fingers around the base of my shaft. He was high on the satisfaction he got from my response to him. I spread my legs wider in invitation and held my breath. Any second, Reid was going to grasp my dick, something I've dreamed about for years. I wished I could remove my pants entirely so he could see what he did to me, but we were in a public park, and I wasn't trying to get arrested in the middle of the best moment of my life. We were all alone, but I wasn't going to take that kind of chance.

His fist closed around me, lightly stroking up to my crown. Reid's eyes widened in surprise when he realized how wet I was. I've never been this turned on in my entire life. My slit leaked like a sieve. He rubbed the sticky wetness around the engorged head, spreading it to aid his movements. His blunt nail slid into my slit, and my hips bucked wildly. My breathing became erratic as I concentrated on his debut hand job.

Something about that made it hotter. It was *ever* only going to be *my* dick in his hand.

Mine was the first and only dick Reid had ever touched—would ever touch. The thought alone was enough to make me blow. "Fuck, Reid, slow down. Take it easy."

He laughed. "I'm just getting started."

"I know, but... I'm close already."

My eyes were glued to the movement of his hand in my pants. Compared to most of the things I'd done with other men, this was rated G, but it was the single hottest sexual act I'd ever experienced. It had everything to do with the guy and not the act itself. Six years of anticipation was enough to make any guy cream his pants on contact.

Reid tightened his grip and stroked down, then up. His fingers not in use grazed my balls. I leaned closer to him, and he closed the distance between us, sealing his mouth over mine. Our first kiss, and he had my cock in his hand. It was too much at once—his soft tongue sliding against mine, the heat of his palm wrapped around my aching cock. Three more tugs and I blew my load over his fist. He milked every drop from me before releasing me and brought his sticky hand to his mouth. The tip of Reid's little pink tongue peeked out from between his plump lips to taste my seed. His pupils were blown wide, either from the taste or the satisfaction of having made me come so quickly, or both.

He licked his entire hand clean before I dove for his mouth again, sharing the musky taste with him. When I pulled away to breathe, my lips ghosted over his ear. "I love you. I'm *in love* with you."

"I love you, too, Hero." He made a contented little sigh, like a kitten, and curled up into my side. "Take me home so we can do that again."

Smiling, I pressed my lips to his downy head. "Reid, baby, we gotta take things slow. I'm not rejecting you. Far from it. I can't wait to do that again, and more, but you're still healing, and I don't want to rush things."

His lush lips puckered in a sexy pout. "But I'm ready. I want to." He looked so hopeful and eager. It killed me to dampen his spirits.

"I know you are, but I'm sure I'm making the right choice, and I need you to trust me. There's a lot we need to discuss before we—advance."

"Like?" Reid looked skeptical, or wary. He wasn't interested in discussing anything except sex.

"Reid, I'm still escorting. Do you really think I'm going to continue sleeping with other guys? Come on, give me some credit. If I quit, and I want to, I really do, it's going to take us a lot longer to reach our goals than we planned. Our house and the camp will take longer to achieve than we anticipated. That's something you need to seriously consider, because I know you've had your heart set on it for years."

Reid looked fierce as he rejected my reasoning. "I've had my heart set on *you* for years, Riley Morgan. I don't care if we live in a tent in the backyard or live out of our car. As long as we're together, I'm happy. As for escorting, I know it's your job and you do it to support us, not to get your rocks off. I would never make you feel bad about your work. It's a responsibility you assumed for my sake. I would be selfish to complain or give you an ultimatum. It's a means to an end."

A snort bubbled from my throat. "Wow, you're a better man than I am because I wouldn't stand for it for a second if our roles were reversed. I can't even imagine my reaction."

Reid huffed. "Be honest, you were never going to let me date someone else. I just can't see it. Would you have accepted it if I chose to be with another guy?"

Never! Not in a million years.

"I guess I'd have to, wouldn't I? I can't tell you what to do with your heart or your life, but I wouldn't have made it easy for you. I'd have completely sabotaged your relationships at every turn. It would have become my mission to make you feel so uncomfortable and guilty, you'd have remained single the rest of your life."

"Riley!" He swatted my arm in outrage. "How dare you! That's such a double standard."

He glared when I chuckled. "I couldn't care less." My fingers stroked his cheek as my lips descended on his. My tongue licked into his mouth slowly, sliding along his in a sensual kiss that left no doubt about my feelings for him. "It was always going to be you, Reid. No matter how long you'd have made me wait. There's nobody else for me. And I'd have made damn sure there was nobody else for you, either."

He giggled against my lips. "So, you'd have won by default?"

"All's fair in love and war, as the saying goes."

Reid smiled, side-eyeing me. "Looks like we made it, look—"

"Reid! If you start singing Shania Twain, I'll tip this hammock over and dump your ass in the sand. Don't ruin a good thing."

My kiss muffled his laughter, and I couldn't help but smile against his lips. He was perfect for me in every way. My sunshine, my Bunny, my *future*. Reid was the center of my world. There was nothing I wouldn't do to keep him laughing and smiling every day.

CHAPTER 16
REID

Griffin hugged me fiercely, his skinny arms slid around my neck and clung until I had to shake him off. "I'm so glad to see you out of the house. I hate to bring it up, but Cy has been so worried about you. He cried, you know, when you were in the hospital. He cares about you so much. It made his day when he found out you were coming over."

Griffin and I were seated at the coffee bar, catching up with each other. Hanging out with him in his bookshop was better for my soul than any therapy. It had to be my favorite place besides home. Growing up, I never had much opportunity to visit bookstores or libraries—I didn't know what I was missing. The smell of coffee and fresh baked treats, the warm ambience created by groupings of plush chairs, new and old books, and sunlight streaming through the floor to ceiling windows. *Fairy*tales felt homey and familiar.

Of course, the biggest draw was coming to see my

best friend. "I guess it's been hard on everyone. Especially Riley. He feels guilty for letting me out of his sight that day. It has nothing to do with him, but I can't convince him otherwise." Sighing deeply, I took another sip of coffee, enjoying the bittersweet warmth that washed over my tongue. "Dr. Webber says time heals all wounds, as long as I don't shy away from them. So, I'm here, and I'm talking, and it's exhausting, but it feels good, too. But enough about me. Tell me something exciting about you."

Griffin laid his hand on my forearm, leaning closer. "Lucky and Cyan are collaborating on a new project. He hired Cy to take pictures and do a short bio of each of the escorts for Lucky's new website Cyan created. A couple of the shoots are going to be here in my shop. Of course, he's going to mention the shop on the website, so I'm excited about generating some extra hype for all of us." My mind drifted until Griffin repeated my name.

"Reidsy! Hello?" He pulled me from my daydream and smirked mischievously. "Whatever's on your mind is much more exciting than my news. Spill the beans."

My eyes widened, which I belatedly realized gave me away. "I don't know what you're blabbing about." I diverted my attention to a very interesting speck on the counter, scratching at it with my nail.

Griffin sat up straighter. "You're going to tell me all about what has put that silly smile on your face! Start talking."

The silly smile spread wider, stretching from ear to

ear. This was my biggest news ever, and I was dying to talk about it. "I did something. Something...um—*sexy*."

The look of surprise and excitement on Griffin's face was priceless. "Oh my gosh, *finally!* You look like you're about to burst. Give me all the details."

"I gave my first hand job. And I had my first kiss! It was amazing. It was—*everything*." I ended with a dreamy sigh.

Whenever I thought about our time at the park, I turned all liquid and lusty. I didn't realize I gave a certain look every time I relived the memories, but Riley noticed several times, and each time, he just laughed and kissed me.

"You, Reid Morgan, are on your way to ditching your virginity, you naughty boy! I'm assuming Riley finally pulled his head out of his ass. How'd that happen?"

With my hand over my heart, I confessed, "In a moment of weakness. We were arguing, and he just shouted it out. We were finally able to admit we've been in love with each other for years. But he wants to take things slow." My eyes rolled hard. "The other day, he took me to our favorite spot, and one thing led to another. I'm telling you, Griff, it was the best moment of my life."

"I bet," he chuckled. "Just wait, it gets even better." Griffin hopped off his stool and hugged me. "Let me know if you have any questions. I'm far from being an expert, but I can point you in the right direction."

~

Word spread quickly about me and Riley. Our so-called friends sent ridiculous gag gifts to celebrate us. Lucky and Hayes had a basket delivered, filled with condoms, flavored lubes, and toys. I didn't understand how most of them were supposed to be used, specifically, but I let my imagination run wild and came up with a few possibilities. Cyan and Griffin dropped off a stack of books: Gay Sex For Dummies (I shit you not), The Art Of Oral Sex, and my favorite, Bottoming For Beginners. My face was red just thinking about it. Murphy left a stack of gay porn DVDs on my nightstand. Hudson had a bouquet of pink and white roses delivered. The card simply said, "Be good to each other." It was a very sweet sentiment. It seemed everyone had a vested interest in my burgeoning sex life.

Deciding to stir the pot, I found a cozy spot on the couch and began leafing through Bottoming For Beginners, making sure Riley would see me when he finished cleaning the kitchen. I wanted to honor Riley's decision to hold off on intercourse, but there were a slew of other things we could do instead. Each time I thought back to the park and our happy hammock time, I popped a boner, eager for our next encounter.

The doctor removed my back brace and cast at my checkup today, leaving me with a soft, removable wrist splint, and it felt freeing to breathe without restriction. My ribs still hurt if I coughed or moved wrong, but I felt primed and ready for more sexy time with Riley.

Riley breezed into the living room, and as he passed me to take a seat on the couch, he did a double take at the cover of my book. "Uh-uh, definitely not. I know what you're doing, and it's not going to work." He cozied up to me and took the book from my hands, laying it face down on the coffee table.

Holding up my hands in confusion, I asked, "What? What am I doing, besides educating myself?" Playing dumb didn't work on Riley. He saw right through my act. I wasn't fooling him for a second.

He narrowed his dark blue eyes. "Dropping hints, doing little things to drive me crazy, so I'll snap. I've had to rub it out three times today to protect myself against you. I'm now immune to your charms."

I couldn't believe he'd admitted that to me. I giggled, delighted that I had such an effect on him.

Riley pressed even closer, his nose buried in my neck. "Anyway, who says you're the only one who's ever going to bottom? I'm Vers, 'ya know. Maybe I need to give you some pointers about topping."

I swallowed hard, my mouth going dry. "Really? You would want me to do...uh, to t-top you?"

Riley tugged me onto his lap, my knees straddling his thick thighs. He gazed hungrily at me. The heat in his stare went straight to my belly, twisting it into knots. His beautiful sapphire eyes mapped my stunned face.

"I can't tell you how many times I've dreamed about having you inside me. That freakishly gigantic cock of yours stretching me, filling me until I scream your name. Yeah, I've spent a lot of hours on that fantasy. Is that something you think you'd want to try?"

I'd never considered it before, but now that I was, my

dick was plumping quickly. "I'm definitely interested in trying that. How do you know my dick is freakishly big?"

Riley grinned like the Devil. "If you think for one minute that I haven't snuck peeks at you every chance I got, you're kidding yourself. And don't even pretend to tell me you haven't done the same."

The blush rising to my skin heated my cheeks. "Maybe once or twice. Accidentally."

"Bullshit," he barked, laughing as he hugged me tight. "Now you don't have to pretend it's an accident. You can explore me at leisure, anytime you want."

Clapping my hands in front of my chest, I exclaimed, "Oh! Can we do that now?"

The smile slipped from Riley's face. He grew serious, leaning back to look into my eyes. "There's something I need to discuss with you first. I heard from the detective today handling your case. The results came back from the lab regarding the tissue found under your nails."

Tension coiled in my stomach, making my muscles cramp. "It's inconclusive, isn't it?" I hung my head in defeat. "That's something I learned in my self-defense class, to be sure to scratch your attacker to collect evidence. I don't even remember doing it, but it must have been subconscious. I guess it was for nothing."

Riley tipped my chin up, studying me fiercely. "They identified the bastards. All three of them. They are going to make arrests, but they wanted to know if you would go down to the station and identify them from pictures. Just as an added precaution to make sure we nail them."

Bright waves of joy replaced the tension, warming

my belly with a pleasant heat. "Yes! Oh God, I can't believe this. I remember exactly what they looked like. I want to do this, Ry. *I need to*!"

"Okay, then that's what we'll do tomorrow morning. I'm so fucking proud of you." He cupped my face in his large hands, holding me like I was something precious. Each one of those looks stacked currency in my self-esteem bank, rebuilding my confidence and self-worth bit by bit. "You're so strong, so brave. You've come so far. I refuse to let those fuckers hold you back. I'll do everything in my power to help you put them away."

I snuggled down into his hard chest, our bodies completely enmeshed, heat building between us, and nuzzled against his shirt, inhaling his familiar masculine scent. "You know what the best part about finally admitting our feelings is?"

"I can think of several excellent answers to that question." He sounded faintly amused, and I realized he was probably thinking about something sexual. Which made me start thinking about sex as well.

"Besides that. The best part is that now I can touch you whenever I want. I don't have to think of lame excuses for getting close to you. Like this." I burrowed deeper into his chest, wiggling my hips in his lap. "I couldn't pull this off before, but now, I can indulge myself whenever I want."

"That certainly is a great perk. And I can stop pretending that the only reason I'm so protective of you is out of some brotherly concern bullshit. It's because I'm in love with you." His lips pressed against mine, sweet and soft, igniting tiny sparks of lust in my groin. When he pulled back, I chased his kiss, and he chuckled.

Sighing deeply, I admitted, "That feels good to know. I always felt like such a burden to you. I hated thinking I was just another one of your responsibilities when I dreamed of being so much more."

Riley playfully bit my nose with his lips. "Never, Bunny. You've got to stop seeing yourself that way. You aren't less than me. This is a partnership. It's not unbalanced in any way. I take care of you and look after you because it satisfies me to meet your needs and know that you're safe. You give to me in ways you don't realize that are just as important, if not more so."

"I do?" I asked skeptically.

"Seriously? Yeah, Reid, you do. Looking out for you gives my life purpose and meaning that I would not have if not for you. I would be just another dumb jock with a chip on his shoulder. When you smile, you light me up. You show me how to be patient and kind, and you give me a reason to be strong. I wouldn't want to get out of bed every day if I didn't wake up next to you. Plus, you're smarter than me in math and English, so you help keep my grades up. And you always clean my toothpaste splatter off the bathroom mirror. You're a definite keeper!"

My bottom lip popped at his teasing. Riley sucked it into his mouth, and I forgot all about his jibe. "Can we go play explorer now?"

Riley laughed, deep and loud. "You want to role play? I didn't realize you were kinky."

"You know what I meant. You suggested that I explore your body at length. I'm game."

"Sure," he said, scooping me carefully into his arms like a southern Belle. "I'm game to let you explore my length, too. Let's go." I laughed as he carried me up the stairs to our room and deposited me on the bed, laying himself out over me. Love, pure and deep, shone in his eyes as he gazed down at me. "So you want to check out my body, huh?"

At a loss for words, I could only nod. "Should I get naked, too?" Damn, I sounded eager. Riley laughed, but I could see the heat in his eyes blazing hotter from just thinking about me taking my clothes off.

"No, Bunny. It'd be too easy to get carried away." He removed his shirt, baring his chiseled chest and abs. My mouth salivated over the miles of unblemished skin, just waiting to be explored, licked, and touched by my hands and mouth. I was contemplating where to begin when he unbuttoned his jeans, sliding them down his thick thighs. This just kept getting better and better. "I'll leave my underwear on for now."

My eyes, round with wonder, must have resembled a deer in the headlights. Riley chuckled and pulled me down for a kiss. "Why don't you start right here?"

I took my time exploring his mouth, nipping his lips and sucking on his tongue. I even licked his teeth. When I felt ready to move on, I trailed kisses along his square jaw and down his neck, sucking until a dark red mark bloomed on his skin.

Riley's breathing kicked up, growing shorter and

heavier. It gave me the confidence to continue. My tongue snaked out, licking his shoulders, his skin tasted clean with a tang of salt. Biting one lightly, I kneaded the muscles in his arms. Riley's biceps were firm and thick, *delicious*. He never had time to go to the gym anymore, but he'd naturally retained a lot of the muscle he'd developed in high school by doing manual labor around the house and at the café.

Working my way down his arms, I massaged his hands and traced each finger with my tongue before sucking each one into my mouth. Riley moaned, loving the oral attention I lavished upon him. The more I touched him, the more excited I became. My dick was as hard as a diamond in my pants, dripping and aching. I longed to feel his hand around it, stroking until I ached no more. It was impossible to tear my gaze from him. His body was front and center in my mind, commanding all my attention.

When I leaned over him to start on his chest, Riley snagged my hips and centered me over his hips to straddle him like I weighed nothing more than a rag doll. "Hi," I whispered as I looked down at him.

"Hi," he smiled as he whispered back. "Are you enjoying this as much as I am?"

I shook my head, confusing him. "No, I'm enjoying this way more than you are."

He bumped his hips against mine for teasing him, but the joke was on him as he moaned. The friction of his erection pressing against mine was too good. I couldn't keep from rubbing against him like a cat in heat as I played with his nipples, rolling them between my fingers, pinching and nipping them before soothing them with my mouth.

Riley was undone, squirming and writhing with lust. With his eyes closed and his lips parted, head thrown back, he was so beautiful, so sexy.

He was my teenage fantasy come true.

The culmination of every wet dream I'd ever had. The star of every one of my jerk-off sessions. I wanted to shuck my pants and ride him as I watched his pleasure broadcast across his face.

But Riley thought I wasn't ready for that, and I didn't want to ruin our moment by arguing. So I kept my pants on and continued to grind on his dick, driving him wild like I always dreamed I could.

"You're killing me, Bunny. I'm so close already," he rasped.

He pulled his briefs down below his smooth balls, exposing his gorgeous cock. "Touch me, please. I need to feel your hands on me."

I hesitated for a second, wanting to be great at this, to bring Riley pleasure and get him off, but not really having much experience at seduction. Naturally, I knew what felt good for me, when I touched myself and imagined it was Riley's hand, so I started there. Grabbing the thick base with one hand, I wrapped my fingers around his shaft and used my other hand to stroke his silky skin up and down. When I passed over the swollen head, wetness seeped from his slit and smeared around the crown, pulling a tortured groan from Riley.

"That's it, baby, so good. Stroke me."

His hooded eyes darted between my face and my hands, taking it all in. I loved making him so needy for my touch. This moment felt so surreal. I'd waited years to make this fantasy come true. Riley kept his hooded eyes trained on my face. The heat I saw in his sapphire irises caused goosebumps to rise over my skin. If I made him desperate with lust, would he throw caution to the wind and make love to me?

Just in case, I doubled down on my efforts. Using two hands to stroke him, it took no time at all before he started chanting my name, eyes closed and head thrown back in rapture.

"Reid, please. A little more. Reid, baby." His breaths came fast and short, telling me how close he was.

Boldly, I brought my mouth to his tip and licked the stream leaking from his slit. He bucked his hips, which pushed his cock further into my mouth. My lips closed around his shaft, and I sucked him deep. He cried out, and I could feel his cock pulse on my tongue as more of his salty semen dripped from his slit. Swallowing it down, I licked my lips and returned for more. He tasted saltier than I expected, and slightly bitter, but it wasn't unpleasant. When I flashed my eyes up to his face, I saw him watching me intently, heat and need swirling in his blue eyes.

Riley brought his hands to my head, tangling his fingers into my hair, and guided my mouth gently, encouraging me to take him deeper into my throat. When I gagged, he moaned, tugging on my hair as he came in a rush down my throat, filling my mouth with his seed. I swallowed every drop, wishing there was more of him to take into my body. Ridiculous or not, I had some kind of romantic notion about having a part of him inside of me.

Riley hooked his hands under my armpits and pulled me up his body to collapse on top of him. He stole my breath with his hungry claiming kiss.

"Oh, God, I can taste myself on your tongue." He kissed me with a desperate fervor I'd never experienced before. "I can't get enough of you."

My dick was still rock hard in my jeans, and I couldn't help but grind against his groin, seeking friction to get myself off. I felt desperate to come any way I could. Riley reached down between our bodies and slipped his hand into my jeans. He took my cock in hand and stroked me with a firm grasp. The heat from his calloused palm satisfied my need for contact. It only took five tugs before I filled his hand with warm cum. The release drained me, in more ways than one. Things seemed to cool down after that. The desperate grappling morphed into sweet kisses and gentle caresses. The sweet way he loved me felt just as good as the sexual release. I was a whore for cuddles, and Riley met every one of my needs. Actually, he exceeded them by far.

"I love you, Bunny. That had to be the most explosive orgasm I've ever had."

Chuckling, I reminded him, "That's what you said last time, in the hammock."

He smiled in return. "That's because it gets better

every time. I can't imagine what you'll do to me when I'm inside you. You always make me feel amazing, inside and out."

"I think we just have good chemistry," I joked.

Riley traced the contour of my cheek. "You think? I think maybe it's more than that. Come on, let's get cleaned up and lay back down so I can hold you awhile and tell you all the reasons why it's more than just good chemistry."

He moved to sit up, but I stopped him. "I'm an idiot for not having done that years ago."

Riley laughed. "I can't imagine you being so bold."

Curiosity got the best of me. "What would you have done if I'd rolled over and shoved my tongue into your mouth?"

"I would've kissed you back and enjoyed every second. Then I would have come up with some ridiculous excuse about why it would be a bad idea to do it again." Riley rolled his eyes and laughed at himself.

My teeth nipped his bottom lip. "I'm so glad we're smarter now."

CHAPTER 17
RILEY

"I'm wide open! Throw me the ball." Greg, a kid with dark brown shaggy hair and eyes the color of molasses, held his hands up in the air, waiting to receive the football.

He was blocked by Colton, a blond boy with brown eyes who was taller than Greg by six inches. Colton intercepted the ball and ran down the field with Greg hot on his heels. Colton might be taller, but Greg was definitely faster. He caught up to Colton and tackled him, snatching the ball from his grip.

Sucking in a deep breath, I blew hard on my whistle, halting the game. "Hey! This is supposed to be touch football. There's no tackling. The center can't afford to pay for any injuries and hospital bills."

I hated to be the nagging voice of reason, but I had to look out for the center and for the boys as well. Colton wanted to play football for his school, but they cut him in the first round of tryouts because he was openly pansexual. Some of the guys on the team were pretty vocal about not wanting to share the locker room with a *fag*. Their words not mine.

The blatant discrimination made my blood boil. What did his sexual preference have to do with running a ball? Why did people have to be such insecure jackasses? The boys stood and hugged it out, laughing as they made their way across the field. My gaze wandered over to the side of the field where a group of kids stood, cheering us on. I searched for Reid but didn't see him.

Reid hadn't visited Over The Rainbow since before the attack. He didn't want the kids to see the damage done to his body from violent homophobic people who hated the very existence of kids just like these. This was a place of love and acceptance and positivity, and Reid felt like a walking billboard for a hate crime. This morning, when he told me he felt ready to return now that most of his injuries had healed, I couldn't drive him here fast enough.

It was an impossible feat to get him off my mind. I found myself constantly distracted remembering our time in bed last night and wondered where in the hell he learned to suck a dick. It wasn't from personal experience—I knew that without a doubt. But damn if he didn't make my toes curl in my socks. What other skills was he hiding up his sleeve?

And his kisses—his mouth was like a theme park, full of wonder and excitement and adventure. Whenever his tongue touched mine, I felt a thrill quicken my heart and stiffen my cock. It was instantaneous and predictable. I'd waited six years to feel his lips against mine, and he sure didn't disappoint. Kissing Reid was my new favorite pastime. I was pretty sure I could get worked up enough to come just from making out with him. Me, a seasoned escort, jizzing my pants from a kiss. I laughed at the absurdity of it.

"Fuck! Ow!"

The ringing and stinging in my head made me double over as I rubbed the sore spot. I'd taken a football to the side of my head because I was lost in a daydream.

"Language, Riley," Colton admonished me, laughing with Greg as they used my words on me. These kids cursed like sailors on leave, and I had to constantly remind them to watch their language. If I instituted a swear jar, the center would have enough money to buy new sports equipment in no time. Colton ambled over to look at my head. "No blood, you'll live. Hey, have you seen Maya lately? She's been ghosting us for over a week now. It's weird. She's usually here every day."

Maya was a trans female who had been a regular at the center since her transition two years ago. I couldn't remember a time I'd ever come here and not seen her, so now Colton had me worried as well.

"I'll check around and see what I can find out. Don't worry, I'll keep you posted. We'll find her."

A week without coming to the center was unusual for Maya. She'd had a rough time since her transition, and I hoped we weren't dealing with anything serious, like running away or being kicked out of her house. The center kept contact information for all their members. If I had to, I could drive over to her house and check on her.

It seemed I wouldn't have to. When I walked inside the center for a bag of ice for my head, I saw Reid and Maya sitting with their heads together at the kitchen table, whispering.

"Hey, Maya. Long time no see. Where have you been hiding? Some of the kids have been asking about you."

Maya looked to Reid in a panic, her eyes bugged out. Were they keeping secrets? If it were important, Reid would tell me. Otherwise, I had to accept that it wasn't my business, which killed me. Reid stood and offered her his hand.

"Come on. Let's take a walk." When he brushed by me, he stopped, pulling me into his arms for a quick hug. "I'll be outside if you need me."

"I do need you. I took a football to the head. It needs kisses," I whined in his ear.

Reid leaned up on his tiptoes and whispered in my ear. "Which head needs kisses?"

He smiled coyly, and it took me a moment to realize he was flirting with me. It was so unexpected from him. Having our relationship out in the open was giving Reid the confidence he needed to come out of his shell around me more and more. I loved this carefree, flirty, dirty side of him.

"Both," I whispered back, kissing his cheek. Reluctantly, I let him go and went in search of an ice pack.

~

As we drove home, Reid dropped a bomb on me. "I don't want to return to work at the café. I don't feel comfortable there anymore. I'd rather find something else, maybe a job that is in line with my degree, where I can help people and make a difference."

Logically, I knew he wasn't pushing me away, but I panicked just thinking how he wouldn't be working with me every day. Things were changing in our lives and in our relationship, and it was a lot to keep up with. I had to let him stand on his own two feet so he could continue to grow and move forward in his recovery, but damn if it wasn't hard for me to give up control. I got antsy when I couldn't lay eyes on him.

Trying hard to sound supportive, I agreed with him. Returning to the café would make Reid a target for retaliation. "I think that's a wise decision. I'm sure it holds bad memories for you."

Reid took my hand and focused his warm smile on me. "They aren't all bad. I've worked side by side with you for two years. We had plenty of good times. But it's time for me to move on. From the café, not you," he amended when he caught my look of panic.

"I fully support your decision. We should ask Charlie if he knows of any internships or jobs in his department that you would qualify for. He's a master at using resources to get what he needs."

"That's a great idea. I'll call him when we get home." Reid gazed out the window, lapsing into silence. Then he added, "I need to find a way to help these kids. I'm not doing enough for them. They need me as much as I need them. It's time I stopped focusing so much on my own problems and started helping others. I think it would also help me as well."

I raised our joined hands to my lips and pressed a kiss to his knuckles. "Those kids don't know how lucky they are to have you in their corner."

I dreaded the next stop on our to-do list today. "Are you ready to get this over with?" We stood, hand-in-hand, outside of the police station, gazing up at the three-story brick building. It loomed over us like an imposing specter, a Pandora's box of bad memories that I feared might trigger Reid's anxiety. "I'll be right by your side the whole time. We do this together." Reid's fingers felt hot and sweaty laced through mine—his clammy palm betrayed how nervous he was. I gave his hand a reassuring squeeze and held the door open for him.

The detective in charge of his case asked us to come in and identify the three suspects they had arrested. They were currently being held without bail on charges of assault, attempted sexual assault, hate crimes, and a few minor charges. The detective informed us that the state was pressing charges on Reid's behalf, so he wouldn't have to testify if he didn't want to. But Reid was braver and stronger than most people gave him credit for. He was angry and wanted justice. He fully intended to testify against his attackers if need be.

We were ushered into a tiny cubicle with a desk, a

potted palm, and two chairs. Detective Vallejo addressed Reid, asking about his health. "I'm feeling much better, thank you," he answered politely. Watching Reid face his fears while keeping his composure made my heart swell with pride.

Detective Vallejo took a seat behind her desk, folding her hands. "Reid, I appreciate you coming down here. I know this isn't easy for you. I want you to take a look at these pictures and point out the men that attacked you." She showed us a black binder that held mug shots of several guys fitting the description of Reid's attackers. Reid zeroed in on them immediately.

"These three. That's them. I'd recognize them anywhere." He pointed to one of a man with dark blond hair. "His name is Troy. He was in my English lit class last year." Reid studied another of the pics. "This one, I don't know his name, but he hit on me in a club a few weeks ago. I rejected him, and he has been harassing me ever since. I filed a report with campus security about him several weeks ago. He came into the café on campus where Riley and I work and harassed me. He called me names, ugly slurs against my sexuality, and threatened me."

My stomach churned with nausea. I let that fucker off the hook. I'd let him stroll right out the door after he threatened Reid, dismissing him as another douchebag who hated gays. I'd underestimated him as an actual threat, and because of my poor judgement, I'd given him easy access to attack Reid. I would not start playing the blame game again, but it was hard for me not to feel responsible.

The detective took the pictures Reid identified and put them in an envelope. Then she pegged Reid with a frown. My heart sank—it couldn't be good news. "I'm going to do everything in my power to put these guys away for a while. But I'll be honest with you, they probably won't get much more than a slap on the wrist and time served. The one you pointed out who has been harassing you? His daddy knows the judge assigned to your case. In fact, his attorney is working with the DA to overturn the bail issue."

"Then we'll get a different judge!" I demanded, outraged at having to play the who-knows-who game of politics.

Detective Vallejo frowned again. "Won't make a difference. He knows all the judges. He's a prosecuting attorney and works with all of them. These boys have money, connections, and no prior arrests. The judge is going to slap them with community service or a short probation stint."

"So they'll be right back on the streets to harass us or worse in no time? Great! Why even bother?"

My anger mounted taller than a skyscraper. I was beyond pissed—I wanted to hurt someone, break something. They needed to suffer for what they did to Reid. There was no way I could just let that shit go, turn a blind eye and swallow the injustice of this. A part of me wanted to burn this city down to the ground—to hunt these fuckers one by one and end their lives.

I don't know how Reid remained calm. "Is there anything I can do to make a difference?"

Her warm brown eyes softened. "Sure there is, Reid. You can persecute them in the court of public opinion. Maybe give an interview or something to try and tarnish their reputations, so it's harder for them to get jobs in this town, or you can press your university to take action against their fraternity or just the students involved. There are ways to be proactive about this, but none of them are going to make the guys serve a longer sentence, unfortunately. This is the part of the job I hate most. I used to work in narcotics until someone close to me was attacked, much like you were. I was angry and so motivated to make a difference in the way they handled things that I switched to victim's crimes. But sadly, I haven't been able to make much of a difference. The laws are the laws, hard to change them."

Reid stood and shook the detective's hand. "Thank you for all you have done for me. Please keep us posted about the court dates." He motioned for me to follow him, and we walked out of the office. We were silent until we made it outside.

As soon as we pushed through the glass doors, Reid grabbed me tight and buried his face in my neck. His slight body vibrated with his silent sobs. He was so strong when he needed to be, but now that he was in my arms and we were safely outside, he could let it all go.

"You did so good, Bunny. So strong. It's going to be okay. I promise you. I'm going to make it okay for you." *Somehow.*

Reid kissed me, his tear-streaked face making my cheeks wet. I tasted his salty tears on his lips and licked them away, wishing I could do the same with his problems.

"Come on. I have tissues in the car."

CHAPTER 18
REID

His hands fisted the denim of my jeans and tugged them down to my knees. Smooth hands wrapped around my flaccid cock, yanking roughly. He was hurting me. All the tugging in the world wouldn't get me hard. His nails raked my soft cock, tearing at the skin. It burned, the sharp sting brought tears to my eyes. I tried to scream, to beg, plead with them to stop. But I couldn't hear my voice. I could only hear their cruel laughter as they egged each other on.

"Stop! Don't touch me!" I screamed inside my head. Any second now, Riley would burst through the door and save me. Any second...

"Reid, baby, wake up. I've got you. Wake up, Bunny." Riley's muscular arms wrapped around me, comforting me. I knew he'd rescue me if I just held on long enough. "Reid, open your pretty eyes, Bunny."

His warm breath tickled my cheek. Slowly, my eyes peeled open, afraid I'd see a dirty alley and a rusty dumpster. But I was safe at home in my bed, snuggled up in Riley's strong arms.

It was just a dream. A nightmare. *Again.*

"There you are. You're okay now, I've got you." He held me as I returned to consciousness slowly, squinting as my eyes adjusted to the early morning light streaking through the windows. "Which one was it? Old or new?"

I knew what he meant. Was my nightmare of an old attack or the most recent one? I hated telling him how much it still affected me after all these weeks. Hated seeing the guilt he still carried. My silence was all the answer he needed.

He rocked me in his arms. "So, new, huh? It's over now. I promise you. Let's get up, and I'll make you breakfast."

"I can't. We have to pick up Maya and drive into Charleston to Dr. Webber's office by ten."

"Alright. We'll get drive-through breakfast, and I'll order something for Maya as well. Come on, let's get dressed." As I disentangled myself from his hold, he tightened his arms around me and leaned over me, capturing my lips in a sweet but possessive kiss. "I love you, Reid. I'll never be able to tell you that often enough for you to understand just how much."

One of the plastic twist ties that banded my heart snapped, loosening its stranglehold on my ability to feel. "Love you, too, Hero. And I'm going to remind you every day for the rest of your life."

~

Maya lived in Cooper's Cove, not far from us, in a gated community with enormous houses and perfectly manicured yards. She was waiting for us outside when we pulled up. Usually, Maya wore tight jeans and fitted shirts that showed off her slim figure. Today she wore baggy cargo pants and a loose t-shirt. She was hiding. As an abuse survivor, I knew firsthand that her choice of clothes screamed shame. She felt ashamed of herself and what they did to her body. I wasn't going to stand for that for one minute. No way would I let them have that kind of power over her.

After we talked yesterday at the center, Maya admitted to me she had been missing all week because she had suffered an attack. She didn't give me many details, but I could piece together what happened for the most part. I had a standing appointment with Dr. Webber this morning, and I encouraged Maya to come with me, begged really, until she finally agreed to join me. I didn't mind giving her my appointment. She needed the help today much more than I did. After placing a call to Dr. Webber and explaining the situation, he agreed to see Maya this morning and rescheduled my appointment for later in the week.

As soon as she climbed into the backseat, Riley greeted her and offered her a bag containing her breakfast croissant and a bottle of orange juice, which she gratefully accepted. After my attack, I had zero appetite, so I wasn't sure if she was accepting the food to be polite or if she was actually hungry. She smiled and thanked him.

Maya was quiet as we drove, focused on her food and listening as Riley and I filled the silence with mundane conversation. When we arrived at Dr. Webber's office, Maya grabbed my hand and whispered, "You're coming in with me, right? Please don't make me go in alone."

I squeezed back, offering the reassurance she needed. "Of course, whatever makes you comfortable."

I hadn't planned on joining her. It wasn't that I didn't want to be supportive, I just worried that the details of her attack would remind me of mine, and after my nightmare this morning, I didn't relish the thought of another setback.

It wasn't long before the door to Dr. Webber's office opened, and he strolled into the waiting room to introduce himself. He acknowledged Riley and I before turning his attention to Maya.

"You must be Miss Taylor. I'm Dr. Webber. Would you like to come in and talk with me for a bit?"

Maya looked to me and back to the doc. "Can Reid join us? Is that allowed?"

Dr. Webber smiled kindly. "Whatever you want that makes you feel safe and comfortable is definitely allowed. There are no rules here except kindness, respect, and discretion. Everything you tell me is confidential. My office is a safe space for you to open up and be honest, so you can begin to receive the help you need."

Maya nodded shyly and followed us inside his office. She took a seat next to me on the leather couch and sort of folded in on herself. It broke my heart to see. Normally, Maya was bold and outgoing, always laughing and smiling with the other kids. I had a moment of clarity when I realized this must be what I looked like when I saw that broken, pained look on Riley's face.

After a basic introduction, Maya explained she had transitioned from male to female two years ago and was currently taking hormone replacement therapy. She briefly described her broken relationship with her parents, who couldn't accept her transition, and her outcast status at school. Maya told Dr. Webber how she started going to the youth center shortly after deciding to transition and how Over The Rainbow was the only place she'd found where she felt safe and included.

"Maya," he said gently, "Can you tell me what happened the night you were attacked?"

The doc had helped her to loosen up just barely, but Maya was sitting up straighter and making eye contact. Her voice sounded stronger and more sure. Until she recounted that night's events. Tears filled her eyes as she told us the story.

"I don't have many friends anymore since transitioning, and things are so stressful and strained at home between me and my parents. So when school lets out, I always head over to the coffee shop down the street from the school. I stay there all day doing homework, studying, or listening to music. I play around online, and sometimes, I just sit and write, like journaling. Usually, I don't head home until bedtime when I can hide in my room."

Dr. Webber offered Maya a bottle of water. She took a few sips before continuing. "Last week, when I was leaving the café, I ran into two guys from school hanging around outside. I tried not to make eye contact with them because I was afraid they'd start harassing me, as usual. I just kept my head down and brushed by them. I started walking home, and after a minute, I heard them walking behind me. At first, I wasn't sure if they were following me, because why would they? I figured maybe they live in my subdivision. But when I sped up, so did they. I got the feeling they were stalking me, and I remember thinking that in every show or movie I've seen where someone is being followed, whenever they turn and look back or start running, that's when the attackers make their move. So I tried to keep my pace and not look."

Maya paused to sip more water. Dr. Webber offered her a box of tissues, which she gratefully accepted, loudly blowing her nose. "I would have ducked into a store, but everything I passed was already closed. Suddenly, I heard them run up on me, and they each grabbed me under one arm and lifted me right off my feet. They ducked into an alley separating the laundromat and the dentist's office. I screamed for help, but we were alone. Nobody heard me."

She broke down, sobbing and shaking. Scooting closer, I put an arm around her shoulders, knowing exactly how scary and overwhelming it felt to relive such a traumatic moment.

"They said such ugly things to me about how if I wanted to be a girl, they'd treat me like one. They were going to teach me what girls wanted." Maya scoffed sarcastically. "Yeah, sure, like all girls just love to be raped. Whatever."

I hugged her until her breathing calmed enough to continue. "It's alright, Maya, you're safe now. We're here for you."

"Thanks, Reid. Anyway, they went off on a whole tangent of slurs. They had me pinned against the wall. His hand was around my neck, choking me as he held me in place. When he pulled my pants down, I fought him, and he slammed my head into the brick wall. Things got fuzzy after that. I must have passed out for a moment. When I came to, I was down on the ground. One of them pinned my arms above my head, the other was—he was—inside me. I must have zoned out again. When I woke, they had switched places and the other guy was inside me. Then they finished, and when he stood up and fixed his pants, he spit on my face and kicked my head. Then I blacked out again."

Maya buried her head between her knees, sucking deep breaths of air through her nose before breathing out through her mouth. We gave her a moment of silence to gather herself together. Dr. Webber and I shared a look of concern. This was worse than I'd feared.

"I don't know how long I was out for that time. When I woke, everything hurt, and I was cold. I realized I was lying in a dirty puddle." She broke down again, sobbing through harsh ragged breaths as she tried to talk through her tears. "They raped me in a mud puddle, and somehow, that hurt worse than the rape. Like all I was worth was dirty water. I didn't even merit a dry spot or a patch of grass. I was wet and cold, and I tried to pull up my pants but I hurt so bad."

By now, I was crying along with her, sharing her grief. Maya's pain filtered under my skin and settled deep into my bones. Plenty of my own similar pain simmered just beneath the surface of my skin. It was all too fresh and raw to hold in.

"I don't know how long I sat there before I could pick myself up and walk home. It took forever because I was moving so slowly. I remember feeling more afraid of going home than I was just before I knew I was going to be attacked. I was so afraid to face my parents that I contemplated some dark things as I walked home."

Dr. Webber gently asked, "Did you consider hurting yourself?"

"Yeah." Maya wrapped her arms around her middle, hugging herself for security. "I thought if I just run away or kill myself, I could just end it all and never have to feel like this again. I could finally stop hurting."

I lent her my support again by wrapping my arm around her shoulders. "Go on, Maya. Get it all out."

She leaned into my embrace, resting her head against me. "My parents were waiting up for me because I'd broken curfew. They could see I was a mess. I told them what happened. My dad said I asked for it because I was a sexual deviant. What does that even mean? Because I was born in the wrong body and I corrected it, I'm a sexual deviant? What the fuck ever!" Anger was replacing her tears, brimming to the surface like water boiling over the rim of a pot.

"My mom said nothing, just ignored me and went to bed. When I showered, I saw blood from my bottom on the washcloth. It ran down the drain in streaks. They didn't use condoms." Maya began sobbing again, hiding her face in my shirt. "They didn't even use lube. I guess they tore me open inside."

She cried it out for a minute before sitting up to blow her nose again. "The next day, I skipped school because I couldn't risk facing them, and I was in no shape to sit in class. I went to the health department instead. They tested me, and the doctor gave me suppositories and ointment for the fissures. Of course, they had to report it, so the police and a social worker came. I told them everything. They drove me home and spoke to my parents. They played along like they were so concerned for me. Total bullshit. When the social worker left, they went to their room and ignored me—never said one word to me about what happened. After that, I contacted my guidance counselor and switched to remote online learning for the remainder of the school year."

Dr. Webber drew a deep breath and regarded Maya with warmth and understanding. "Maya, thank you for trusting me. First, I want you to know that I am a safe space for you to vent. You are brave and strong, and you are safe here. Second, I want you to know that if you'll allow me to, I'm going to help you process this, and together, we will get you to a place where you feel strong again. I know that you've known Reid for a while now, and I can vouch for him that he is trustworthy and safe if you feel comfortable opening up to him. You are not alone, you are not to blame, and you are supported and accepted by the people you have chosen to surround yourself with."

He paused for a moment, choosing his words carefully. "As I've been told by Reid, you have many friends at the center. They care about you and worry over you. If you'll let them, they would like to help you heal by showing their support to you. Don't shut them out. Accept inclusion and help whenever it is offered." He stood and asked, "If it's alright with you, I'd like to give you a hug. It's perfectly acceptable to say no. I just feel that sometimes hugs are the best medicine."

We all laughed a little as Maya accepted the hug. It surprised me when she wasn't the first one to pull away. The girl was probably touch starved because her parents showed her no affection. I had to agree with Dr. Webber. Sometimes, hugs really were the best medicine.

Dropping Maya back at home when her feelings were so raw made me feel sick. The worst thing for her right now would be to have an argument with her parents and trigger her feelings of self-hate and shame. So Riley and I took her for ice cream and dropped her off at the center so she could surround herself with supportive people.

"Call me anytime if you need me. Or if you just need to talk. I'm always here for you." Riley seconded that and gave Maya his number as well.

The ride home was emotional for me as I processed Maya's trauma. It held so many similarities to mine. Except for one major difference—I had Riley.

"Ry, I never would have gotten this far in life if not for

your constant love and support. I could love you for the rest of my life and still not be even with you for what you've done for me."

Riley laid his hand on my thigh. "Nonsense. Everything you said is true for me as well. We were even a long time ago. I really admire how you handled Maya. You are the best person to help her. We're all lucky to have you in our lives. Me most of all. And if you let me, I plan on spending the rest of my life showing you just how grateful I am for you."

When we stopped at a red light, he leaned over and kissed me. It was soft and sweet, and I never wanted it to end. But he just promised me a lifetime of kisses like this one, so I reluctantly let him go.

CHAPTER 19
RILEY

It was almost absurd how quickly our moods changed from somber to playful as soon as we walked through our front door. The mass of cars clogging up our driveway and a good portion of the street in front of our house should have been a dead give-away. The whole gang was here. We hadn't all gathered together like this since Reid was in the hospital, and I was glad this time was under better circumstances.

Everyone clustered in the backyard around the fire pit, despite the cold weather. Lucky grilled burgers and hotdogs. Griffin was in the kitchen baking, probably dessert.

"What's going on, Griff? Are we celebrating something?"

Griffin pretended to sniff the air. "Can't you smell it?"

Reid looked perplexed as he, too, sniffed the air. "The brownies?"

He flapped an oven mitt at him. "No, silly. Love is in

the air. We are finally celebrating you and Riley coming out."

Reid and I exchanged confused looks. "Uh, you're about six years too late. Reid and I came out when we were fourteen. But I do like brownies."

Griffin laughed like I said something funny. "No, not your sexuality, dope. Coming out about your relationship. *Coming together*, finally!"

"That merits brownies and a barbecue?"

Reid looked skeptical but excited. I'm sure he thought celebrating our mutual feelings was a fantastic idea. He and Griffin weren't best friends for nothing, they were like-minded.

"Of course! It merits everything. This is so exciting! Lucky and Cyan have had a bet going forever. Whoever caved first won a hundred bucks. And they had to deduct twenty for every year you wasted since we met you guys. So, they're waiting to hear your story to see who won."

A headache formed at the base of my skull, and I groaned. Reid squealed, obviously growing more excited by the second. The dull ache behind my eyes tightened painfully when Reid suggested, "We should play a couples game, like 'how well do you know your partner' or something similar."

Griffin shook his head. "That's a horrible idea. You and Riley have been together six years already. You'd blow everyone out of the water."

"Yeah, what he said," I agreed with Griffin, hoping to change Reid's mind.

"And anyway," Griffin explained, "There's another

game about to begin. The guys are holding a hotdog contest."

It was Reid's turn to groan. "Like, where they shove a bunch of meat in their mouths all at once to see who can swallow the fastest? No, thanks, I'm not interested." I laughed because competitive games were Reid's hellscape. He looked miserable just considering it.

"Nah, if it were just that, it would be no contest. Cyan would take the cake. He can swallow a lot of meat." Griffin arched his brow to insinuate his double entendre. "They came up with a few new ideas. How deep can you swallow a hotdog whole? Couples' games where one partner holds it between their teeth and the other eats it, ending with the sexiest kiss. Oh, and Murphy's brainchild, holding the wiener between your knees and racing across the yard."

I pegged Griffin with a look of incredulity. "You're shitting me, right?"

"Nope." He smiled. "Not shitting you." He was still chuckling as me and Reid stepped through the sliding glass doors that led outside.

As soon as we crossed the threshold, the guys erupted in catcalls and whistles. "The lovebirds have finally arrived!" Lucky held up his beer, toasting us.

After Reid and I took our seats at the patio table, everyone converged on us, hovering over the table when the seats were all taken. "Okay, we've waited long enough. Tell us how it happened. We want the whole story. The Full Monty. Don't leave anything out," Cyan issued.

"Especially the naked parts," Murphy added.

"No, you can skip those," Hayes amended.

"What? They're right across the hall from me. I can hear everything. It's hot." Murphy grinned a dirty smile. I wouldn't put it past him to listen in at our door, hand cupped to his ear.

Lucky smacked his little brother upside the head. "Go on, lay it on us."

It was going to be a long day. "You don't care how it happened, you just want your money. Which one of you had bets on me?"

It made me uncomfortable to discuss our relationship under a microscope because I still carried so much fear that I would eventually screw up badly enough to push Reid away. *Permanently.*

Lucky raised his hand, smirking like a schmuck.

"Well, you're both out of luck. We kinda cracked at the same time. Sorry to disappoint you." Not true, I loved to disappoint them.

"It's true," Reid seconded. "We were in the middle of a heated argument. Our guards were down, and it just slipped out."

Cyan persisted. "Yeah, but who slipped first? Someone had to stick their foot in their mouth first. I'm sure you didn't say it at the same time, did you?"

Now it was my turn to raise my hand like a schmuck.

"Yes!" Lucky hollered. "Pay up, loser." He knocked Cyan's arm, holding out his hand for his payout.

Cyan brushed him off and grabbed another soda. "Whatever. I'll settle up with you later. Let's eat."

We ate burgers, the smoky flavor from the charcoal kickstarted my flagging appetite, and we saved the hotdogs for the games. Our friends wanted to hear about all the details of our relationship that they never asked about because they felt it wasn't their business. I felt it still wasn't their business, but Reid answered good-naturedly.

His smile was all teeth, and I had a feeling he loved this so much because I was his favorite topic. "We realized we've always been in love with each other. We kept quiet for different reasons that made sense to us at the time. I'm glad we finally figured it out."

Murphy wistfully eyed each couple seated around the table. "Everyone's so happy now that they're married off. Do you think I'll ever find the right guy?"

"I didn't know you were looking," Cyan said, as surprised as I was by Murphy's unexpected comment.

"I'm not. But when I'm finished having fun, I hope I'm as lucky as you all were."

"It's going to take a hell of a man to handle a spitfire like you. I can't wait to meet him." I laughed, clapping his back playfully.

"When you're ready, the right guy will be waiting for you, Murph. You'll see. He'll knock you off your feet before you even know what hit you," Lucky said.

Murphy grinned and primped his hair. "I hope not. I want to be prepared, so I look my best."

Lucky laughed. "You always look your best." He cupped Murphy's cheeks, making his lips pucker, and blew him a kiss.

"Damn straight I do. You never know when Mr. Right will walk through the door."

Hudson's arrival cut our conversation short. "I hope someone saved me a burger because I'm starving."

He greeted Reid and me first, kissing us both on the cheek. "Better late than never, guys. Did you get my flowers?"

"We sure did, but it wasn't as much fun as the collection of gay porn Murphy gave us." I was only teasing. Hudson's gift was thoughtful and appreciated.

"I hope you sanitized those DVDs before you touched them," Hudson joked, winking at Murphy.

When everyone finished eating, the games got underway. The hot dog relay was a disaster. Murphy teamed up with Hudson since they were both partnerless. The couples raced across the yard while holding a hotdog between their thighs before passing it off to their partner, hands free. I doubled over in laughter as Hudson squished it to bits between his knees accidentally and was disqualified, causing Murphy to seek revenge against him in the next game. Their rivalry amused me to no end. It felt so good to laugh after such an emotionally charged day.

Next was a game where you held the dog between your lips or teeth while your partner tried to take as much of it as he could into his mouth at once, no chewing. The dog had to remain whole. It was a play on deep throating and Cyan took first place, surprising no one. Murphy, in a fit of pettiness for having been disqualified in the last round, sought retaliation. He seized the hot dog between his teeth and when Hudson, a straight man who had never had anything longer than a baby carrot stick in his mouth, tried to swallow the hotdog, Murphy shoved his head forward, causing Hudson to choke on the wiener. It was like watching a train derail, I knew it was going to end badly but I was helpless to look away.

"Mmm, you sound so sexy when you gag, Cupcake." Murphy joked, playing dirty and getting Hudson riled up and angry.

Hudson glowered. "That's okay, my little Cream Puff. The games aren't over yet."

Ever since Lucky's birthday party last year, Hudson and Murphy constantly exchanged the worst sort of nicknames imaginable. The endearments became more outlandish every time they got together. They had an ongoing rivalry that just wouldn't quit, but it sure was entertaining to watch.

Throughout the party, I kept an eye on Reid, making sure he was okay. Though he chose not to participate in the games, I felt relieved he seemed to be enjoying himself.

For the last game, the contestants attached a hotdog on a string and tied it to their belt loop. They stood over an empty beer bottle and the object was to drop your hotdog into the bottle without using your hands. The game was actually a lot harder than it looked because with each movement of your body, the string swayed with momentum, missing the skinny neck of the bottle each time.

Following a round of ridiculous smack talking where

I made a joke about my meat being too thick for such a tight hole, the game began. After several failed attempts to bottle their meat sticks, Hudson squatted impressively low over his bottle, sliding his wiener effortlessly into the bottle's mouth between his thighs. Reid and Griffin, who were not participating in the game, cheered wildly for him, fist-pumping the air and clapping. The rest of us called foul.

"That's cheating! It's not supposed to be that easy." Murphy yelled indignantly. He would try and steal Hudson's win at all costs, to no one's surprise.

"Actually, nobody specified any rules, so I'm thinking it's allowed," Griffin explained patiently. I snickered, knowing nobody was going to argue with him.

Hudson clapped his mammoth hand on Murphy's thin shoulder, making him flinch. "Calm down, Pop Tart. You're just upset that I used common sense and you have none. Also, I think you're jealous that I can squat lower than you. It's too bad. I bet the boys you date would appreciate that."

"Stuff it, Breeder. They appreciate all my unique skills." Murphy looked pissed.

Hudson dismissed his immaturity. "Just because I don't dip my stick in men doesn't mean I don't know how to dip my stick. Straight men have unique skills, too, Butter Bean."

"Gee, Hudsy, I'd love for you to take me upstairs and prove it. Show me what you know. Maybe you can teach me something new."

Cyan and I nearly fell over laughing. That effectively

sealed Hudson's lips. It seemed that whenever their rivalry became too heated, Murphy would flirt with Hudson inappropriately, causing Hudson to clam up and become defensive or quiet. For whatever reason, Hudson did not seem to appreciate Murphy's ribbing and innuendo. I think it made him very uncomfortable. Reid had a theory about why, but I would not entertain his foolish ideas. Hudson was usually the most easy-going laid-back guy, but whenever he was around Murphy, he seemed to have a hair up his ass. Not that I could really blame him. Nobody knew better than me how annoying Murphy could be, except maybe Lucky, but the guy had a heart of gold. I couldn't figure out why he clashed so hard with Hudson.

Fucking finally, everybody left, and I could take Reid upstairs. I was practically pushing him up the steps with my hand on his lower back, urging him along faster.

"Why are we in such a rush?"

Because it's bedtime? Bedtime equals sexy time. How could he not expect me to be in a rush? "I had so much fun playing wiener games, I thought we could play a few more." *Together. Alone. In bed.*

Reid giggled, suddenly moving much faster. "I need a shower. I smell like smoke and charcoal from the grill."

I hurried ahead of him to the bathroom, turning on the shower so the steam would warm up the cold tiles. Reid came in behind me, stripping off his shirt.

"Are you joining me?"

I stepped right up to him, taking his lips in a slow sensual kiss as I tugged his pants down his hips. "Would you like that?"

We'd never showered together before. No matter how many times I'd dreamed of sliding the curtain aside and joining him, it had never happened. Now my dick couldn't stop thinking about it.

Reid blushed, and I loved that he still had a reason to. "Yeah—y-yes. I'd love that."

Crouching low, I removed his shoes and pants from each leg, stood, and kissed him again, with more passion this time. His mouth opened for me, and my tongue slid inside, tasting every crevice. His mouth tasted salty from the hotdogs, and I sucked the flavor from his tongue, enjoying the way he melted into me. Each time his tongue retreated, I chased him deeper, sucking his tongue between my lips and drawing him back into my mouth.

Pulling away, I gazed down the long length of his lithe body. "You're so beautiful, so perfect. You were made for me."

I stripped out of my clothes quickly and ushered him into the shower. The steam was already thickening the air, condensing on the tiled walls and fogging up the mirror. I let Reid take the hot water first as I stood close behind him. Grabbing for the shampoo, I poured a dollop into my palm and began massaging Reid's scalp, running my fingers through his corn-silk locks.

He purred with pleasure, leaning into my touch.

"That feels incredible. It's relaxing, but I'm getting excited."

He had no clue what his simple, honest admission did to my libido. Everything Reid did or said drove me nuts. A simple lingering look from his topaz-blue eyes could set me on fire.

He tipped his head under the spray to rinse the suds from his hair, and I draped my arms around his body, massaging his soft skin with a soapy cloth. My lips sought out the column of his long neck as I washed him, sucking and biting my way down to his collarbone. My tongue traced the outline of his delicate bones as I feasted on his sweet skin. Reid writhed in my arms, grinding his pert little ass against my fully hard cock.

Dropping the cloth with a wet plop, I spread the soap with my hands, gliding over every inch of his body. I teased his tiny nipples into hard peaks, addicted to his body's response to my touch. He had the most sensitive nipples, and I loved to torture and tease them. My right hand delved lower to dip inside his navel, making his stomach contract under my touch. Reid's body was sensitive everywhere.

God, he drove me crazy. He wasn't pretending for my benefit or putting on a show for me. Reid was literally falling apart under my hands because my touch and the pleasure it brought him was the best thing he'd ever felt before. *I* did that to him. *I* made him feel that way. He had no idea how good he made made me feel.

Despite his newfound strength and confidence, I needed him to need me, to rely on me. I wanted to be his muse. His greatest source of inspiration and courage. Because I needed to know that my place in his life was solid. As unshakable as the ground we stood upon. Essentially, I needed reassurance that Reid and I were forever.

My hands roamed lower, past the thatch of blond curls to grasp Reid's hard cock. He melted against me, sliding his arms around my neck.

"Don't close your eyes, baby. Look down, watch me touch you."

I stroked his shaft slowly, loving the easy soapy glide of my hand over his velvety skin. His heat seeped into my hand. God, he was so thick and long. Absolutely gorgeous. The perfect cock on the perfect man. Everything about Reid was pure perfection, from his face to his body to his heart and soul.

I'd never know what I did to deserve him.

Tightening my grip, I stroked him quicker, drawing out the sweetest whimpers from his parted lips. "Feels so good to touch you like this. I've waited so long." I'd bet he was leaking from his slit, but I couldn't tell for sure because suds camouflaged it.

"Ry, please. I need more. I need *you*."

"Come here, turn around and step up here. I've got you."

The shower had a built-in tiled bench seat in the corner. Only big enough for one person, but I had an idea. When Reid was standing on the bench, his cock was at the perfect height to hit my mouth if I bent my head slightly. He tapped his hardness against my cheek, giggling at his boldness. In one slurp, I sucked it fully into my mouth, his eyes going wide with shock as I took him to the back of my throat. For a long moment, I held him there, letting him feel the muscles of my throat contract around his swollen crown.

Reid gasped, one hand braced on the wall and the other tangled into my hair as he guided my mouth back down, encouraging me to take all of him into my mouth with each pass of my lips. Reid was larger than most of the guys I'd blown, but this was my job. I'd learned a few tricks.

Reaching up, I massaged his smooth sac, rolling his balls between my fingers. He spread his legs further, inviting me to explore. I took his invitation and ran with it, spreading my soapy fingers around his taint, pressing slightly as I sucked him to the root.

"Touch me, Riley."

Reid whimpered as he looked down on me, watching with blown pupils as I stroked and sucked him. He looked wrecked with lust.

My fingers pressed further back, tracing around his tight hole. He would need to loosen up a fuck ton before I could slide my finger inside of him, even with the soap to ease my way.

The more I teased him, the softer his ring became, until I felt it give way under my fingertip, allowing me to breach him. I increased my mouth's suction as I slid inside, hoping to distract him with pleasure. Once I was in, the soap helped my finger to glide smoothly, and I found his prostate with no trouble. Pressing on the bundle of nerves as I took him to the back of my throat pushed Reid over the edge. Two minutes had to be a new record for me as Reid cried out, plunging even deeper into my mouth as he shot his load down my throat. He collapsed over me as his legs gave out, and I wrapped my arms around his hips to support his weight. Carefully, I set him down on his feet and held him tight as he settled.

"Can I have a taste?"

He kissed me before I could answer, stealing my tongue and sucking it into his mouth. I wasn't used to Reid being the dominant in any area of our life, but I could get used to it in the bedroom easily. His velvet tongue slid against mine as he explored the flavor of my mouth. Heat swirled in my belly, and it wasn't from the temperature of the water. It surprised and delighted me that Reid was playful and curious about sex. He seemed eager to learn and try new things. I had always assumed sex would be a sensitive subject for him, possibly even triggering for him, but so far, Reid seemed to thrive from the passion we shared.

He wanted to experience everything, and there was nothing I wanted more than to teach him.

CHAPTER 20
REID

"It's been a while since we've been able to talk one-on-one. Tell me where you're at with everything going on. How are you processing everything?"

Dr. Webber studied me with patient eyes, giving me time to group my words together. "I feel good. Strong. My moods have been steady, and I haven't hidden away in more than a week. Mostly, I guess I feel hopeful."

"Hopeful. I love that word. Hopeful about what, specifically?"

The city skyline visible through the big picture window drew my gaze. There was a whole world out there waiting for me. "Everything. My future, a new job, Riley, Maya's recovery. Right now, everything feels like it has the opportunity for a happy ending."

"Everything does, Reid. If you stay positive and in the present. How are your online classes going?"

"Great. I've maintained my grades. But I'm not any

closer to wanting to return to campus just yet. I can't face them. Things still feel so unresolved."

Dr. Webber reached for the travel mug on his desk and took a sip. "Give it time. No one is rushing you. Are you still attending the self-defense class?"

Smiling enthusiastically, I nodded. "I learned a new move to fend off an attack from behind. I tried it on Riley and put him on his as—butt. It was epic. He's so much stronger than me, but I was able to defend myself."

"I wish I could have seen that." He smiled ruefully. "I bet it felt amazing, didn't it?"

"Amazing doesn't begin to describe how good it felt. Poor Riley." I snickered, recalling the look of astonishment on his face when he hit the floor. It was comical.

The doc checked over his notes. "Let's back up a second. You mentioned you were feeling hopeful about Riley. Can you tell me what you meant by that?"

Heat bloomed across my cheeks, spreading down my neck like a rash. "Riley and I, we... um, we... we had a fight. And we said things. We didn't mean to, but we said we l-loved each other. Like, are in love with each other. For years." My eyes fixated on a spot just over Dr. Webber's left shoulder as I spoke, feeling too shy to meet his eyes. "So, we're together now."

Just like that. Simply wrapped and tied in a neat package with a bow. No angst. No drama. No sleepless nights wondering if we ruined our lifelong friendship.

He said nothing at first. Then a slow smile crept across his face. "Well, well. It's about time, isn't it? You've only been dancing around each other for six years now. Isn't it incredible what a little honest communication can accomplish?"

My face flamed with heat. "Imagine that." I let out a little laugh that sounded super fake.

"Congratulations. We'll put a pin in that topic and circle back later. Let's hear more about this new job you mentioned."

"I just don't see myself returning to the café. Besides it not being safe, there's just too many memories from that night that I don't want to see every time I turn the corner. Besides, I'd like to find something in line with my future where I can make a difference helping kids. I've talked with Charlie about this, and he's looking into possible opportunities where he works with the Department of Children and Families. Also, I've been looking into some other avenues online and was reading about the Guardian ad Litem program. I'd love to pursue that. I want to be a voice for the kids who need representation in court. More than anyone, I care about what they're going through and how they feel."

Dr. Webber spread his arms open. "Reid, I'm so tickled that you're moving in this direction. I can't think of a better choice for you. It's clear to me you will make an enormous difference in the lives of so many kids in need. If you need references, besides Charlie, please don't hesitate to ask me. I want to ask you now about Maya. I know you've been a shoulder for her to cry on or lean on, and I want to know how that's affecting your recovery."

Inhaling deeply, I held the breath in my lungs for a

moment, feeling my chest expand before letting the air whoosh out. "At first, it was rough. It totally brought everything back, fresh and clear in all its ugly reality. But honestly, watching how Maya deals with it and copes with her trauma inspired me to keep my head up. She wakes up every day and chooses to be positive. She chooses to get dressed and leave the house and smile and maybe laugh. I've learned a few things by watching her. Supporting Maya has definitely helped me cope with my own issues."

Dr. Webber's kind brown eyes shone with pride. Choosing him as my therapist was probably the smartest thing I'd ever done. Dr. Webber was exactly what I needed when I searched for a professional to help me through this tragedy.

"Wonderful. Now, let's call Riley in here. I'd like to ask him a few questions, if you don't mind."

My shoulders shook with suppressed mirth, thinking how much Riley hated sitting in the hot seat, answering questions about his feelings for me.

Opening the door to his office, I motioned for Riley to come inside. He took a seat next to me on the leather sofa, looking back and forth between me and the doc. I was sure he wondered why he was called in here.

Dr. Webber gave Riley a genuine smile. "How are you, Mr. Morgan? I hear congratulations are in order."

Riley smirked in return, leaning back to get more comfortable. His guard dropped now that he realized he wasn't in trouble. "Sure are."

"How do you feel it's going?"

Dr. Webber gripped his pen and notepad, and I wondered if he was actually taking notes or just giving Riley a hard time to humor us.

"Uh, pretty great, actually."

Riley looked at me as if checking to make sure I was satisfied with his answer. My lips stretched wide as I smiled adoringly. He was usually so composed and confident, especially where I was concerned. But now he was more docile, second guessing himself, and nervous. It was unexpected, and I loved that he still surprised me after all these years together. I wondered if it was because our relationship was still so new.

"I'm glad to hear that. Now, turn to Reid and look into his eyes and tell me again how great it's going."

That sounded like an odd request. Riley must have thought so, too, because his eyes looked wary as he faced me. But, as the doc asked, he gazed into my eyes and his immediately softened, his nervous energy fleeing. Riley's emotions surfaced as he held both my hands in his larger ones.

"Being with Reid, out in the open, being honest about our feelings for each other, it's better than my best day."

"And what was your best day?" Dr. Webber laid his pen down and simply watched us with a soft smile.

Riley's gaze never faltered from mine. "The day I met Reid. That was my best day. But now, every day is better than the last."

Erasing the distance between us, I leaned toward Riley and popped a chaste kiss on his pink lips.

Then Riley turned back to Dr. Webber, still holding one of my hands. "I have a question for you, but it's kind of personal."

"That's my specialty. Ask me anything." Dr. Webber adjusted his glasses higher onto his nose and grinned at us.

"So, Reid and I, now that we're together, we want to, um, express our... feelings toward each other. But not with words. More with our actions. Express our feelings *completely*. In your professional opinion, is that something you think Reid is ready for, considering what he's recently been through?"

The doc lifted his legal pad to his mouth to cover the snicker pulling at his lips. "Are you asking me if I feel Reid is ready for a sexual relationship?"

I could count on one hand the times I'd seen my big strong hero blush, and I popped a finger on my other hand, adding to the tally.

"Yeah, I guess I am. I don't want to do anything that might set him back or trigger him negatively."

"Have you asked Reid how he feels about it?"

Riley glanced quickly at me and then back to the doc. "Yes. Of course, I've discussed it with him."

"Endlessly," I grumbled under my breath. I was positive they both heard me, as Dr. Webber's smirk spread into a full-fledged grin.

"And what did Reid say? Or, better yet, what did you hear?" Dr. Webber asked patiently.

"Reid said he was ready and that he thought he would be okay, since he would be with me."

Dr. Webber raised his eyebrows, waiting for Riley to self-assess and come to the correct conclusion on his own. "So what part of that is tripping you up? It's my opinion that a person knows their own body and mind better than anyone else can. Say, for example, if you are feeling pain in your stomach and you go to the doctor. He runs tests and X-ray's and says he can't find anything wrong, so you must be fine. But you go home and continue to feel pain. You're convinced something isn't right and seek a second opinion. And you continue to advocate for yourself until you resolve the problem. You knew something wasn't right because nobody knows your body better than you do. Correct?"

Riley and I both nodded our heads in agreement. The analogy made perfect sense.

"It's much like that for Reid. He still has a long road to travel in therapy, but he knows his mind and body better than you or I or anyone else does. If Reid says he's ready, then I trust his decision. Sure, there might be a moment when he's triggered, but you'll be there with him to get through it. The process of feeling something hurtful and working through it with someone you trust is therapeutic. You would probably be doing more harm if you continue to reject him than if you move forward with *expressing your feelings with actions instead of words.*"

I couldn't help but giggle when he repeated Riley's words with such exaggerated emphasis. "Thanks, Dr. Webber. I just remembered we left the stove on. We have to rush back home."

I probably ruined the lie I was trying to sell with the

laughter I failed to suppress as I tugged on Riley's hand, leading him towards the door in a great hurry.

"Stop being so excited in front of the doc. It's embarrassing," Riley groaned, covering his face in his hands.

I loved that a man who was paid for sex for a living blushed about the prospect of having sex with me. It highlighted the differences between his clients and our relationship and made me feel like I was sitting on top of the world. Everything Riley did made me feel cherished and unique.

When we were alone in the car, Riley reached across me to buckle my seatbelt in place. He turned to face me, and I knew we were about to have a serious moment. I packed away my humor and excitement, waiting to hear what he needed to say.

"Bunny, just because the doc gave you the green light doesn't mean we're going to run home, grab the lube, and hop in bed. We agreed to go slow. I know it's killing you. Hell, it's killing me, too, but we don't have to rush this. We've been building up to it, learning each other's bodies, what feels good and what doesn't, and it's been amazing and thrilling and fun. This is the good stuff. The stuff we've dreamed about for years. I don't want it to be over in a snap. I've waited so damn long for you, built it up on a pedestal, no, a fucking skyscraper, and just jumping in bed on any given Tuesday or whatever just feels—anticlimactic."

Everything he said made sense—I felt it deep in my heart, knowing it was as special to him as it was to me. He was waiting for the right moment to make magic together, and it would be magical, I had no doubt. It may sound ridiculous, but Riley and I? There was no way we could come together and it not be *unforgettable*. Volcanic. Atomic. Like fireworks on the Fourth of July —*breathtaking*.

Making love with Riley was going to be life changing. I could wait a little longer for life changing—it was worth the wait.

"So, when will we know when the time is right?"

"We'll just know, Bunny. We'll both feel it and know."

He kissed me like he needed the breath from my lungs to stay alive. His tongue wrapped around mine, silky and warm, claiming me, promising me with his lips that our moment would come, and it would feel as incredible as this kiss. I sighed into his mouth, sharing his breath, breathing it back into my lungs.

"I love you, Hero. You're worth waiting for. Six years is nothing... I'd wait a lifetime for you."

That night, as I exited the bathroom, Riley stood in front of our closet, choosing a shirt. My feet halted in the doorway as I towel-dried my hair. He turned around, reading the hesitation on my face.

"Reid, I promised you I was only accepting non-sexual dates. I meant what I said—I would die before I broke a promise to you."

Nodding, I inhaled a deep, fortifying breath. I trusted

Riley with my life, so why was I second guessing him now? It was just old insecurities rearing their ugly heads. Now that I had Riley the way I wanted him, I had too much to lose, and I was not willing to gamble with his affections.

Riley slipped the navy blue dress shirt over his shoulders and secured the buttons. “I’m taking a woman out tonight. We’re going to her coworker’s wedding. I’ll be home early.” He tightened the knot in his tie and crossed the room to stand before me. Dressed in nothing but my towel, my feet rooted to the floor, I forced a smile on my lips. “Maybe I’ll bring you home a slice of cake.”

“Just bring yourself home, that’s all the sweet I need.”

He looked incredible when he dressed up. His classic, rugged good looks clothed in refined threads made me want to undress him.

Riley dropped to his knees in front of me, tugging my damp towel down with him. He wrapped his lips around my semi-hard dick, sucking the crown with force. My toes curled as tiny electric shocks zinged down my thighs, making my legs quiver. Riley licked up and down my shaft and around the swollen head, teasing me until I begged for his mouth.

“Suck me, Ry. Please.” My hands tangled in his hair, applying just enough pressure to let him know I wouldn’t allow him to get up again until he finished.

He took me to the back of his throat and swallowed, making me whimper with need. When his lips slid back down my hard length, he did so slowly, causing me to want to ram my dick deep down his throat. Taking mercy on me, Riley set a fast, steady pace, licking into my slit every time he slid off. As I spilled down his throat, I shouted, sagging against the dresser for support.

"Mmm, that'll taste great with the cake later." He peered up at me and winked, a drop of my cum smeared on the corner of his mouth. Swiping it away, I sucked my finger into my mouth, tasting myself. Riley and I moaned at the same time as my eyes closed, savoring the flavor and the visual of watching him blow me. "We might need a repeat of that when I get home, if you're still up."

I'll be up, in more ways than one. You can bet on that.

Riley stood and brushed the wrinkles from his pants, then folded me in his arms. His breath tickled my neck as his lips, swollen and wet from sucking me, made contact with my skin.

"I'm going to start taking you out on proper dates. Real dates where we dress up and go to dinner somewhere nice, or to a movie or something. Would you like that?"

"I like anywhere I am with you, as long as we're together. It doesn't have to be fancy, Ry." Smiling, I closed my eyes and absorbed the pleasure of being in his arms.

Riley dragged his nose down the length of my throat. "I don't know what I ever did to deserve you. I must have suffered greatly in my past life. Maybe God thought he owed me. But I'm never going to take you for granted." He looked directly into my eyes, his sapphire irises darkening. "You're a priceless treasure, Reid Morgan. And you're all mine." He kissed me sweet and soft, drawing out the slide of his lips over mine.

Long after he walked away, I stood there with my eyes closed and my lips parted, feeling everything his declaration evoked in me. Like a balloon floating through the air, I felt weightless—a pink, sparkly cloud of bliss.

While Riley danced the night away, I cozied up on the couch and painted my nails a pretty Christmas red. For the first time in—forever, I felt mostly comfortable being home alone. Dr. Webber suggested I view this as *me time*. Time alone to hear my own thoughts, connect with my feelings, and pamper myself. Taking his stellar advice, I devised activities to get to know and like myself better. Online quizzes, reading self-help articles, and cooking a nice meal for myself were just a few of the new things I'd incorporated into my routine.

When I was home alone, I'd gotten used to leaving the TV on for background noise to fill the silence—only half-listening to a baking show as I scrolled through online shopping sites for Christmas presents for my friends and Riley. For Aunt Sadie, I bought a freesia-scented perfume she said her frenemy, Mabel Mitchum, was allergic to. Lucky and Murphy's aunt is an evil genius.

With Cyan in mind, I ordered a new pair of obscene pajamas with roosters on them. The shirt said, 'I love cocks'. They would probably become his new favorite pair. I still hadn't decided on Griffin's gift, but I ordered Murphy a box of neon condoms and a t-shirt that said, 'I'm not gay but my boyfriend is'. Even though he was single, I knew he'd love it.

My phone rang, and Ryan's name flashed across the screen. Lately, I hadn't seen much of him because I'd been taking online classes while I healed. He recently took over my job at the café, working with Riley, who was less than thrilled. I'd gotten used to hearing Riley grumble about his clumsiness and ineptitude.

In my mind, I could hear Riley's voice complaining like it was yesterday. "He spilled hot coffee on my shoes! I bet he did it on purpose." And, "I spent an hour stocking that shelf, and he just *accidentally* bumps into it, knocking everything over." Followed by, "I swear to God, he flirts with every guy who walks in the door. He says it's for better tips, but I think he's just a total slut." I reminded him we don't slut shame, which you'd think he'd remember as an escort, but he just glared at me.

They just needed a couple more weeks to work out their kinks before they became great friends. Well, not *great*, but *sort-of-kind-of* friends.

"Hey, Ryan, what's up? How's the Manga Maniacs coming along?" He was still trying to get me to join his anime group at school. I'd come a long way, but I just wasn't ready to mingle in a group—I was getting there.

"Great! I hope I can get you to join me for the next one after Christmas break. How are you feeling?"

"Better. My ribs are still sore, but I'm healing fine.

Before you called, I was painting my nails and Christmas shopping. What are you up to?"

"Actually, I'm calling with a purpose. Now, hear me out, okay? I have a friend in my creative writing class who is a journalism major. He says he's in Murphy's class. He heard about your attack. I swear I didn't say anything, but it kind of spread around campus on its own, 'ya know? So, he approached me knowing we're friends. He wants to do an interview with you, even if you decide to remain anonymous. He's trying to shed light on the harassment and attacks from Alphas and Alpha allies. I read over some of his notes, and it's far more widespread than you probably realize. Reid, you could help someone by telling your story. You could make a difference for all of us at school. So, just think about it, okay?"

So many different feelings flooded my mind at once. "Uh, yeah. I'll think about it." Thankfully, he couldn't see the tears gathering in my eyes. "I need to talk it over with Riley. But I'll let you know soon."

After we hung up, I muted the television and sat in silence for a long time, dissecting my feelings about telling my story. It came down to a matter of fear. Fear that others might shame or judge me. Fear that they might pity me or see me differently. When I finally decided to return to school, I didn't want to see any of that on the faces I came across. It would kill me, weaken me. I didn't need another reason to hide, and their judgement would do that to me.

On the other hand, by keeping quiet, I was also

hiding. It boiled down to whether I had the strength to stand up for myself—or would I cower to my fears. Then I thought, why was I doing all of this? What was the point? The therapy, the self-defense class, the self-esteem exercises, it was all designed to help me face my fears and be strong. Stronger than I'd ever been. Hiding wasn't a possibility anymore. No matter how scary the thought of being interviewed was, I had no choice—I had to speak up and tell my story, even if they all judged me.

It was time to raise my voice and speak out.

CHAPTER 21
RILEY

The sun shined so bright, it impaired my eyesight, turning everything white. With Reid's hand tucked into mine, we walked down the sidewalk, talking, laughing, when suddenly things became dark, all the light bled out of the sky. Cold shadows blanketed us, suffocating the air from my lungs. Then somehow, Reid was standing alone as I watched impotently from a distance. Big hands, many hands, pulled roughly at him, dragged him down. Holding Reid against his will. I could hear him scream for me, but I was useless to help him. He was lost to the darkness, enveloped by a hazy black fog that choked him.

My lungs seized up, and I couldn't scream—couldn't move—frozen with fear and indecision as I watched him succumb to his greatest nightmare.

I came awake abruptly, hands flailing and legs kicking out as a terrified scream finally tore free of my throat. "Ry, I'm here. I'm safe. You're safe. Everything is okay now, Ry." Reid's slender arms held me, and I turned into his warmth, clinging to him even tighter.

It was the same dream I'd dreamt many times since Reid lay helpless and broken in the hospital. "I had the dream again. I could feel your fear, the way you froze up and couldn't save yourself. That's how I felt in my dream —I froze—I couldn't save you."

"Hero, you save me every day. You have since I was fourteen. You keep the darkness away. You pull me out of my shell and encourage me to stay in the light. You take care of me and love me when I feel lost. That's how you save me. Please, don't underestimate the impact you've had on my recovery, on my entire life."

Rolling over his body, I laid myself out and starting with his pillow soft lips, I worked my way down his stomach, planting kisses in between my words. "I admire your strength and courage... It takes a lot to smile after what you've been through... I'm in awe of you."

Reid wiggled his hips to draw my attention there. "If you go a little lower, you'll really be in awe of me." He giggled.

Taking him in hand, I wrapped my lips around his impressive length and worshipped him with my mouth, milking him dry in under three minutes. Hearing Reid cry out my name was music to my ears. It soothed something inside me, some basic need to care for him and meet his needs. To bring him pleasure and make him happier than anyone else was able to.

"How about we go downstairs for pancakes and anime? Celebrate our Christmas vacation in style."

Reid smiled dreamily. "Sounds perfect."

Reid told me about the interview over breakfast. For a moment, I hesitated, only because I didn't want him to regret doing it. What if there was a backlash from people who allied with Reid's attackers? Tomorrow, we were leaving to spend the weekend with Charlie and celebrate the holiday, so ideally, it would need to be done today. Reid called Ryan back and made plans to meet for lunch. I planned to be glued to his side, holding his hand as he retold his devastating story.

We were in for a surprise when we arrived at the Apple Blossom Bistro. Reid had more support than he bargained for. Cyan and Griffin were seated at a table next to Lucky and Ryan. A man I didn't recognize sat next to Ryan. He must be the journalism student. Reid took a seat while I ordered us coffee. When I sat down, the man introduced himself.

"Hi, I'm Terry, Ryan's friend. I'm a journalism major at Waltham, and I've been interested in writing this story for the better part of a year now. After the first Rainbow Rally, my eyes were really opened to the problem on campus with bullying against queer students. The further I delved into my research, the more I uncovered actual physical attacks, hate crimes, violence, and it wasn't just towards the students. The faculty was being victimized, too. The common denominator I find in everyone's story is that they are afraid to speak out because they fear either retaliation from fraternity members and students or, in the case of faculty members, retaliation from the administration, going all the way to the top. The whole cart of apples is rotten to the core."

He paused to sip his coffee. "The reason the rally was so successful, in my opinion, was because everyone came forward together. There is strength in numbers. I thought maybe by Reid telling his story, along with several other personal accounts, others might come forward as well. The administration can quiet one or two students, but they cannot turn a blind eye to the majority of queer students and faculty all speaking out at once. Lucky is here because he agreed to tell his story about how he was attacked at a frat party last year. Cyan is going to corroborate that and describe the harassment they endured when they lived on campus."

I laid my hand over Reid's thigh, squeezing reassuringly. "I can add several accounts where Reid and I were harassed and threatened at the café on campus. Ryan, you were there a couple of times during those incidents. Maybe you can tell your side of it."

"Definitely. Anything I can do to help."

Ryan was doing his best to support Reid—I might not like him, but I appreciated it. Maybe I could try to cut him a break next time I was stuck working with him. *Maybe.*

We finished off two more coffees while Terry gathered everyone's stories. It was harder to hear them all grouped together at once than to trickle in here and there over the past two years. I hadn't realized just how many people were affected. It always seemed like Reid and I took the brunt of their hate. But that was just me being more worried about Reid than I was about anyone else. By the time we left, I felt better about my risk assessment regarding the interview.

Ryan was correct. There was strength in numbers, and it seemed like the students and faculty at Waltham that fell somewhere on the rainbow spectrum were fed up and ready to stand up and speak out. A united voice would sound very loud in the quiet darkness that had blanketed Waltham University for so many years. It was time to shine a light, turn up the volume, and take out the trash.

Reid seemed nervous as we drove to Charlie's house. The bouncing knee, nail biting, and constant fidgeting with the radio dials were dead giveaways. "What has you feeling so nervous, Bunny?"

Reid chewed his bottom lip. "I don't know. Do you think Charlie will be happy for us?"

Releasing the steering wheel, I reached over to tug his bottom lip free of his teeth. "Of course, he will be. He probably has our wedding planned out already. Our friends have said they've always seen our connection. Apparently, we wear our hearts on our sleeves. There's no way Charlie hasn't seen that. He knows us better than anybody."

"I guess you're right. Maybe I'm just nervous because we've gone through so many changes lately. I wonder if he'll still see me as the same old Reid he knows and loves."

When he resumed bouncing his knee, I laid my hand across it to steady him. "Well, you are and you aren't, but the new and improved shiny version of Reid Morgan leaves nothing to be desired. He'll only love you more. I can't wait to show him our gift. Bet you ten bucks he cries, the old sap." Smirking fondly, I recalled how Charlie cried at our high school graduation.

Reid cocked one eyebrow, looking thoughtful. "You know, he's not that old. Not really. I wonder why he's still single. He never dates. He's one of the best people I know. Maybe he just doesn't put himself out there for a reason."

"Maybe it's none of our business."

Reid agreed with me, shaking his head. "You're right. I just want him to be happy, like we are. But I have too much on my plate to interfere with his love life."

We arrived just in time for lunch. Charlie greeted us warmly, shuffling us off to our room to drop our bags and settle in. We were in for a surprise as we were greeted with our first clue that our news wouldn't surprise Charlie. The room I shared with Reid when we stayed overnight at Charlie's house was small. Previously, it held a bunk bed that had a double mattress on the bottom and a twin on top. The room I was staring at now looked nothing like it had the last time I was here.

"You like? I recently gave this room a makeover. I

figured you aren't boys anymore. Maybe you'd prefer something more mature looking."

Gone were the bunk beds and race car decals on the walls. Nightstands flanked a pillowy looking queen bed. The new furniture was charcoal colored wood. A navy spread covered the bed and the walls, previously a bright blue, were now painted a soft grey.

"Wow! What a difference." I loved the calming colors he chose but wondered what made him decide on only one bed.

As far as we knew, Charlie was not aware that Reid and I shared a bed. Whenever he came to do a welfare check at our foster homes, he always saw the empty bed I never used. There were plenty of times other kids came in and filled that bed, but I wasn't sure if Charlie knew that. Apparently, Reid was thinking the same thing. "There's only one bed. I guess I can sleep on the couch?"

The twinkle in Charlie's eyes belied his words. "You should sleep wherever you're most comfortable." He turned on his heel and returned to the kitchen, leaving us alone together.

"Do you think he knows?" Reid whispered. I shrugged my shoulders, not knowing what to say.

Lunch started off awkward. The tiny eat-in kitchen was too small to hide our secrets. The spark of our chemistry hovered in the air between us, broadcasting our couple status loudly.

"So, Reid, how's your therapy coming along? Do you feel it's helpful?" Charlie peppered us with questions between bites of his panini and fries.

"Very helpful. I've realized so many things by talking with Dr. Webber. Thank you for putting me in touch with him. He's a wonderful listener. Recently, I referred a friend from the center to begin therapy with him as well.."

"I'm so glad to hear it. Tell me about school. How's the transition from in-class to online going?"

They talked while they ate, catching up with recent events. Then Charlie turned his all-too-knowing eyes on me. "What's new, Riley?"

Reid kicked my shin under the table. He wanted me to be the one to out us. *Coward. Why me?*

Because it's your job to protect him, a little voice screamed in my head. Reaching for Reid's hand, I laced my fingers through his. "Charlie, Reid and I have something important to share with you." I lifted our joined hands to my lips, kissing his knuckles. "It's taken us a long time to figure things out and to be able to be honest about our feelings for each other. I'm in love with him."

Reid bounced in his seat like he couldn't contain all the joy he felt. "And I'm in love with Riley. I've wanted this since I met him. We're happy, Charlie. Really, truly happy. I know it might be weird for you because you see us as brothers, but what we have is so much more than that."

Charlie just laughed. He sounded beyond delighted with our news. "Brothers? No, Reid, I don't see you two as brothers. Just because you are both my boys doesn't automatically make you brothers. You and Riley share a brotherhood. That's different. Your coloring, height, and age may be the same. And you share a surname, but what you two have is thicker than blood. You and Riley have a strong foundation of love, loyalty, trust, and faith in each other. You provide for and protect each other. You are partners, best friends, brothers, and soul mates. And now you are lovers as well. It was inevitable. I couldn't be happier if I'd won the lottery."

He stood and rounded the table, standing behind us. Charlie wrapped an arm around each of us, creating a three-way hug. "Actually, I did win the lottery the day they assigned me your cases. You two are my boys. *My sons.* I love you both so much. There's nothing I wouldn't do to ensure your happiness. I'm just so ecstatic you've finally come together after all these years." He kissed the tops of our heads and ruffled our hair. When he took his seat again, he looked ten years younger.

I couldn't begin to count all the favors and gifts Charlie has given us over the years. It felt incredible to be able to give him something in return.

"Okay, so now that we have that happy news out of the way, let's talk about your new job, Reid. I've lined up a paid internship for you in my department. I'd like for you to start after the new year. Basically, you'll be assisting the social workers, making coffee, copying documents, setting appointments, and filing and answering phones. Once you familiarize yourself with the paper trail and routine, we'll train you to sort cases by priority. Sort of like triage in a hospital. The most critical situations receiving top billing. We're so overloaded with calls and cases and welfare checks that we're afraid someone will slip through the cracks. When someone calls to report a concern, you'll be the one interviewing them on the phone, gathering all the details and taking notes for the caseworker."

Reid's face lit up, shining with excitement and hope. "I'll really be helping! Oh my God, I can't wait!" He threw his arms around my neck, squealing in my ear. "Ry, I'll be an assistant case worker! Almost like a real one. I'll be helping kids, Ry!"

Shifting my weight, I craned my neck in his tight hold to peer at his exuberant face. He had never looked more beautiful than he did right now. Reid positively glowed with happiness. A rosy blush infused his cheeks, and his topaz eyes sparkled bright blue. He took my breath away. I dove for his mouth, kissing him with urgency, needing to soak up some of his joy and show him just how much love I had for him. Charlie faded into the background as my lips fused with his. Reid was all I knew. His lips were everything, his hands were everywhere. We were all that existed in that moment.

It might have been five minutes or an hour before Charlie laughed. "I'll just start on the dishes." The scraping of his chair's legs across the tiled floor interrupted our kiss. Gazing into Reid's eyes, foreheads pressed together, I breathed his air. "I love you, Bunny. You're going to do amazing things. I'm so proud of you. I love your big, bottomless, loving heart."

He chased my lips, becoming lost in our kiss, until Charlie interrupted. "Get a room, boys."

CHAPTER 22

REID

"Did you get the box of stuff from the garage?" I asked Charlie, barely able to contain my excitement.

Charlie smiled at me indulgently. "It's sitting behind the tree. You two get started, and I'll get the hot chocolate."

Charlie's tree sat undecorated by the big bay window in his living room—it's branches naked and plain. Growing up, Riley and I never took part in anyone's holiday decorating rituals. We were never asked, or it just wasn't a big deal in the houses we lived in. Usually, the foster homes that housed large groups of kids didn't celebrate with gift giving because it became too expensive and time-consuming.

Most often, the kids were dragged along to charitable gift giving organizations throwing parties for underprivileged kids where we each opened two or three gifts that weren't even close to anything on our wish lists. Usually, the toys weren't even age appropriate and the clothes never fit right.

After we met Charlie, we started coming over every year and celebrating with him. He always saved the tree decorating for our visit. The fanfare and hoopla of Christmas was something I looked forward to all year. Tradition and sentimentality was my thing—baking Christmas cookies, watching holiday movies, wrapping gifts and choosing the prettiest paper, I loved everything about it.

Riley seemed satisfied just being able to celebrate with us. He always said I was his gift—every single year.

Now that I'd seen him naked, touched his soft, smooth skin and tasted him, I pictured him without a stitch of clothing, tied with a big red bow, sitting under the tree with his legs spread in invitation. The provocative vision made my skin flush with heat. Having Charlie sitting not three feet away made my hard-on really awkward.

Charlie laid out a plate of sugar cookies we'd baked together after lunch and mugs of steaming hot chocolate. We did most of the decorating while Riley sat back and watched, snapping pictures with his phone.

"Ry, remember this one?"

The round red ornament I held had his name spelled out in glitter glue. We each made one for Charlie as a Christmas gift the first year we came over to celebrate. Riley scrambled off the couch to join me, taking the ornament I offered. Every year we hung them side-by-side on the tree, right in front. I placed my hook right next to his, like little glass love birds nestled together on the tree, and turned my face up for a kiss. Instead of a sweet peck, he took me in his arms and dipped me back, taking his time to devour my lips. Sighing against his mouth, I melted in his embrace, lost to my holiday fantasy.

Charlie cleared his throat, snickering behind his mug. "Who's ready for a Hallmark movie?"

The correct answer to that is *ME*. Nobody was interested in the sappy rom-coms but me, but they always watched anyway, for my sake.

Riley's solid shirtless body next to mine was too much to resist as I rolled into his side and slipped my hand around his waist. His skin felt warm under my hand as I trailed my fingers up and down his spine, waking him gently.

"Mmm," he moaned sleepily. "So good."

"Yeah? You want more?" I had reservations about getting frisky in Charlie's house, but Riley was so damn tempting. Maybe if we were really quiet...

"No, the smell. Bacon and coffee. So good." Riley slipped out of bed and headed for the bathroom.

The food? I must be losing my touch if the shine was wearing off our relationship after only a few weeks. Riley chose bacon over blowjobs. Climbing out of bed, I followed him to the bathroom, sliding up behind him, bringing his back flush to my chest.

"Merry Christmas, Hero." My lips grazed the shell of

his ear. Goosebumps rose across his skin.

He finished rinsing out his mouth and turned his head, kissing me with more passion than I was expecting after his earlier rebuff.

"Merry Christmas, Bunny."

The kitchen was my favorite room in Charlie's house. Painted the palest yellow, the color reminded me of morning sunlight—warm and cheery. He claimed the white cabinets were a nightmare to keep clean, but I thought they looked elegant. Charlie set the cherry wood table with steaming mugs and heaping plates of eggs, toast, and bacon.

"Merry Christmas, boys. Sleep well?"

Nobody missed the gleam in his eye before he schooled his features. "Much better than those bunk beds. The new room looks great, Charlie. Thanks for making breakfast. This looks delicious."

After we helped Charlie clean the kitchen, we settled in the living room to open presents. Over the last few weeks, while I was home recuperating, I had worked hard to assemble Charlie's gift. Weeks ago, I told Riley about my idea to create a picture album of photographs and memories of our time with Charlie over the years. Excited to be a part of it, Riley made three trips to the store to print out pictures from our phones.

Selecting his present from under the tree, I handed him the box wrapped in gold paper. Charlie picked off the red bow, smiling. "For me?" He unwrapped the box carefully, removing the album. Flipping the cover open, his smile spread wider as he turned each page. "Oh my

God, boys. I can't believe you made this. It's us! Everything from holidays to foster picnics and beach days. Oh, I remember this! First time I took you boys sledding. We had to drive up to North Carolina for the weekend to find snow. Oh, the Star Wars movie! I remember Reid choking on a popcorn kernel. Riley, you whacked him on the back so hard he gagged and threw up on your shoes." Riley laughed with Charlie as my cheeks flamed bright red.

"I wanted to die that day. Just let the earth open up and swallow me whole. I was so embarrassed."

Riley smiled tenderly at me. "I can understand why, now that I know you harbored a secret crush on me back then. I'd be mortified, too. But I didn't mind my pukey shoes. I was too worried about you to care. After I realized you'd be okay, I was flying high as a kite from having saved you from choking."

How could we have been so stupid to waste so much time when we both wanted the same thing?

"This is perfect, guys. I love it." Charlie's eyes misted with liquid emotion. "I know I say things like how proud of you both I am and how much I enjoy our time together, but I rarely say that I love you. But I do. I cherish you both so much, just like you were my own."

"Love you, too, Charlie." I hugged him tight, lingering for a moment in his arms.

Charlie turned to Riley. "Love you, Charlie. You're the best thing that ever happened to us."

"And in turn, you boys are going to be the best thing that happens to so many lonely kids once you get your camp up and running. You really need to consider a year-long camp instead of just summertime. What are those kids supposed to do the rest of the year? Maybe a day camp for after-school activities and sports. Help with tutoring, counseling, life skills—the possibilities are endless. Those kids need all the help you can give them, every day, all year long. Something to consider, you know?"

I looked to Riley, my eyes already twinkling with excitement and ideas. Charlie made a good point. A year round camp was much more productive than just three months in the summer. Were we ready for something this big? Our dream was growing out of control before our eyes. The authentic life experience I would gain in my new job would be invaluable, but I had an enormous amount of things to learn if I hoped to run a successful camp someday.

Riley handed me an envelope. Confused but excited, I tore it open. "I thought we agreed, no gifts this year."

Riley's mouth twisted awkwardly. "I know, but I couldn't resist making you smile."

Inside the envelope was a slip of paper with a message from Riley. 'Congratulations! You are subscribed to CrunchyRoll for one year.'

Without warning, I threw myself on him, knocking him over as I draped my arms around his neck. "Really?! Oh my gosh, I can't wait to get home and watch something." The gift and the sweetness of his gesture thrilled me. He knew me so well.

"What's CrunchyRoll? Is it a gift card to a sushi restaurant?" Charlie looked lost.

Rolling my eyes, I scoffed, feigning disgust at his lack of knowledge. "No, Charlie. It's a streaming service for anime. I can log on from any device and stream most any anime show. All my favorites are on there. Thanks, Riley!" I raised up off his chest so he could sit up. He looked so proud of himself for choosing the perfect gift.

"Well, it sounds way more exciting than my gift. I don't have anything for you to open, but I did a thing."

Riley looked wary. "What'd you do, Charlie?"

Charlie shoved a cookie in his mouth, taking longer than he needed to chew and wash it down with a sip of his hot cocoa. "I added both of you to my health insurance plan. For the last three years, you two have been paying for your own insurance and that's great, but it's a very affordable plan that doesn't cover much. You have huge deductibles and copays. Reid, your hospital bills weren't covered completely, and neither is your therapy. With my insurance, everything is covered, and you can continue therapy for as long as you need to. I would feel so relieved knowing that if anything happens, you're both covered and can afford the help you need. So, no arguing about premiums. It's all covered, and you each have one less bill now."

A sudden burst of pressure rose up my throat, clogging my airway. My eyes burned with unshed tears, blinding me. "Thanks, Charlie. I really appreciate it. Excuse me." Desperate to escape, I raced to the kitchen, needing solitude. If I was going to breakdown, I'd rather do it in private.

Riley waited a whole five minutes before he joined

me, a new record for him. Dr. Webber explained to him that he needed to give me space to feel my feelings and self-soothe before he jumped to my rescue to fix me. Or save me. His giant hand landed on my shoulder, squeezing softly.

"Are you okay, Bunny?"

The tears that distorted my vision made it seem as if I was looking through sheets of wavy bubbled glass. "Yeah, I'm not upset. Just overwhelmed, I guess."

Riley wrapped me in a bear hug, and I breathed in his warm, fresh scent. It calmed me quicker than anything else could.

His lips whispered into my hair. "Talk to me, baby. Tell me what affected you."

Wiping my eyes on his T-shirt, I lifted my tear-streaked face. "It's just, no one's ever cared before. This is different from donating a jacket or a backpack to a needy kid. What Charlie did for us goes so much deeper than that. Nobody has ever offered to pay a bill every month to ensure our health and safety, just for their own peace of mind. Just because their life wouldn't be the same if we weren't okay. It's—it's *love*. Real love, pure and selfless. It feels good, but it's also scary. What if he's not here one day? What if we lose him?"

Riley cupped my cheeks in his large hands, his thumb swiped my tears. "That's a possibility for anyone in our lives. But the thing with Charlie is, I think even if he isn't always with us, we'll be able to feel him. Feel close to him. That kind of love doesn't leave just because the person does. *It's infinite*. Why don't you take my hand,

and we'll go back in there and tell Charlie just how much his gift means to us."

"It's not his gift, it's him. I want to tell him how much *he* means to us. Somehow, we got so lucky to find the people we needed. Like our friends and Aunt Sadie, and Charlie."

"And each other. You're the only one I really need, Reid. More than anyone else." Riley claimed my lips, sliding his tongue along mine. When he kissed me like that, possessive and demanding, I forgot time—I forgot my name. Sometimes, I even forgot to breathe.

It was like I could only motor along so far in life before I needed another kiss. They were the fuel that kept me going.

My phone rang as we were packing our bags to head home. Ryan's name flashed across the screen. I hesitated to answer, not wanting to upset the good mood between Riley and me. Nothing drove his mood to the gutter faster than mentioning Ryan's name. But I wondered if it had anything to do with the interview. Curiosity made me answer the call.

"Hello?"

"Reid, I have great news!"

I excused myself while we talked. The call lasted fifteen minutes—that's all it took to change my life. I found Riley loading our bags into the car. "Ry, can you come inside so we can talk?"

He popped his head up over the trunk. "Yeah. You okay?"

"I'm perfect. I just want to tell you and Charlie at the

same time."

When I had them both settled on the couch, I relayed Ryan's news. "So, Ryan called. The interview was released yesterday online on the school's website, as well as posted in many extracurricular group forums and has by now circulated widely. Terry, the guy who interviewed me, has been receiving calls and emails all day from students who contributed their personal stories of abuse and harassment from Alphas and some of their allies. Including several faculty administrative employees who were allies of theirs and supported their hateful rhetoric. Terry encouraged each one of them to file a police report. Many of them did. They also filed reports with the school. Everyone is coming forward." A torrent of tears overtook my voice then, shredding it until I was too choked up to continue.

Riley knelt before me and wrapped me in his arms. "Bunny, don't you see? You made a difference, for yourself and for so many others. You changed everything." He pulled back, looking into my drowned eyes. "God, you're so fucking amazing. So brave. And you did it all on your own."

Tightening my arms, I squeezed him tighter, burrowing into the safety of his embrace. "I'm never on my own, Ry. Everything I do is with your support. Two halves of a whole, remember?"

Riley rubbed his stubbly cheek against my smooth one. "Always, baby. Forever."

Riley lowered his head, his lips seeking mine, sealing them together. Our tongues danced together in the wet heat of his mouth. The kiss was slow and sensual and reaffirming. I wanted to crawl inside of his mouth and live there for the next few hours, but now wasn't the time with Charlie sitting next to us.

"I can't believe my voice isn't alone anymore. I'm not the only one screaming out loud, being ignored."

Riley grinned and shook his fist. "Hell yeah, your voice just got a whole lot louder. We should call the detective handling your case and see what she says about the new charges."

In a hurry to get going, I jumped up and tugged on his arm. "Come on, we'll call from the car. I want to get back home."

What I left out, for Charlie's sake, was that I needed to be alone with my Hero, in our bed, with nothing separating us. Not clothes or distance or well-meaning family. Just Riley and me together.

I needed to feel calm and centered, and only Riley could do that for me.

Detective Vallejo called us before we even reached the highway. "Reid, you won't believe it!" She parroted most of what Ryan had already said. "We've got them this time. I'm going to make these charges stick, Reid. There are too many accounts here, too many witnesses and victims for them to slither off my hook. As soon as I have a court date, I'll let you know."

It wasn't a guaranteed conviction, but it was enough of a validation to make me feel like I mattered—like my trauma was real and visible and worthy of justice.

It was enough to make me feel human again.

CHAPTER 23
RILEY

My lips sought his to quench the thirst from going without his mouth for so long. Our tongues twined, causing a rush of saliva to end the drought. My lips brushed across his slowly, exploring and teasing, awakening his early morning desire. Reid hitched a leg over my hip, mashing his morning wood tightly against mine. He humped against my groin as his mouth danced with mine. Everything about the kiss and the dry hump was sloppy and hungry and full of need. I was starved for him, impatient to get inside of his tight little body.

After weeks—*no, years*—I finally had a plan for that. Reid's birthday was less than two weeks after mine. We always celebrated together, one birthday at the halfway mark. Mine was next week, and I had an idea to take Reid to the romantic bed-and-breakfast where Lucky proposed to Hayes and Cyan took Griffin.

I intended to spend an entire weekend focused on

Reid, make it all about him—his happiness, his pleasure, and finally, *finally,* make love to him. Was there a more romantic setting? Every year, when we celebrated our birthdays, we would remember our first time together. Only, I planned to do more than just initiate his body. I had a plan that would join him to me for the rest of our lives.

Reid climbed on top of me. "Ry, do that thing where you stroke our cocks together." He leaned down to lick my lips. "I need you so bad."

God, he killed me when he was needy like this, desperate for the release my cock could give him. Without hesitation, I shoved my pants down, and he copied me as I retrieved the bottle of lube from the drawer in the nightstand. My slick hand worked our slippery cocks together, up and down in my tight fist. Reid straddled above me, naked down to his hips, was a sight hot enough to make me spill right then. His pale skin stretched taut over barely defined abs, small pink nipples tightened into hard peaks—I wanted to lick and taste every inch of his delicious skin. His smooth supple flesh made me want to trail hickeys and love bites over the unmarred canvas of his perfect, untouched body.

Reid tempted me in the best and worst ways. It was usually a toss up whether I wanted to worship him or defile him. He whined, bringing my focus back to our double hand job. Reaching between his slim, pale thighs with my other hand, I caressed his balls, kneading them in my slippery palm.

"Feel good, baby? You needed this, didn't you?"

He bit his plump lip. "Need you, Ry," Reid huffed, panting like he'd run a marathon. "Love it when you touch me."

His hips bucked back and forth as he fucked into my hand. It was difficult not to imagine he would move his hips just like this if he were riding my cock, buried deep inside his tight little ass.

The visual danced through my mind as I pumped our cocks together. It proved to be too much, making me spill over my fist. Reid whimpered, his wide, glassy eyes focused on my cum as he reached his breaking point. He cried my name as he came, his cum joining mine as it pooled around the base of our cocks in a milky puddle.

Oblivious to the mess, Reid leaned down and attacked my mouth in a sloppy, sated kiss. Then he grabbed my hand, bringing it up to his mouth, and giggled as he sucked my fingers clean. I loved he was still shy about doing filthy things. I prayed he never lost that shade of innocence.

Reid's phone rang, vibrating on the nightstand next to the bottle of lube. He was still straddled over my hips when he leaned over to check it.

"It's Ryan. I wonder what he could want so early in the morning."

"Fucking cockblocker," I grumbled. Probably wanted the same thing I did this morning, a piece of Reid.

Reid only chuckled. "Technically, we're finished, so he's not cockblocking you. Don't take it personally." He answered the phone, still smiling at me. "Hey Ryan, what's up?" He was silent for a second as he listened. "Seriously? No way! Really? Yeah, I'll think about it. I need to discuss it with Riley, of course, but I'll let you know. Thanks, bye."

I wanted to strangle him as he patiently put the phone back on the bedside table and reached for tissues to wipe the sticky mess from our groins before tucking himself back into his sleep pants.

"You gonna tell me what that was about? Or do I need to call him back myself?"

His lips twitched, fighting back the smile dying to come out. He scooted down to my thighs so he could tuck my soft cock back into my pants and made a long, drawn-out process of tying the drawstring of my pants into a bow. I swatted his hands away.

"Reid!"

He laughed, finally giving life to his smile. "When the collective accounts of abuse started flooding in, the news picked up the story. The school had no choice but to get involved. They suspended each student arrested and expulsion is pending the outcome of the trial. Also, the Alpha Sigma Rai fraternity is disbanded and no longer a recognized chapter at Waltham University."

"Holy shit! Are you serious?" I tried to sit up, but his weight on my thighs prevented me from raising up much higher than my elbows.

Reid bounced on my lap. "Ry! They did it! They're gone!"

My fingers dug into his hips to keep him still. "They? No, you did it, Bunny. You started the ball rolling, and it picked up speed when everyone joined in, but it was you, baby. *You* did this."

"I'm going to send Terry a gift basket."

"A gift basket?" I scoffed. "Hell, I'd blow him." Reid looked at me, unable to believe what I just said. He smacked my chest. "I mean, if my lips didn't already belong to you. I'm sure he'd love a gift basket."

My arms snaked around his waist, and I hugged him tight, peppering kisses along his cheeks, down his neck, and across his chest, closing my teeth softly around his nipple.

Reid dissolved into giggles, squirming on my lap and giving my dick ideas about going another round. "So what was it you said at the end, when you told him you'd consider it? Consider what?"

"Returning to campus after the Christmas break. Instead of completing the semester online. I think I could do it, Ry. With the Alphas gone, I think I would feel safe enough to go back to class. And of course, you'd be with me the whole time."

Relief flooded me. "Of course, baby. Right by your side."

I despised this new schedule we'd fallen into, where I had to say goodbye to him each day while he stayed home alone and I went to school without him. Every time I looked over to the empty seat beside me in class, my heart squeezed, remembering the reasons why he couldn't be there with me. And now that I worked with Ryan instead of Reid at the café, I went pretty much the entire day without his sunny presence beside me. It was like missing a limb. His return to campus would lessen the ache considerably.

~

Four days later, we were headed down the highway, on our way to Georgia's Tybee Island. Awake before the break of dawn, I tiptoed around our room, packing two duffle bags in secret, and stealthily stowed them in the trunk of our car while it was still dark outside. We were ready to hit the road by the time the sun came up.

Reid had no idea what I had planned. He thought we were spending the day laid up in a hammock at his favorite park by the river. It wasn't quite time for our birthday celebration, but I was trying to sneak this trip in before we had to return to school. Reid became suspicious when I passed the exit that led to the park.

He turned his head, glancing back at the turnoff. "You passed it, Ry. You can turn around up ahead." He fiddled with the radio as I passed the U-turn and kept on driving. By the time he glanced up and paid attention, we were passing the sign that said we had exited Cooper's Cove and invited us back real soon. "Ry? Where are we going? Is there another park you wanted to try out?"

Excitement fluttered in my chest, anticipating his surprised reaction when I revealed our true destination. "Maybe. It's farther out, though. Might take a while to get there. Lean your seat back and relax while I drive."

I didn't want him paying attention to the signs on the highway telling him we were headed to Savannah.

Two hours later, we pulled up in front of the historic B&B. I gently shook Reid's shoulder to wake him.

His pretty face, so peaceful and relaxed in sleep, was turned toward me, and I took a moment to watch him unguarded. A face that I'd loved for six years. A face that expressed the many facets of his personality. A face that could get me to do just about anything to put a smile on it. I brushed his bangs from his forehead and kissed his sweet lips. His eyes remained closed, but a coy smile slithered across his lips as he snaked his arms around my neck, holding my lips in place for another kiss. This one deeper, his silky tongue sliding into my mouth.

I pulled back, my lips hovered over his as I mumbled against his mouth. "Wake up, Sleeping Beauty. We're here." As he sat up and surveyed his surroundings in confusion, I grinned like a loon. "Stay right there. I'll get our bags and your door." The romantic gestures would begin the second he stepped foot outside the car and would last until we got back in it to go home.

When I opened his door and held my hand out for his, he looked up at me in wonder. "Riley? There's no park, is there? Where are we?"

"Remember the B&B that Lucky and Hayes went to? And Cy and Griffin? We're here!" My hand gestured toward the sunny yellow two-story house decorated with gingerbread trim and gabled roofs.

Reid squealed, throwing his arms around my neck and climbing me like a tree, despite the bags draped over my shoulders. I almost lost my balance as I braced myself, laughing at his excitement.

"Oh my gosh, this is so romantic!"

We checked into our room and deposited our bags in the closet. Reid's cheeks flushed bright with excitement as he bounced on the corner of the bed, testing the springs.

"This is where Lucky and Hayes got engaged. And where Griffin lost his vir—you know. It's a special place that holds some kind of romantic magic. Do you think it will for us?" Reid looked so hopeful.

Closing the distance between us, I laid him back, climbed over him, and kissed him slowly, teasing every corner of his mouth. "I'm sure it will, sweetheart. Is that what you want?"

I knew what I had planned for him and what I wanted to happen for us, but I had to make sure he felt ready.

"God, yes! I'm so ready, Ry."

I laughed—his insistence was precious. Reid always came across as this sexy mix of innocent and eager. It was like a siren's song to my soul.

"I'll keep that in mind. Let's go explore the beach. I have a picnic lunch prepared for us if you're hungry." Against my will, I let him go and led him from the room as he glanced back with longing at the plush bed.

"Come on," I teased. "It will still be there when we get back." He followed reluctantly.

~

Reid's phone chirped as I laid out our picnic on a wool blanket in the sand. "Bunny, I know we just received huge important news and there's a lot going on back home, but can we maybe silence our phones for a few hours? I want you all to myself."

Reid muted his phone and chucked it into the basket, humming with excitement. "What?" I asked, curious about his change of mood.

He spread his hands wide. "I love this. All of it. You and me, alone all weekend. Romantic picnics and moonlit walks on the beach. I like having you all to myself, all your focus on me."

I plucked a juicy grape from the picnic basket and slipped it between his lips. Reid licked my finger as I popped it in his mouth. "You always have my focus. You're the center of my world." He blushed, dipping his head. My fingers stroked his smooth jaw before I tipped his chin up and stole a kiss. "I like the sound of a moonlight stroll tonight."

The upside of coming to the beach during the off-season in the dead of winter was the privacy. We had miles and miles of unpopulated beaches all to ourselves. Tybee Island resembled a ghost town during the winter. Only a few of the locals remained year round.

Reid and I touched and kissed constantly, needing the contact after not being able to touch for so many years. If only there was a way to connect our bodies as one unit where we could live inside of them together forever.

Two minds, one body, one heart. *One shared life.*

We wrapped up our lazy picnic and borrowed bicycles from the inn. We rode around the island like a couple of kids, exploring and laughing and making memories that I hoped would last us a lifetime. This was the first time Reid and I had ever gone away together, alone. Without social workers, chaperones, foster parents or Charlie.

This was *our* trip, *our* time, and I wanted to make every minute count.

After a sexy, soapy shower, we changed our clothes and headed down to the dining room for a romantic candlelight dinner. A huge wooden table dominated the elegant space. The crystal chandelier that dangled over the dining table was shaped like a piece of coral. It was a breathtaking conversation piece made by a local artist. We had the room to ourselves, as there was only one other couple checked in. With our glasses filled with sparkling cider, we toasted to another year together and a new beginning. A delicious chocolate cake followed dinner. I fed Reid several bites of the decadent, rich treat. His lips lingered on the tines of my fork in a suggestive way, plumping my cock. If I didn't take him down to the beach soon, we'd be heading upstairs instead.

"I think it's about time for that moonlight stroll."

We walked hand in hand along the shore as the icy water kissed our bare feet. The moon shone bright and full, the perfect backdrop for the most important night of my life. Reaching into my pocket, my fingers curled around the circle of metal. I drew it out and covertly slipped it on Reid's finger. It took him a moment to realize what I'd done. He looked down at his hand, his eyes stretching wide like saucers. The pale light of the moon reflected off the diamond's facets, making it sparkle like glitter. Reid covered his mouth with his hand in shock, unable to believe what his eyes were seeing.

"Ry?"

His beautiful eyes glistened with unshed tears as I dropped down to one knee in the sand, taking his ring finger in my hand again. "I have loved you from the first day I met you. I will *always* love you. But it's not enough to just tell you. I need you to be mine in every way. Will you marry me, Reid? Will you spend the rest of your life loving me? Will you promise me forever?"

Reid sank to his knees in the sand, my arms wrapped him tight and close. He buried his face in my neck and sobbed silently, his tears soaked through my shirt, into my heart.

"You still haven't said yes, Bunny."

"Yes," he choked through his tears. "Yes, forever."

I held him while he drained his tears, never wanting to let him go. Reid straddled my lap as I rocked him soothingly.

He lifted his tear-streaked face. "I don't want to wait any longer. Let's get married while we're here. We can go to the courthouse tomorrow and make it official."

Nothing would make me happier than to leave this island married to the man I've loved my entire life.

"Really? That sounds perfect, except I don't think I want to say my vows in a courthouse. Our whole life, all the bad shit, took place in a courthouse. We deserve better than that."

Reid frowned, deep in thought, as he chewed his lip. "You're right. Let's do it now. Right now, right here."

Could I be this lucky? But I worried that Reid would have regrets if he felt rushed. "What about Charlie and our friends? Shouldn't we share this with them?"

Reid wrapped his hands around mine. "We will, eventually. We can have a little party when we get back home. But this is *our* moment. I only want to share it with you. Since the day we met, it's always been just me and you, and that's the way it should be now. *Just us*."

Fuck, he said all the right things. A rush of warmth suffused my heart. "You're right.Tomorrow we'll make it legal, but today, is just for us. "

Reid brushed his lips over mine and licked into my mouth. I could feel the love he tried to pour into the kiss, to show me what was in his heart. He needn't bother, I knew. It was identical to what was in my heart.

"You go first," he suggested.

Tugging Reid to his feet, I sucked in a deep breath of fresh salty air and took an inventory of everything in my heart, letting the words spill out. With his hands tucked in mine, I promised, "I, Riley Morgan, swear I will love you, Reid Morgan, until my dying breath. I vow to respect you, cherish you, and protect you every day. I will do my best to keep you safe, ease your fears, and make you smile, and I will try my best to never let you down and always, *always* show you how much you are loved."

"Fuck, Riley, I love you." Tears continued to fall from his beautiful topaz eyes.

"I love you, too." I snuck a kiss to his lips before he continued.

"I, Reid Morgan, take you, Riley Morgan, to be my husband. I vow to love you, respect you, and be faithful to you all the days of my life. I promise to try my best to obey you and compromise with you when we disagree and to never purposely hurt you or disappoint you. I will *never* lie to you. I swear that my body and my heart belong only to you until my dying breath."

"Obey, huh?" I snickered, wondering how long he'd last before breaking that vow.

Reid looked offended that I'd doubt him. "I said I'd do my best." But then he smiled, conceding my point.

Clasping his hands tighter, I brought them to my lips and laid a kiss over the back of each one. "I now pronounce us married. Now kiss your husband."

My nose rubbed against his, bringing our foreheads together. Reid slipped his tongue into my mouth, licked my tongue, and then retreated. Grinning against my mouth, he nipped at my bottom lip. It seemed he wanted to play. I'd give him a kiss he'd hopefully remember for the rest of his life.

I caught his lip between my teeth and sucked until he parted his lips. My tongue snaked inside, searching for his, and sucked his tongue into my mouth, lapping at it until his hands found my cock. He rubbed me through my pants as I fucked his tongue. The noises Reid made had me on the verge of coming. He sounded so hot and needy. If I listened to a soundtrack of his sex noises, I could probably come untouched just from imagining the things I was doing to him to elicit such sounds.

The kiss went on and on, trading the inside of his mouth for the inside of mine, sharing fluids, sealing promises, and celebrating our future. "I'm dying to get you upstairs, but there's one more thing I wanted to do before that."

Reid looked ruined, debauched in the best ways. "I'll give you fifteen minutes."

My lips curved into a half smile. "I only need ten." Searching through my phone, I pulled up our song from a playlist. The music surrounded us as I tugged him into my arms. We danced beneath the moon's light as I whispered the words in his ear. Bryan Adams' *'Heaven'* described us perfectly. Every time I heard it, I thought of Reid and everything we've been through since we were kids until now. "You have been my partner for six years. Since the day we met, you've been the only boy in my heart. That's never going to change, Reid. We've been married in every way that counts. The only thing a marriage license is going to change is that it will be recognized in the eyes of the law."

Upstairs in our room, I stripped Reid bare and laid him down on our bed. Starting at his soft pink feet, I licked and kissed a blazing wet trail up the entire length of his body, ignoring his cock and paying special attention to his mouth. He rubbed his hard length against my belly, seeking friction. His sticky precum pooled in my navel. I dipped my finger to collect it and spread it across his lips. His soft pink tongue joined mine as we licked it clean.

"I want to take my time with you, but I don't think I can."

God, I've waited so long. Sitting up, I grabbed the bottle of lube from the nightstand and coated my fingers. My tongue dominated his mouth as I massaged his hole, opening him slowly. He writhed like a fish on a hook, pushing my self-control to the brink. I slipped my finger inside, gliding in and out, twisting, driving him wild. When I added a second finger, stretching him impossibly further, Reid keened like a baby kitten, soft and needy.

"Turn over, baby."

Reid rolled onto his stomach and spotted Benny the bunny propped against his pillow. He turned him face down and plopped a pillow over him to hide his innocent plushie eyes as I did filthy things to his companion.

My greedy lips sucked hickeys all down his thighs as my fingers found their way home again, teasing until he begged for relief. "Ry? I want to ask a question but it's—"

"Reid, we're married. You can ask me literally anything."

His glassy, dilated eyes found mine. "What would happen if you sucked a hickey around my hole? Would it turn purple like the rest of my skin?"

I don't know what the sound was that came out of

my mouth, but I didn't recognize it. It sounded painful to my own ears. "We're going to find out right now."

Gripping his slim hips, I spread his cheeks apart and dove for his smooth pink hole. My tongue feasted on his delectable skin until he humped the mattress beneath him. I sealed my lips around his pucker and sucked hard, keeping the pressure constant until I was sure his skin had to be dark purple.

Licking my lips, I lifted my mouth to inspect the damage, and sure enough, I'd marked him well. Seeing the evidence of my claim against his perfect, pale flesh made my cock leak like a broken faucet. "*Mine*," I growled between his cheeks as I kissed it better. Reid squealed as I slid my arms under his waist and rolled him to his back.

"I can't wait, baby. Gotta have you, now."

There would be no condoms between us. When I stopped sleeping with my clients, I was tested, and I was ready to share myself with Reid completely—no barriers.

The head of my swollen cock nudged his tiny hole. "I'm sorry if this burns a little, but I promise you, the deeper I go, the better it will feel." My hips surged forward, and I pushed inside his tight body little by little as he held his breath. "Breathe, baby."

When I was fully seated, I felt him clench around me, adjusting to the fullness. The rapid squeeze of his muscles, coupled with the warm sheath of his channel, nearly brought me to my knees. Moving slowly, I drew in and out of his body, taking my time to feel every flutter and pulse of his ass. It took a moment for his face to unclench, but when I saw his pupils dilate, I knew he was ready to take more.

As I tunneled deeper into him, his body bucked with the force of my thrusts, moaning wantonly with each stroke. Reid clawed at my back, tugged on my hair, and bit my lips. He babbled mindlessly with pleasure, making little sense.

"I-I'm so... it's, oh, so full." My lips feasted on his nipples, sucking and biting until I'd made them sensitive and raw.

I might be obsessed with his small rosy nipples. Everything about Reid's body was the standard I held all men to. The way his sharp hip bones jutted in stark relief, his slim waist and small, plump ass—*utter perfection.*

We rolled, and I sat up, pulling him along with me until we reclined against the headboard. Reid straddled my thighs, and I wound my arms around his back as he wound his around my neck. We were completely intertwined, and my cock was lodged as deep as I could plant it inside him. With each stroke and thrust, I could feel a tingling euphoria spread through my body, warming my blood like wildfire. Lust burned through my veins until it peaked, pushing me right to the edge of my limits. It drove me to push faster, tunnel deeper and harder into Reid's body. The sounds he made, the look of pure bliss on his face, told me he could take everything I gave him and more.

My butt cheek cramped, and when I changed my angle to relieve the pressure, it sparked something inside of Reid, driving him impossibly higher as he cried out, raising his hips and pushing back against me to get my cock deeper inside of him. When my cockhead rubbed over that spot again, he clenched around my shaft, and I cried out. My balls shrunk and tightened up against my body. I could feel the warmth of my seed as it raced through my shaft and shot into his tight heat, flooding his channel with my cum.

Reid squeezed his eyes shut and clung to my neck as I continued my frenzied pace, driving into his tight hole unforgivingly. I could sense he was close, and I wanted to rock his world like he did mine. My cock was over sensitive and starting to soften, but I kept pushing, trying not to lose my momentum. Reid moaned my name over and over as he fisted his cock furiously. One last powerful thrust had him spilling his seed over his belly. One long rope sliced across my chest, and I dragged my finger through it and licked it clean—his blue eyes glued to me as I sucked. Reid meshed his chest against mine, smearing his seed on my belly as he claimed my mouth in a possessive kiss so hot and primal, it had me considering a second round.

Total satisfaction replaced every doubt I might have ever held about us ruining our relationship with sex. "Don't ever forget that you're mine, and I won't ever give you a reason to regret shackling yourself to me for life."

Reid laid his head on my shoulder. His tongue chased a bead of sweat that rolled down my throat, and he licked the salty flavor from his lips. "I've never regretted it, Ry. I don't think I ever will. I can't believe you just did all that to me. After reading all those books, I thought I knew what to expect, but I had no idea."

"You mean Bottoming For Beginners didn't have all the answers?" Reid laughed into my neck, his lips vibrating against my skin, tickling, making my body come alive again. "That was... unlike anything else, ever."

I stared into his eyes as my heart melted into a sticky puddle of goo. "Mr. Reid Morgan, *my husband*."

Reid sighed like he hadn't a care in the world. "Mr. Riley Morgan, *my husband*."

EPILOGUE

RILEY

Reid leaned back in his seat and sighed, a smile played around his lips. "I'm so glad this semester is over. This coming Spring semester is going to be a fresh start for us."

The sun shone through the window, highlighting the platinum streaks in Reid's silky hair. "I bet you're excited about putting in more hours at the center this summer. I can't believe they approved it for our work study. The credits apply toward our degrees." I loosened the knot on my tie. "I wish we had time to go home and change before heading to Over The Rainbow."

Reid shook his head. "Sorry, no can do. If we're late for Maya's first group, she'll kill us. Her and Colton have worked so hard to organize this and get it going. I'm not going to be the one to disappoint them."

Maya and Colton had worked tirelessly to organize a TGNC support group open to every interested resident in the city. The transgender and non-conforming support group catered to minors and adults of every gender, race, sexuality, creed, and age. There wasn't anyone who wasn't welcome.

"I'm glad we invited them to our wedding reception party-thing. They make the cutest couple, don't they?" Reid had hearts in his eyes everywhere he looked. It was most likely a side effect of being ridiculously in love.

"Reid," I warned, "don't go playing matchmaker. Let them find their own way. Everybody has their own story, and Colton and Maya need to write their own without your meddling interference. They have enough obstacles to overcome as it is. Let them take it slow and easy."

His big, round eyes didn't fool me. "What? Me? I'm not doing anything—I mean, planning anything. I just think they're cute, is all. Nothing wrong with admiring someone."

Reid was the picture of innocence, if innocence looked like they were hiding a quiver of Cupid's arrows beneath their jacket.

"Uh huh. Have I told you today how much I admire *you*?" Like a sap, my eyes softened whenever I looked at Reid.

"Only twice. I could do with a few more compliments." Reid leaned over the console, placing a quick kiss on my smiling lips.

"How do you feel about the outcome of the trial this morning?" I'd been monitoring Reid's reaction closely, ready to offer support when needed.

Reid's long, slender fingers twisted in his lap. "Five

years in prison is a long time and not long enough. Knowing they aren't free to hurt anyone else is more satisfying than feeling justified that they were found guilty. But in a few years, they'll be right back out on the streets again, committing the same crimes. So, has anything really been resolved? I feel so ambivalent about it all." Reid stared out the window at the passing scenery.

I turned the radio down. "Reid, look at me, baby." Reid focused on me, his expression neutral. "There's no way for you to know what those guys are going to experience during their time away. Maybe they'll come to terms with their actions and resolve some of their hate. They will be surrounded by gay culture for a long time inside that prison. I can't accept that you believe things don't happen for a reason. All the suffering they caused, it can't all have been for nothing."

"Maybe you're right. Maybe some good will come of this. I can't imagine what or how, but I need to remain hopeful, not spiteful."

"Reid, sweetheart, you have the most forgiving heart of anyone I know. You couldn't hate anyone. That's what makes you such a beautiful person."

His arms flailed excitedly. "Darn it! You always do this to me. You say something nice about me and then it makes it impossible for me to keep secrets from you," Reid sputtered, exasperated.

My brow arched in question. "Secrets? I thought you worked it into your vows that you wouldn't ever lie to me?"

Reid smirked knowingly, looking mighty superior.

"Lies and secrets are two separate things."

"Yeah? Well, they're close cousins. Don't get hung up on the details. What are you keeping from me, Reid?"

"My research paper for my social work degree. I came up with an idea, maybe kinda. But you aren't going to like it."

"Hence the secrets. Spill the tea, Bunny. What's your grand idea?" My intuition told me I was about to regret asking.

"I was toying with the idea of a one-on-one rehabilitation project for violent offenders and their victims. Of course, it would be entirely on a volunteer basis, considering whether the victims or inmates are interested in participating or not."

"Absolutely not!" I was adamant that Reid not go within spitting distance of his attackers. Or any other violent offenders, for that matter.

Read tried to defend himself. "But you haven't even listened to the details yet! Another thing we worked into our vows was that we promised to try and compromise when we disagreed."

"I believe only *you* vowed that, not me," I pointed out with a superior smirk. He sighed like it was painful. "Okay, tell me the details of your brilliant plan."

"You see, I believe some inmates use their time inside to reflect on their poor choices. Maybe their conscience gets the better of them. Or maybe they're removed from the environment that was causing their violent behavior and they have a change of heart. I thought it might be productive for victims to sit down with their offenders in a controlled, mediated, secure environment, and let them know how their actions affected their victims personally, maybe even physically, health-wise. Long-term consequences and such. And if the victim is willing to offer forgiveness or understanding, it might go a long way to helping the offender? I thought maybe they each had something to offer the other in terms of healing."

"Are you done?" Reid nodded, waiting for me to give my opinion. "*Absolutely not!*"

Reid turned his body to fully face me. His eyes pleaded with me to be fair. "That can't be it, Riley! You're going to have to compromise with me on this. I truly believe I'm onto something. It may not work in every case, but for those that are ready and able to sit down with each other, I think there's a lot of good that can come of it, and I'd like to study the research." He pried my right hand off the steering wheel and clutched it tightly. "I think I was meant for more than just helping foster kids find a place to belong. Maybe I'm also meant to help abuse victims and survivors to have a voice and to heal through telling their stories and recognizing themselves in others."

Fuck! His bleeding heart was going to be the death of me. There wasn't a single thing I hated more than this idea, but I was fooling myself if I thought I could deny Reid anything he set his beautiful heart on.

"I hope you think I look sexy in a prison guard uniform, because I'm coming with you."

Reid's satisfied smile was worth the compromise. "You look sexy in everything and nothing at all. Thank you for trusting me."

"Trust is the glue of life. It's the most essential ingredient in effective communication. It's the foundational principle that holds all relationships. *Stephen Covey.*"

"Oohh, impressive. I'm glad to see you paid attention in our modern philosophy class," Reid snickered. "Every kind of peaceful cooperation among men is primarily based on mutual trust. *Albert Einstein.* See, I paid attention, too."

Sassy and sexy. He wanted to play? *Perfect*—I loved to play with Reid. "Can we begin preparing when we get home later? I have a pair of handcuffs and a taser." My eyebrows wagged playfully, and Reid laughed. The carefree sound was a balm to my battered soul after months of watching him suffer.

"I don't know what kind of sex acts involve a taser. That seems way outside of my comfort zone. But we can definitely use the handcuffs."

I could work with that. "Can you call me Sir?"

Reid trailed his finger down my arm. "I'll call you anything you want, Hero." The hearts were back in Reid's eyes again, coloring his world with a rose-colored tint. "Hey, Ry? What if we fell in love and got married on a beautiful beach, and every night we had dirty, hot sex, and every morning you made love to me. And you didn't have to sleep around anymore and I got to work with Charlie every day helping kids. And we decided to expand our dream of a summer camp into an every day camp. Only, it wasn't a dream because it was really happening for us. What if everything we ever fantasized about became real? And there was nothing left to dream of because it all came true?"

If I wasn't already married to him, I would ask him again right now. Every day he reminded me why I was the luckiest bastard in the world. "Then I guess we need to dream bigger, Bunny. We have to keep reaching for the stars."

Want to see more of Reid and Riley? Claim your copy of Happy Campers today! This is a free bonus chapter available exclusively for newsletter subscribers.

Do you want a sneak peek of **Curious Relations**? Keep reading!

The fourth book in the *Hearts For Hire* series is an enemies with benefits, bi-awakening, escort romance between brothers-in-law. Murphy and Hudson pull no punches when it comes to their antagonistic, heated bromance.

Join my Facebook Reader group, **Raquel Riley's Romantics**, to stay up to date on everything happening in Cooper's Cove!

Visit my website for signed books, digital downloads, merchandise, and much more! **www.raquelriley.com**

CURIOUS RELATIONS: HEARTS FOR HIRE BOOK 4

MURPHY

I bounced into Limericks Bar and Grille feeling light, looking forward to a fun night with my friends. A night off from work where I could just be me, Murphy Maguire —the brother, the friend, the fun-loving, happy-go-lucky goofball. Tonight, I didn't have to be sexy and alluring. I didn't have to work to convince some man to get into my pants for a high price. All I wanted was to kick back and relax and celebrate my big brother's twenty-second birthday.

As soon as I walked into the rowdy sports bar I noticed the guys occupying a large table in the back. They waved me over, shouting my name to be heard over the crowd. This place was always loud. The jukebox competed with the game playing on the television, and there was always someone singing along with the music or laughing a bit too loudly. The atmosphere was lively. I liked to come at the end of the night, when the noise died down and Shannon Calhoun, the resident bartender and co-owner, had already gone home for the night. Being underage, I had zero chance of getting a drink with alcohol in it while he was still on duty. If he saw a man buy me a drink, he'd snatch it right out of my thirsty little hands.

"Hey, you made it! Grab a seat. Wings and drinks are on their way out." Lucky looked slightly flushed. He must have been pre-gaming his drinking tonight.

Directing my attention to Hayes, I asked, "Where's your brother? Did he decide he was too cool to hang out with us?" I tried not to sound bitter but I think I detected a note of disdain creeping into my voice.

"He's over by the bar." Lucky pointed across the room. Limericks had a bar side and a grille side. The grille catered more to dancing, food, and pool tables. The bar took up most of its half, a large oval shaped counter with green leather stools, surrounded by large flat screen TVs broadcasting different sports.

My eyes followed his direction, landing on a tall blond Viking sitting at the bar. Hudson had a girl draped over his arm. She clung to him and laughed at something he whispered in her ear. Every time I saw him here he was on a date with a different girl. This one had long brown hair and wasn't wearing much of a dress. Her shoulders were bare and her ample cleavage was on full display. Ugh, women! Boobs, vaginas, periods. Gross, gross, gross! I guess if you're into that sort of thing, it's all good, but it doesn't do shit for me.

"Hey, everybody quiet down, the Morgans are calling. I want to hear how their trip is going." Cyan shushed the entire table. They called through video messaging and we gathered around the phone so we could see their faces. My roommates had been gone for two days and I was already feeling lonely and forgotten. I hated being alone. I needed people, company, and laughter. Someone to talk to and to fill the silence. I didn't do well on my own for long.

"Hey guys, how's the trip going? Isn't that place the best?" Cyan asked, full of excitement.

Reid waved a paper in front of the camera, blocking the screen. "What's that, a parking ticket?" Cy asked.

"Move that paper, we can't see your face," Lucky said. Reid continued to wave the paper around. He kept flashing his hand in front of the lens as well.

"Holy shit! You're married!" Griffin screeched, his face in shock, mouth forming a huge gaping O shape. Everyone caught on quickly, looking closer at the paper. "That's a marriage license. You're wearing a ring, Reidsy!"

"Get the fuck out!" Cyan shouted.

"About damn time!" Lucky added. "Hudson! Come here. You have to see this!" Lucky waved Hudson over to our table, his date trailing behind him.

"What about us? You didn't wait for us to witness it?" Hayes sounded genuinely hurt.

Riley's face popped into the frame, crowding Reid out. "This was just for us. Maybe we'll throw a party for everyone when we get home."

"So, this is for real? You're legally and officially

married?" Cyan seemed to be having a hard time believing the new couple eloped without giving notice.

"Really real. As real as it gets. We are the misters Morgan." I couldn't tell who was smiling bigger, Reid or Riley.

"You were always the misters Morgan. That's not something that changed just because you married," I pointed out.

"Don't sound so sour, Murphy. You'll find yourself a man. Someday. Maybe in about thirty years, when you finally grow out of your awkward teenage phase." Riley snickered at his ridiculous humor, as if he was supposed to be funny or something. *Or something. Jerkwad.* "By the way, we're staying a few more days, so don't expect us home tomorrow. We're on our honeymoon."

My roommates shared their congratulations, well wishes, and bad marital advice before hanging up.

Hudson introduced everyone to his date, Laura, except me. When he got to me, his face pinched. "Nice of you to join us. Whose bed did you crawl out of to grace us with your presence?" Discreetly, I shot him the bird by pretending to itch my nose with my middle finger. "Laura, this is my soon-to-be brother-in-law's kid brother, Murphy."

Kid brother? Way to make me sound prepubescent! Sometimes I got the feeling everyone saw me as a joke or an annoying cling on, something to be discarded under their shoe. Especially Hudson. I swear that man went out of his way to hate me.

Long after my friends went home, I stayed, moving

over to the bar after Shannon Calhoun called it quits. I found a few lonely men willing to buy me drinks and turned on the charm. Hudson was still there with Laura, practically participating in sexual foreplay right there in public in the middle of the bar. He ogled her cleavage and she rubbed against him like a cat in heat. *Disgusting*.

With my head resting on the sticky bar top, I didn't see Hudson approach. "You planning on sleeping here?"

I picked my head up and scanned the room, looking for his date. "Where's your girlfriend?" Was I sneering? *Pathetic*.

"Laura went home, called an Uber. She's not my girlfriend, by the way. Just a bit of fun for the evening."

My lips curved into a smirk. "Well, I don't know about you, but my idea of fun involves joining my date when they go home."

"Yeah, she said something about wanting to get to know me better first. Apparently she's a 'nice' girl." Hudson emphasized the word nice as I snorted.

"Not in that dress. Nice girls don't wear a size four when they're really an eight. Trust me, that girl is playing you for a commitment."

"Probably. Can I take you home?" This was beginning to be a regular occurrence with Hudson. I was starting to suspect he hung around until closing just so he could drive me home safely. Not because he's a nice guy, but because he felt responsible for me in some convoluted way just because our brothers were getting married.

"I don't want to go home. It's too quiet there. The

honeymooners won't be back for a few more days and I don't wanna be alone. It creeps me out," I whined.

"Well, you're welcome to my couch, but I can't just leave you here, so make a decision."

"Your roommate won't mind?" Was that hope staining my voice?

"Nah, he's already asleep. He won't even know you're there until tomorrow morning when you're ready to leave. I'll drive you back home after breakfast."

"Lead the way, Bon Bon." Hudson rolled his eyes. He was probably sick of hearing my ridiculous pet names. But he gave as good as he got, always concocting something twice as stupid to call me.

"After you, Swizzle Stick." He held the door open with a flourish, pretending to be a gentleman.

I've never seen the inside of Hudson's apartment before. It was a trendy loft in an industrial area. Brick walls and scarred oak floors gave the open space warmth. There wasn't much in the way of decoration, just some couches and an enormous TV, but it was nice. "I like your place."

"Thanks. I don't know how much longer I'll be here. My roommate is getting married in a couple of months. If I don't find another roommate soon I'll have to downsize. Let me go get you an extra pair of my pajamas. There's cold water in the fridge."

I made myself comfortable on the couch, palming the remote. Hudson was back in a flash, holding out a pair of blue and black plaid sleep pants. "These might be a little big but they'll do. If you need anything just knock on my door. I'm down the hall on the left." Then he retreated to his bedroom, leaving me alone with an infomercial about cleaning products. It didn't hold my interest, but I needed the background noise to help me sleep.

Grabbing a throw pillow, I stuffed it under my head and covered myself with the blanket draped over the back of the couch. The pillow was comfortable and the blanket soft, but the leather beneath me was cold. It would take a few minutes for my body to warm it up. Despite Hudson's hospitality, I felt uncomfortably out of place, but it beat going home to an empty house.

Sometime during the night, I got up to relieve my bladder. The pipes made a strange noise when I turned on the water at the sink. The wrenching metal that echoed through the ceiling vent was reminiscent of a jail cell door clanging shut or someone dragging a lead pipe across a concrete floor. I really needed to stop watching horror movies before bed. Hudson's door was cracked slightly as I walked past it. It only took me a second to make my decision not to return to the couch and be attacked by Freddy or Chucky or one of their besties.

I opened Hudson's door and slipped inside, quietly tiptoeing to the empty side of the bed. He didn't even stir when I climbed in, pulling the covers over my head to stay safe. He would probably laugh at me if he could see what a wuss I was acting like. I didn't care, better safe than sorry. If an axe murderer broke in here, I wouldn't think twice about using Hudson as a human shield. If it came down to him or me, his ass was getting sacrificed, not mine.

I tried to think of cute safe things like kittens and rainbows and spring flowers in bloom until I fell back to sleep. Hours later, I was rudely awakened by Hudson's loud mouth.

"Fuck, Murphy! What are you doing? Get the hell out of my bed." Hudson bolted upright, looking enraged.

He'd rolled his body to the far side of the mattress, hugging the edge. "I think it's pretty obvious what I'm doing."

"Trying to molest me? Your leg was tangled up with mine."

"What? No!" Damn, I missed out on touching his legs? Were we spooning? "I was trying to stay alive. Your loft is straight out of central casting for horror movies."

Hudson ran his hand through his short blond hair. The blunt ends stuck out in every direction. "Out of all your shitty ideas, this has to be the worst one."

His rejection stung even though I wasn't even trying to come on to him. To cover the hurt, I fell back on my good friend, slutty sarcasm. "If you give me five minutes, I'll prove to you it's a great idea."

"God dammit! You're like a lost little puppy looking for a master. I don't want to hold your fucking leash anymore. Go home!"

I was too stunned to think of a comeback. Tears stung my eyes as I crawled out of his bed. A wave of sadness washed over me, bringing all kinds of buried emotions to the surface, burning my throat and eyes. I've never handled rejection well. It's my biggest insecurity, but Hudson's words cut extra deep. I felt too humiliated to examine the whys right now. I just needed to grab my clothes and get the hell out of here as fast as possible.

I shuffled to the door with my head hung low when Hudson's voice stopped me. "Murphy, wait. I'm sorry. I didn't mean that. I just—I was caught off guard when I woke up."

I refused to look at him, instead staring at my feet with my hand on the door knob. "It's fine. Not like I expected much different from you." Pulling the door open, I placed one foot over the threshold.

Hudson's question stopped me. "What's that supposed to mean?"

Oh, he's the insulted party now? *How convenient.* "I'll be gone in a minute, don't worry about it."

He just couldn't let it go. Hudson jumped out of bed and followed me into the living room while I hunted for my wallet and keys. "Look Murphy, someday you're gonna find a good man, the one meant for you. But it's never going to be me."

Where is a sinkhole when you need one? Why can't the earth open up and swallow me right now? This is the part where my asinine flirting comes back to bite me in the ass. He can take his goddamn pity and choke on it! In a pathetic attempt to salvage my pride I dumbly predicted, "And someday you're going to realize how much you want me, but it'll probably be too late by then because I'll have settled for someone else."

"God, I hope so," he mumbled. Unfortunately for

him, the acoustics in the loft were great and the sound carried to my ears.

"Thanks for the rescue last night. Next time you see me drowning in a bar, just look the other way and pretend you don't know me."

Palming my phone, I opened my Uber app and ordered a ride as I took the elevator down to the lobby. Time to do what I did best—get lost in other men's beds.

DEAR READER

Thank you so much for reading **Coming Together**, the third book in the Hearts For Hire series.

If you enjoyed Reid and Riley's romance, **please leave a review** to tell other readers how much you loved them. Telling your friends and spreading the word on social media helps people find their new favorite book.

With love,

Raquel Riley

Next in Series

Two roommates. One gay, one straight. Will their flirtatious game lead to love or loathing?

Hudson Brantley

Murphy loves taunting me, but two can play at that game. When he takes things too far one night, I decide to turn the tables on him. But what if my little joke ends up being not so funny?

What if it ends in true love?

Murphy Maguire

I only meant to tease him, but Hudson has no problem calling my bluff. What starts as a dare quickly turns into an enemies-with-benefits arrangement. Until I start wanting more...

Can I convince Hudson to give us a chance at a real relationship?

Curious Relations is an age gap, enemies with benefits, bi-awakening gay romance with a happily ever after, a rowdy bachelor party, and male escorts. This is the fourth book in the Hearts For Hire series.

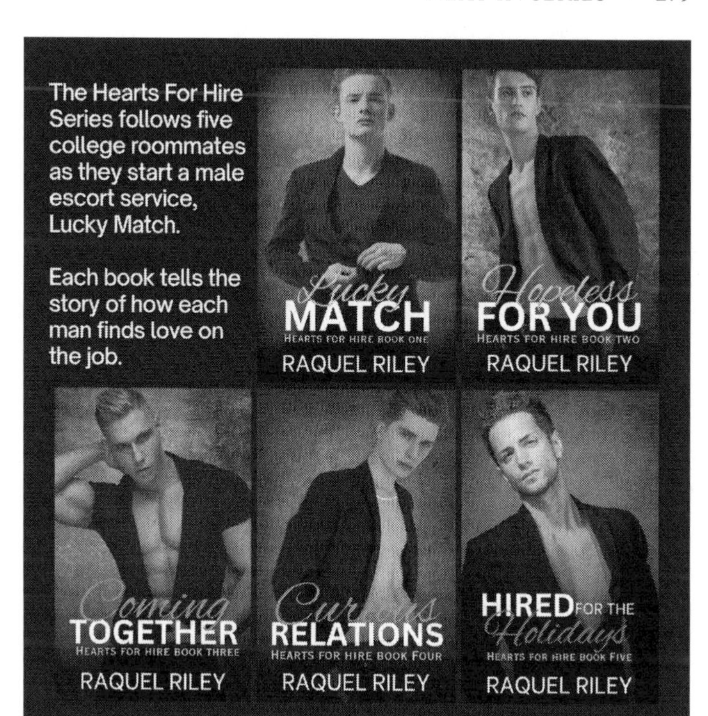
The Hearts For Hire Series follows five college roommates as they start a male escort service, Lucky Match.
Each book tells the story of how each man finds love on the job.
Lucky MATCH
HEARTS FOR HIRE BOOK ONE
RAQUEL RILEY
Hopeless FOR YOU
HEARTS FOR HIRE BOOK TWO
RAQUEL RILEY
Coming TOGETHER
HEARTS FOR HIRE BOOK THREE
RAQUEL RILEY
Curious RELATIONS
HEARTS FOR HIRE BOOK FOUR
RAQUEL RILEY
HIRED FOR THE Holidays
HEARTS FOR HIRE BOOK FIVE
RAQUEL RILEY

ABOUT THE AUTHOR

Raquel Riley is a native of South Florida but now calls North Carolina home. She is an avid reader and loves to travel. Most often, she writes gay romance stories with an HEA but characters of all types can be found in her books. She weaves pieces of herself, her family, and her travels into every story she writes.

For a complete list of Raquel Riley's releases, please visit her website at **www.raquelriley.com**. You can also follow her on the social media platforms listed below. You can also find all of Raquel's important links in one convenient place at **https://linktr.ee/raquelriley**

ACKNOWLEDGMENTS

Tracy Ann, your feedback is so appreciated! Thank you for your continued praise and support of my stories, and for keeping me organized and on task.

Also, thank you to my **ARC/street team** for your insightful input and reviews and outstanding promotion.

A huge thank you to the **86'ers!** You crazy bunch are guaranteed to make me laugh at least fourteen times a day.

I can't forget the **Secret Circle!** You bunch keep me accountable and sane and cheer for every one of my accomplishments, both big and small.

Last, but never least, thanks to my family for being so understanding while I ignore you so I can write.

Made in the USA
Columbia, SC
22 December 2024